PUSH COMES TO SHOVE

J.L. O'Faolain

Dreamspinner Press

Published by
Dreamspinner Press
5032 Capital Circle SW
Ste 2, PMB# 279
Tallahassee, FL 32305-7886
USA
http://www.dreamspinnerpress.com/

Push Comes to Shove

Cover Art by Shobana Appavu
bob@bob-artist.com

ISBN: 978-1-62380-030-7

Printed in the United States of America
First Edition
October 2012

eBook edition available
eBook ISBN: 978-1-62380-031-4

To the Internet's greatest geeky superhero!
You know who you are.

PROLOGUE

HE HEARD the footsteps before the guards got anywhere near his cell. There was no question of who they'd come for. All of the cells surrounding his were unoccupied. He didn't bother looking up from his book as the black guard stepped into view. Why they had come was anyone's guess. He assumed the warden was attempting to reassert his authority after the recent string of riots. All of them had been planned. He was aware of each one several days in advance but had opted not to participate, not even when the trio of Latin Kings dragged one man into his block to gang-rape him. He'd simply rolled over and gone back to sleep.

He couldn't recall the name of the man watching him. Learning the names of the guards seemed pointless, since they all came and went. The sense of disgust coming through the bars from the one watching him now left a sour taste in his mouth, but he smiled in response to it. They all hated him. It was a given, but most of the staff working in the East Arlenton Correctional Facility shared a special dislike for his presence.

No one, least of all himself, would say he was a model prisoner. Anyone put in the same cell as him would end up going to the infirmary within a week's time. Mind you, these same prisoners were people the warden typically hated or wanted to see hurt for some reason. It had been a game among the other members of the institution to see how long it took for him to go over the edge. Some prisoners tried to get transferred to his cell in order to prove how tough they were. The ones outside looking in placed bets with whatever they had. Sometimes the guards got in on it.

Then he had an accident, and the warden made the uncontested decision to place him in an unused section that had once served as the prison's special confinement quarters. Since then, there had been no more problems.

Of course, by contrast, he'd been bored out of his skull.

Still, overall, he preferred being left alone. There was no one trying to stab him from the lower bunk while he slept, or some three-hundred-pound muscle head shouting loudly about how he would soon be his next bitch. The silence got tedious after a while, but it made reading a lot easier.

A loud clang rattled through the air. The guard was tapping his baton against the bars, trying to get his attention. He considered ignoring the man, but curiosity overruled his better judgment all too soon, so Sun Tzu's *The Art of War* went down with his place marked on the bed atop Machiavelli's *The Prince*.

Silently, he watched the guard from the top bunk, not moving. "You've got a visitor," the dark-skinned man said stiffly, as though the very idea went against the very laws of nature. "Fix yourself up first."

Smoothly, he came down off the bed to the floor. "I'm ready," he said, in a soft voice that surprised most people. "Let's go."

It was much louder once they left his area of the jail. The other prisoners were making noise over something that didn't concern him. Several guards banged their batons against the bars, trying to calm things down, to no avail. When he strode past, the volume dropped like a stone in a clear pond. Confused, a number of inmates on the far end of the block stuck their heads out to see what was wrong. At the sight of him, they all moved back into their cells without a word. None of them looked up as he moved quietly past.

He assumed they were bringing him to the regular area where visitors spoke to inmates through phones from behind bulletproof glass. He'd only seen them once, at the station where he'd been held prior to his trial and subsequent sentencing, but figured they must have them here as well. Surprisingly, the guards steered him into a private room where several narrow tables stood with chairs all around. A woman in her late forties was waiting for him near a window in the far back, going through some papers she'd just taken from an open briefcase next to her. The suit she wore was simple, but tailored to fit the nice curves of her wide hips. It spoke of the conservative attitude following the economic crisis of the last few years.

Any other observations he might have made were lost as he felt his cock thicken in his prison uniform.

It had been a long time. She most certainly could sue him over it if she liked.

The guards left him in the seat across from her, still chained up. The woman noticed this as they started to leave and called out.

"You can take those off," she said politely but firmly. "I doubt I'll be in any trouble."

The guard smiled at her like she was a little girl wanting to cross the street by herself. "With all due respect, ma'am," he replied, the sarcasm in his voice apparent, "this one is nothing but trouble. I'd keep those cuffs on if I were you."

"I'm well aware of this gentleman's...." The woman paused then. "Quirks," she settled on finally. "You can uncuff him."

There was no room for dispute in her voice, so the guard came back and slowly began the long process of taking off the many chains binding his hands and feet. When it was finished, the guard stood at the head of the table, holding the chains up so he would see.

"I'll be right outside."

The words were bold, yet they rang hollow. It was an empty threat, since he could have killed the guard right now without standing or breaking a sweat. They both knew this, and the guard knew he was wasting everyone's time. Ignoring the woman, the black man turned and walked away, clinking with each step he took.

"Charming fellow," he retorted once the door was shut.

"Indeed," the woman replied after a moment's hesitation. "I suppose you must be wondering what this is all about?"

Shifting uncomfortably from his erection, he gave her a once-over again before voicing his assessment. "You're a lawyer," he said. "You work for some kind of charity, or a nonprofit organization. I'm guessing you were sent by someone very powerful, or a group of very powerful someones, who don't want the general public to know what they're doing. Also, you skipped lunch to come here."

He had caught her off guard. She recovered very quickly, but the surprise never completely left her face.

"'How did you know?'" he went on. "That's the usual question that follows."

The lady seemed to hesitate, but then rose to his challenge. "I could have been a lawyer's assistant," she pointed out.

He laughed. "No lawyer would hire an assistant over twenty-five," he countered. "You're very professional. Everything about you says that. You've been doing this for quite some time. The briefcase, the paperwork, even the way you riffle through them—all of that says experience. No self-respecting woman of your intelligence would settle for being an assistant for so long."

"You might be surprised," she said, before adding, "Sadly. Still, you weren't wrong. I am a lawyer, and I do work for a nonprofit organization. Care to explain how you knew that?"

"Your suit," he answered calmly, pointing. "Lawyers from commercial firms, firms that deal with the rich and powerful every day, like to show off how much money they have. They need to fit in with the bigwigs. Lawyers who work for charity try to present a more conservative approach, particularly these days. Your suit looks very professional, but nondescript. You could be from any number of law firms, here to see anyone in this facility. That was how I figured your bosses didn't want word of who you were visiting here to get out. You're trying to blend in, but in a place like this, you still stick out like a sore thumb."

"How so?"

The smile on his face was sardonic. "This is a men's prison," he said. "Take a wild guess."

She returned the smirk with one of her own. "How did you know I skipped lunch?"

Behind them, high up on the wall near the barred window where sunlight streamed through, was a clock ticking away the time.

"It's after twelve," he said, giving the timepiece a nod. "This is when most people on the outside eat lunch. You're here, so I took a stab in the dark."

"I actually did eat lunch before I came here," she informed him, trumping him. "At nine-thirty this morning. Ramen noodles don't do much for me, though, so I'm going to grab something on the way back."

"Must be nice," he mused. "If you decide to swing by the cafeteria on the highway just off the interstate, avoid the meatloaf. It is neither meaty, nor loaf-y, in any sense of either term."

"I've been there before," she said while going through her papers again. "Once was enough for me."

After a moment, he leaned back slightly so that his erection was a little more noticeable. "So," he went on. "Now that we've broken the ice, as I assume people still say, care to explain what you're doing here paying a visit to East Arlenton's most notorious?"

"I came to ask if you would like to be released."

Her tone was utterly deadpan. The chair he was in fell back to the floor loudly. He felt the ire from the guard outside. It mixed with the hunger coming from the female lawyer, making him both peckish and grumpy in turn. He hated swimming in other people's emotions. It was one aspect of his powers that he felt was overrated. Still, the woman intrigued him, and the guard's fuming amused him.

"That," he admitted, "I didn't see coming."

"I work for the Real-Life Superhero Association," she stated, setting the papers down in front of her. "Perhaps you've heard of us?"

"I have," he replied, knowing she was joking. "Vaguely."

"We were wondering if you would be willing to come work for us," she explained. "The RLSA has started a recruitment drive, and some of the senior members feel it would be in both our best interests to have you on board."

A frown marred his otherwise handsome, youthful features. "You can't be serious."

"Deadly," she replied in a flat voice. "It has taken us quite some time to get even this far. The state was adamant about keeping you locked up, but recent events have led to one of the local senators showing support for our cause. Should you agree to cooperate, you would be released on good behavior for a probationary period. Two of our members would serve as your probation officers, helping to reorient you back into society as a prominent member of the superhero community."

"I see," he said, leaning back in his chair again. "So I get out, am given a job as the Association's poster boy, and your people get to show the world that capes and masks are a good thing."

After a second, she nodded. "Basically."

His chair came back down loudly again. "And suppose I don't want to leave?"

"You want to leave," she countered. "I'm not blind, either. This place is suffocating you."

"But becoming a productive member of society doesn't sound like much of a challenge," he replied easily. "Or a lot of fun."

Smiling, she leaned forward toward him. "We know that the warden has been using you," she whispered. "You've had several inmates with prices on their heads placed in the same cell with you. All of them were offered a deal if they could dispose of you and make it look like a random prison fight. You injured all of them critically without killing them. You've also been before a parole board and denied release shortly thereafter."

His eyes narrowed. "The Association has been spying." He tsked. "Naughty."

"We're heroes," she stated, rising up again. "Not cops. It's obvious how the world works. We're trying to do something about that."

Neither of them spoke for a moment. Much as he hated it, the idea was beginning to show merit.

"Doesn't the RLSA already have a poster boy?" he asked after a moment, thoughtfully. "Why would your people need me when you've got him?"

"He's still only one man," she replied. "He can't be everywhere."

"More than a bird? More than a plane?" he quoted. "'More than some pretty face on a train?' I guess it really isn't easy being Superman."

"I really wish you would consider this."

He surprised her a moment later. "I'll consider it," he said, giving her his best smile. "But only on one condition."

The worry on her face made him chuckle softly. "Tell me your name," he added, mitigating her fears.

"Oh." Shaking her head, she offered him her hand. "Susan Walters," she introduced herself. "Sorry about that."

"Nice to meet you, Ms. Walters," he said, taking the hand she offered. "You already know who I am, though, I'm sure."

"Actually, I don't." Taking her hand back, she extracted another paper from her briefcase. "Nothing in your record has your birth name. I compiled documents from your police records, prison transcripts, and news reports on the Deadly Seven, but nothing in them gave your real name."

"You already know it," he insisted. "Just call me Wrath."

CHAPTER
ONE

"JUST like that!" the photographer called out excitedly. "Turn toward the camera a bit. Make sure your face is in the light."

Nervous, Push did as the photographer asked while beads of sweat popped out of his forehead underneath the dusty cap of brown hair. He had never been comfortable on camera and had to remind himself continuously that this was for a good cause while the photographer clicked away. The front of his costume had been raised up slightly to expose the rock-hard abs underneath. Not that the spandex did much to conceal them. His blue uniform conformed to the contours of his body so tightly that he might as well have been wearing nothing at all.

But, he wasn't going to argue with a professional about what looked good on a calendar.

"Excellent! Now, lower your chin a bit."

Push did as he was told. "Raise the shirt up a little bit more," said the photographer, giving signals with his hands. "Now, Push. Give us that smile we wanna see!"

Impishly, he squinted his eyes slightly and grinned, raising the corner of his mouth into a smirk just as the flash went off. Spots swam in front of his face, but he held the pose. Next, the man wanted him to pull the front of the shirt up over his shoulders. The fabric was a new type of spandex with memory cloth woven into it, so it held up very well, both during fights and for when photo shoots demanded he look sexy.

Push felt ridiculous.

Over and over, he turned, flexed, and posed however the photographer demanded. At five feet and six inches, Push wasn't the epitome of manly sexiness that the camera guy insisted he was. True, he kept his body in tight shape, but it couldn't compensate for how small he looked in comparison to the average guy on the street. Adding to this, the studio was very cold. Goosebumps kept popping out over his arms and legs, a testament to the fact.

When he was down to his underwear, the photographer started insisting he remove the goggles. Fortunately, before he could explain, Annette came to his rescue.

"The goggles stay on," the RLSA personal assistant said firmly. "They're a part of his identity."

The photographer started to object, but Annette had his contract with the studio in her hand between blinks. "It's stated right here," she reminded the willowy cameraman. "The goggles remain on at all times."

Annette looked over at him then. "And in any case, I think we're about done for today. Push has a meeting to get to, and there's no way we can publish the underwear photos in the calendar. The council was adamant that we keep things PG-rated."

Push was already picking his clothes up off the floor. "Coming," he said. "Has anyone seen my telescopic bo staff?"

"You left it over by the door," she reminded him, while the photographer silently fumed next to her. "Hurry up. Scratch still has to do his shoot before we meet up with the Cape Cabinet."

Push glanced up while wrestling both legs back into his pants as Scratch strode across the carpeted floor into the space set aside for the shoot. Standing there awkwardly under the bright lights just at six feet, Push's best friend lifted the sides of his long coat out, showing off the T-shirt he wore underneath. The logo on it was of a set of billiard balls in a pool rack. Superimposed over them were the words "Big Balls." Scratch's shaggy mop of dark brown hair went well with his cocoa-tanned skin and taut swimmer's build.

"Um, did you want me to start off with the coat on?" Scratch asked in a thick Jersey accent.

The photographer ignored him. "I still say we should have done both of them together," the man said in an airy voice to Annette. "The fans would love it!"

"Maybe next year," she said dismissively. "You'd have to change the whole setup, and we don't have the time for it."

Scratch was still standing under the bright lights. "Keep the coat," Annette told him, almost as an afterthought. "At least for right now."

"Well, we might as well get started then," the photographer grumbled, moving back over to his camera. "Now, look right into the lens and give me your best 'sad kitten' smile."

Push snorted before going back to dressing himself. His costume consisted of a simple pair of spandex jeans, short-sleeved shirt, utility belt, boots, and a jacket for cold weather or when he needed extra pockets. He'd gone with a light web-color rendition of royal blue as a base, then added darker, traditional royal-blue stripes racing down vertically. The stripes veered diagonally past his pecs before straightening out again down the—even he had to admit—tight abs. The same stripes raced down the sides of his pants for an added effect. The costume was simple, practical, and easy to fight in. It was for this reason that Push had resisted changing it, despite Annette's demands that he try a new look.

Annette wandered over as soon as he got his pants on. "He's getting better," she noted, referring to Scratch. "I thought he would be a lot more anxious. You've both come a long way."

"I still can't believe you talked both of us into doing this," Push muttered, dragging his shirt down over his head so he wouldn't see Scratch posing.

"It's for…."

"Charity," he finished, cutting Annette off. "I remember, but we both feel silly for doing it. You'll never fully convince me that people will buy calendars of crime-fighters posing half-nude."

"This whole thing started because people wanted full-nude shots of crime-fighters," Annette reminded him as Scratch began to inch out of his shirt. "The Cape Cabinet eventually reached a compromise with the public. They are still a little worried about the Association being shown in a less than tasteful light."

"Right," said Push, averting his eyes before another flash went off.

"We still haven't heard anything back yet from the New York City Comic-Con," she went on, watching Scratch a little too closely now. "It looks like a toss-up between you and Grant Morrison for the twelve-thirty panel. I think they might be leaning toward Morrison, though, to tell the truth."

"I'd still like to go to Comic-Con," Push mused. "I'd probably have more fun as part of the crowd, though, instead of as a guest speaker."

"It's important we maintain a positive image," Annette insisted as another flash went off. Scratch was down to his faded jeans and the customized brown leather leg guards now, and the photographer was insisting he open up the fly.

"Comics are the reason we're—Hold it!"

The photographer spun around as Scratch froze. "Sorry," she said, before glaring toward Scratch. "Scratch, why aren't you wearing underwear?"

Scratch looked down at his zipper, which was halfway down. Against his better judgment, Push looked on as his best friend blushed. "Um, I forgot?"

Annette sighed. "The pants stay zipped," she told the cameraman. "We're not letting him flash the American public with his junk."

"I wouldn't have complained," the photographer insisted as Scratch zipped back up. Push felt a twinge of disappointment as well, but said nothing as the photographer went back to work.

"Aren't the two of you roommates?" she wondered, giving him a look. "You of all people ought to have warned him about that."

Push remained defiantly silent as he watched one of the assistants rub oil over Scratch's muscles. "Excellent," the photographer said excitedly. "Now, pout your lips ever so slightly."

Scratch held his face as the camera went off. "Beautiful! Keep going!"

FORTY-FIVE minutes later, the photographer was satisfied with the pictures he'd taken. Because of Scratch's commando status and the photographer not thinking ahead and bringing a selection of undergarments for him to choose from, the jeans stayed on. Push thought it was hysterical, but also suspected his friend had planned all of this deliberately. Scratch had been the more enthusiastic of them about the calendar shoot, but that didn't mean he was above pulling a stunt like that.

In a few months' time, their faces would grace the months of January and December, respectively. The Cape Cabinet was still nervous about the prospect of superheroes working as part-time calendar models, but their stance these days was that any press was better than none. And despite his apprehension, Push was actually looking forward to seeing how things worked out. At the very least, it would be something he could look back on and laugh about.

Unfortunately, now that the shoot was finished, they had the Cape Cabinet to deal with. Push had never liked these meetings. The Cabinet was composed of some of the founding members of the Real-Life Superhero Association. The Association, as some preferred to call it for simplicity's sake, had been formed back in the late seventies, but before that, they had been what people today called the Genesis of Capes.

It was such a stupid name.

At least the stories weren't dull. Back in the sixties, a handful of police reports mentioned sightings of the Hooded Judge in the Washington city of Spokane. A man in a modified judge's robe wielding a sledgehammer was going around assaulting muggers. In the beginning, no one had taken it very seriously. Then the Hooded Judge was blamed for the murder of a man who had been accused of molesting a young girl. The girl in question was able to verify that someone fitting the Hooded Judge's description was seen leaving the man's residence on the night of his murder.

These days, people debated back and forth as to whether it was actually the Hooded Judge in the first place. None of the reports painted an accurate description, and new evidence following the murder suggested the man had been innocent.

But the damage was done, and the manhunt started. While the search for the Hooded Judge went on, a young journalist and comic book aficionado came to Spokane to cover the event. Jack Montgomery, who would later become famous as the Spangled Runner, ended up being inspired by the Hooded Judge despite opposing his methods. According to the stories, he made a costume for himself, started doing charity work while in the guise of his superhero alter ego, and promoted his activities with the help of a comic fanzine he sometimes helped work on with his friends.

And things, as they say, took off from there.

The Spangled Runner made it clear from the get-go that he did not support vigilantism in any respect. His superhero identity was simply a means to inspire young children the way that the comic book heroes of his youth had. The idea spread like wildfire all the same, until the Real-Life Superhero Association began in 1978. From that point on, ordinary citizens were invited to join the ranks of the ostensibly nonprofit organization, provided that they passed the training program. Even though most superheroes today were still more about feeding the homeless and giving rides to stranded people on the side of the road, the project had expanded to include individuals with specialty training.

Push and Scratch's territory was police consulting and bounty hunter work.

There was talk that certain RLSA members would be granted Federal Marshal status, but Push didn't see that happening anytime soon. Despite the support they'd been given, especially in the last decade or so, people were uncomfortable with the idea of costumed crime-fighters. No one was more against the idea than the police. Push suspected they were worried people would begin to see them as incompetent.

Sadly, their fears weren't completely unfounded.

The ride back to the RLSA's main office was relatively quiet. Traffic was reasonably low for once, and Annette managed to avoid fussing over him by keeping her cell phone glued to her ear. He was her favorite project, and it irked him to no end.

Push, it just so happened, was gay.

Da-da-dum!

He always felt as though ominous music or thunderclaps should follow that declaration. Push had been out of the closet before he joined the RLSA. In fact, the moment he entered the fold, they began promoting it as a means of showing how "forward-thinking" they were. At times, in the past, he had entertained thoughts of quitting. Mind you, it meant a lot when people wrote to him talking about how big of an inspiration to the gay community he was. Quite a bit of his fan mail came from teenagers, some of whom were still in the closet with their family and friends. These days, however, he felt more like a celebrity model than a crime-fighter. It definitely wasn't what he'd signed on for.

The Real-Life Superhero Association was located inside an office building in downtown Chicago. Jameson, their driver, dropped them off at the front door. Annette was still glued to her phone as they entered the air-conditioned lobby. Several of the receptionists gave him and Scratch a wave as they crossed the expanse to the elevators at the far end. One thing about this place was that most people were nice. Of course, they might have been that way only because Push was so well-known. Scratch caught his fair share of the spotlight by being Push's partner, but he was a superb crime-fighter in his own right, and it bothered Push that his friend got overlooked. Scratch, however, didn't act concerned by it. It was just one of the many ways he was such a hero to Push, personally.

The Cabinet room was located on the twenty-third floor. Margaret Liu, the chief secretary in charge of this floor, was on the phone when they stepped out into the hallway. A man dressed like Captain Ahab, with a hook covering his left hand and a fishing pole in the right, was standing in front of her desk looking riled.

"The costume is much better," she said to him quickly while her hand covered the receiver. "You still need to work on the name, though."

The stranger frowned as though he'd bitten into something sour, then stormed off toward them. As they passed one another, Push overheard him mumbling.

"Don't see what the big deal is," he growled quietly. "I've got the fisherman motif. What's wrong with a name like Master Baiting?"

Scratch's straight face didn't hold once the man was gone. "Um, he can't be serious, right?"

"I'm sure he was," Annette replied. "How's it going, Margaret?"

"Lousy," she hissed, slamming the phone down hard. "I can't find the file on that serial killer from Biloxi, the computers have gone down on me twice today, my lunch still hasn't arrived yet, and this guy from Nevada won't stop calling!"

"What's wrong?" Annette wondered, peeking around the counter to check out Margaret's computer screen. "Oh, is this part of the recruitment for the new X Project?"

Margaret nodded wearily. "The guy claims he has a legitimate superpower and wants to sign up. I've checked his records, and he seems to be legit as far as his claim goes, but that isn't what worries me."

"What is it?" Push asked, curious.

"The man's name is Charley Filsworth, and he was born with an incredibly high acid content," Margaret explained. "His bodily fluids are poisonous to most people, and his urine has such a high corrosive level that it can dissolve solid objects. Apparently, he's taught himself how to control his acid content with diet so that the acid levels in his urine are even higher."

Both Push and Scratch laughed. "I'm just imagining what his costume would look like," Scratch said when Annette glared.

"Oh, crap!" Margaret screamed, jamming both thumbs into her temples. "Don't even suggest that! Now I can't stop thinking about it!"

"As if your day wasn't bad enough already," Annette said pointedly, glaring at the two of them.

"Think about something else," Push suggested. "Think about pink and purple elephants!"

In response, Margaret cried out again. "Ack! Now I can't stop thinking about that guy urinating on a pink and purple elephant."

"Nice going," Scratch teased.

"Everything is ruined for me forever," Margaret moaned, before pushing a button. "They're already waiting on both of you. Go in before you say something even worse. Annette, when you have a chance, see if you can find out where my lunch went to. I'm starving!"

In response, Annette pulled out her phone while Push and Scratch headed toward the room with the RLSA sigil on the door, the meeting chamber for the Cape Cabinet.

"I'm ordering something for you from the deli down the street," Annette said before the doors closed behind them. "It should be here in fifteen minutes."

Push smiled wryly before glancing around. He'd been here before, but that had been a while back. The meeting room for the Cape Cabinet was big and covered in a sandalwood-finish paneling that always gave off a woody smell. He guessed it was to make people feel more relaxed. The entire chamber was decorated with trophies, medals, letters of commendation, photos of the council members posing with various people, and even newspaper clippings dating back several decades. Everything was arranged in such a way that none of it stood out right off the bat. If you stood there long enough without focusing on the people across the room, though, it became clear. The meeting room was one big tribute to how awesome the cabinet members were.

The members in question were sitting in their designated seats on the other side of the room. Separating them was a vast expanse of carpet that had the RLSA logo woven into it. It always reminded Push of photos he'd seen of the president's office in Washington D.C. The Cabinet themselves sat behind a great oval counter bending away from the room entrance. On the wall behind the counter was a separate door through which they came and went. Each Cabinet member was given a specific seat. In front of them were the various names they went by. The identities of the Cabinet had been made public knowledge years ago, but to much of the world, even the parts that hated them, they were known by their hero signatures.

There was Patriot Arrow, who always wore his bow-and-arrow ensemble, even to meetings. To his left was Booster Hawk, still wearing his signature black-and-gold outfit in defiance of a tabloid who called it "out of style." Rocket Grasshopper smiled as Push came forward. Push had never gotten the impression the man liked him, despite Rocket having been nothing but outwardly friendly toward him. Mr. Answer pulled his fedora down slightly and kept glaring toward Scratch, as if anticipating an attack.

Urban Knight was showing off his latest fashion statement. The man changed outfits every other year or so. Push couldn't remember if this was his eighth or ninth one since he'd joined the RLSA. Shadow Devil sat perfectly still next to him. Out of the entire Cabinet, he was the one Scratch had the least amount of information on. Between the two of them, Scratch had always been the resident expert on the Cape Cabinet's back story. To this day, the only thing Scratch had been able to put together on Shadow Devil was that he'd operated out of Las Vegas for a time before the council formally banded together.

The final two members on the far right were Star Lantern and Silver Dollar. Silver Dollar, as Push recalled, had been a volunteer bank guard before the days of the Association, while Star Lantern got her start working at a power company that had been under fire from environmental terrorists in the sixties. Sitting together, the Cabinet should have looked ridiculous. They could have easily passed as a bunch of elderly dorks at a comic book convention. It was the looks in their eyes that really gave it away. These people had seen a lot through the years, and it showed in the parts of their faces Push could see. None of them were the sort he would want to mess with, and he was the one with the superpower.

That, and they were the reason he got paid every other week.

"Nice to see you both," Rocket Grasshopper said, his eyes lingering on Push longer than necessary. "Prompt, as usual."

"We've called you both here on a matter regarding the X Project," Mr. Answer interjected. "I hope neither of you require a briefing on the subject?"

"No, sir," they each answered.

"Good," Patriot Arrow said. "The recruitment process for X Project has been slow. Given the circumstances, the RLSA has decided to look elsewhere for its candidates. We believe we've located a potential applicant, and would like for the two of you to show him the ropes."

"Who is it?" Scratch wondered.

"He is being transported to Chicago even as we speak," Silver Dollar informed them. "If all goes well, you'll be introduced in a couple of hours."

"There is," Shadow Devil began, after glancing down toward the others, "something rather significant you should know first. Our applicant—"

A knock at the door cut him off. "Sirs," Margaret said, sticking her head into the room. Going by the tone of her voice alone, she sounded very upset. When Push looked back, however, her face was a complete blank. "We just got an emergency call from the transport vehicle crew. They were attacked outside of Grand Rapids. The…."

Margaret's eyes darted from the Cabinet to Push and Scratch, then back again. "The subject," she said crisply, "has disappeared."

The entire Cabinet froze. "What was the nature of the attack?" Silver Dollar demanded. "Where did it come from?"

"External," Margaret replied, stepping fully into the room. "The vehicle was run off the road by an eighteen-wheeler and then ambushed. One of the guards called from his cell phone before the ambulance took him away."

Scratch looked at Push and mouthed the word "Guards?"

Push darted his eyes quickly at the Cabinet in response.

"If the subject escaped," Mr. Answer postulated, "he would have most likely gone to the nearest city."

"Agreed," said Patriot Arrow. "Push and Scratch."

Both turned back to the Cabinet in response.

"You will search Grand Rapids for any sign of our missing volunteer. Head to the site of the attack first, just on the off-chance he is nearby, then proceed to Grand Rapids. We'll have a hotel suite waiting for you, as well as information on the missing X Project member."

Push and Scratch nodded before heading for the door. Margaret moved out of the way to let them pass, and Push gave her a nod in acknowledgment before leaving. Neither of them said a word, not even as they traveled down the elevator to the basement. It wasn't until they were out of the elevator in the long hallway that spilled out into the basement garage that Push spoke aloud.

"Guards, huh?"

"And they kept using the word 'transport'," Scratch added. "Also, why not give us the, um, 'information' now?"

"Good questions," said Push as they strode into the garage together. "Unfortunately, there's not going to be much time for them. We're here."

Someone had undoubtedly alerted Iron Mechanic while they were on their way down. The six-three black man with arms as big as Push's head stomped forward, leaving his crew behind to fiddle under the hood of the Cherry Buster.

"How you boys doin'?" Iron Mechanic asked, shaking both their hands. "I hear you gotcher selves volunteered to a mess out near Grand Rapids, eh?"

"Looks that way," Push said. "We could use a car. Mind if we borrow one of yours?"

"And it's gotta be fast," Scratch added. "And, um, comfortable, too."

Iron Mechanic gave one of his crew members a signal, then turned back to face them. "I think I can help you boys out," he said, grinning from ear to ear. "Come this way."

The Mechanic led them down through the maze of vehicles. The RLSA had been collecting and modifying cars and trucks for years. The Chicago garage was the official location, but each RLSA office across the country had a private garage where they stored vehicles for professional use. Push had ridden in a few of them before. His personal favorite was the Blackdog, a modified Camaro, but Push noted that it wasn't in its usual parking space.

Iron Mechanic seemed to guess where his thoughts were. "Had to send it to the lower basement level for repairs," he explained, leading them deeper into the garage. "Flashbolt brought it back with two punctured tires, a broken headlight, and a cracked rear window."

"God," Scratch swore. "That man cannot drive to save his freakin' life."

"I love that car," Push moaned. "What the hell is Flashbolt's problem?"

"If he keeps that shit up, he'll be walkin' to his next assignment," Iron Mechanic assured them. "I've done told those capes upstairs, he can't keep comin' down to my garage expecting to walk outta here with whatever he wants, then bringin' it back in twenty pieces."

"It's a wonder he still has his license," Scratch muttered as they rounded a corner. "Maybe the story about him and that senator was true after all."

Push laughed but then stopped short when he saw the vehicle Iron Mechanic was pointing at. The man had led them into a side area of the garage where five cars were parked in a row and gestured to the truck in the center. Neither Push nor Scratch could believe it.

"It's already been outfitted," Iron Mechanic said. "We confiscated it about a month ago from a drug bust. I was gonna give it a whole new paint job, but Booster Hawk and Patriot Arrow insisted I keep it the way it was. Now, it may look slow, but that baby has eight gears of speed under the hood, and the keys are already in it."

The truck in question was painted a bright neon shade of canary yellow. The windows had been tinted dark, and on the back of the tailgate, the words "Pussy Wagon" had been emblazoned. The same words covered the roof as well, and though Push could not see clearly from the angle he stood at, he bet they were on the hood too. Bright pink flames decorated the bottom and sides.

It was an eyesore on wheels.

Iron Mechanic was already gone when Push looked around. "He cannot be serious," Push groaned, though it was clear the mechanic intended for them to ride out of there in the seizure-inducing monstrosity. "The worst part of Quentin Tarantino's films has just come to life before my very eyes!"

Scratch, meanwhile, was laughing his ass off. "I love it," he wheezed between gasps. "Let's go."

Push was walking back toward the main part of the garage. "Iron!" he shouted angrily. "What gives, man?"

"Sorry, Push," the Mechanic said without turning around. "We've got thirteen slated for re-mods, five for repairs, and half of the ones remaining were put on hold for later missions. Out of what's left, that's the best I can give you."

Push was quietly cursing under his breath as he strode back toward the Pussy Wagon. Scratch was already inside on the passenger seat, strapping on his seat belt. The truck had an extended cab in the back, and the interior smelled new. Either it wasn't very old, or Iron Mechanic had taken special care in outfitting this one.

Probably the latter. It was known among the RLSA that Iron Mechanic had an active social calendar when he wasn't fixing cars for superheroes. The man might not have seen much street action recently, but his bedroom had the coming and goings of a Chicago train station.

It was enough to make even Push jealous.

The onboard computer came to life the moment Push turned the key in the ignition. "Please identify yourselves," a female voice demanded.

Scratch quickly reached over and punched in both of their security clearance codes. "Thank you," the voice said, more softly now. "Designates Scratch and Push, you have been authorized by the Michigan State Police to ignore all traffic lights and road signs for the duration of this mission. In addition, strobe lights have also been permitted. You may activate them now."

Scratch punched the button to activate the built-in strobes as Push steered them out of the garage. Rush hour traffic was waiting for them the minute they pulled out of the garage hub. Without blinking, Push brought the truck up onto the curb, driving over the sidewalk into the perpendicular lane they were cut off from.

"What?" he asked. "We were told to get there as soon as possible and ignore all traffic lights."

"Um, I didn't say anything," Scratch replied. "I'm just wondering if the Cape Cabinet meant for us to ignore the road."

"It was implied," Push insisted, pressing down the gas before shouting, "Move aside, slowpokes! Pussy Wagon coming through!"

THE drive down the interstate toward Grand Rapids was uneventful, save for the shocked looks they received from a handful of families on road trips. At one point, they were passed, perhaps inevitably, by a Corvette full of what appeared to be college co-eds. More than one of them pointed and laughed. Scratch just smiled and gave the girls a light wave before the Corvette blazed on past them.

"We're coming up near the crash site," Scratch said while double-checking the GPS readout. "Just a few more miles up ahead."

The place was still crawling with cops as they approached. Push was already reaching into his jacket for his ID as they slowed to a stop. One of the officers on the scene approached as Push lowered his window.

"Association members Push and Scratch," Push said in lieu of a greeting. Scratch was holding up his ID badge as well. "We heard there was some sort of attack on a transit."

The officer shifted uncomfortably for a moment before turning around. "Sarge!" the young man called out across the road. "You'd better come see this."

The sergeant waddled toward the truck a moment later. The overweight man was sweating despite the cold weather. Push noticed that the man kept giving the truck once-overs in time with his footfalls.

"Can I help you boys?" he asked.

"We were sent to check on a possible operative who disappeared when the transit was attacked," Push explained, putting his ID badge away.

The sergeant chuckled. "Nobody said anything to me about a cape-flapper being on this," he replied, pointing to the wrecked black van behind him.

The van in question was armored and looked like it had caught fire. Now that Push had a proper view of it, he noticed that the ground surrounding it was scorched as well. The tar of the road had burn marks, almost like skids, except that these didn't bear the pattern of tire treads. Before the sergeant continued, Push recognized the van for what it was.

"This here was a prison transport vehicle," the man finished.

"Our mistake, then," Push said, giving the man a nod. "We'll be on our way, if it's all the same to you."

"Smart move, boys," said the sergeant, wearing a stiff grin as Push rolled the window back up.

Scratch was looking back the entire time as they drove off. "That was a prison transport van," he repeated. "They were carrying a prisoner."

"The Cabinet said it was an X Project recruit," Push reminded him, turning sharply onto an exit that would take them into Grand Rapids. "No wonder they were so tight-lipped about it."

"Either they think we're idiots...."

"Or they didn't want word to get around in the Association about who it was," Push finished, slowing down a little as they came off the exit ramp. "Knowing the Cabinet, probably both!"

Scratch began messing with the GPS computer as Push drove. "I'm searching for the hotel they booked us," he explained. "The Cabinet said there would be a dossier on the X Project applicant. If we're going to find him, we'll need to see that first. Right now, we don't even know for sure if it's a man or a woman."

"Sounds great," Push said, keeping the lights on as he drove the Pussy Wagon in and out of the row of kamikaze drivers. "Bring up the audio so the computer can navigate me."

Scratch fiddled with a few more buttons, then whistled. "Sweet," he said. "Um, we've got a hotel room at the Amway Grand Plaza Hotel!"

Push rolled his eyes in answer, but followed the computerized voice as it began guiding him through the city toward their destination.

The Amway Grand Plaza was everything the name suggested, exterior-wise. As they drove into the parking lot, Push felt himself beginning to warm up to the idea of driving the Pussy Wagon, especially as he saw a few appalled expressions on people's faces. To the valet's credit, he said nothing as Push climbed out of the truck, not even about the way they were dressed. After all this time, the sight of people in circus outfits was losing some of its shock value.

Of course, none of that meant they would have an easier time checking in. There was a line at the reception area, and no one volunteered to let them go on ahead. If anything, Push noticed more than a few civilians clam up as they drew close. One old woman gave Scratch a look of pure disdain before practically shoving her nose into the back of the suited man in front of her in defiance. Push and Scratch simply waited for the line to thin down.

"Do you have any luggage?" a nice-looking receptionist asked the moment they stepped up.

"No," they each answered.

In response, the woman reached under the counter for their room key and handed it off to them without another word. "Your room is located on the thirtieth floor on the north side. Thank you, and we hope you enjoy your stay."

"She was cute," Scratch noted as they headed for the elevator.

"I'll get her number for you later, if you'd like," Push offered, as they waited for the elevator car to clear out. "She looks like a screamer to me."

"Thanks," Scratch replied gratefully. "But I'll pass."

Push frowned and waited until they were in the elevator and had pushed the button for their floor before speaking again. "In case you change your mind, same rules as before apply," he stated. "No more than an hour, and try to wait until we're done here."

"I'd buy you that He-Man action figure you've wanted for the last year in exchange for two," Scratch said, having apparently changed his mind in the time it took for the elevator to rise. "It's been a little while."

"For that, I'll give you two hours and first dibs on the shower."

"Deal."

Their room was down the second hall on the left. Push had to admit, it was a very nice place. He'd never been comfortable with the Association setting him up in such swank housing, but as Scratch once put it, they might as well enjoy things while they lasted.

Scratch shrugged out of his long coat first, tossing it aside on the bed. It made noticeable clacking noises as the mattress shuffled under the weight.

"I'm always afraid one of those will go off when you do that," Push said worriedly as he laid his own jacket neatly folded on the bed spread.

"That only happened twice," Scratch reminded him. "And you were nowhere near me when they went off. Besides, it was just the smoke bomb and glue grenade. I've never had the eight-ball explode on me accidentally."

"I'm not reassured," Push insisted.

A state-of-the-art laptop had been left on a table near the window. Push went over to it and brought the machine online while Scratch relieved himself in the bathroom. When he emerged a few minutes later, Push had all the information they needed on-screen.

"You're not going to like this," Push said, looking up as Scratch came toward him.

"When do I ever?" Scratch countered. "How bad can it be?"

"This bad," he said, turning the laptop around so Scratch could see.

Scratch frowned down at the profile picture on the screen. "I know the face," he mused. "But I can't place it."

"Wrath," he explained, moving the laptop back to where it faced him. "The youngest member of the Deadly Seven, remember?"

"Shit!" Scratch exclaimed, taking a seat next to Push so he could read alongside him. "He was on that transport? What were those idiots thinking?"

"A better question might be, what stunt did they have to pull to get him out?" Push replied ominously, moving his finger around the touchpad. "The last I heard, Wrath was denied parole each time he faced the board. How does the Association expect us to babysit a former contract killer?"

"You're the one with the superpower," Scratch reminded him. "I guess they figured you were the right one for the job."

"Wonderful," Push grumbled as he scrolled through the documents. "It's all here, at least. Information about the trial, where he was captured, his work with the other Deadly Seven in New Orleans before the police finally busted their operation."

"Does it say anything about his real name?" Scratch wondered. "I heard that was a big deal back when he was on trial."

"Nothing," Push said flatly. "In fact, there's nothing in here about his life before he joined the Deadly Seven."

A few more minutes passed with them silently perusing the files. "Here's one other thing," Push said hopefully. "The prison fixed him with a tracer before he left the facility."

"If he escaped," Scratch said warily while Push brought up the tracking software, "then he's probably found it by now."

Sure enough, the grid registered no blips. Push swore as he shoved the laptop away. "Let's go through what we know so far, then," he said. "We know that the escort was a prison transport, and that it was carrying a dangerous criminal."

"Who's been in jail for the past ten years or so," Scratch added. "He's probably hungry right now."

"He'd need money," Push pointed out. "And a place to stay. There was nothing in the files that suggested he has connections to people in Grand Rapids."

"Um, who operates here in Grand Rapids?" Scratch wondered, bringing the laptop over to him. "If we can get in touch with anyone who has info on the local crime syndicate, they might be able to point us in the right direction."

"Mind-Bender," Push said at once. "He's the hypnotist, remember? I introduced you to him at the convention last year. He kept wanting to hypnotize me."

"He's listed right here in the directory," Scratch said, nodding. "And it has his cell phone number. Feel like giving him a call?"

Five minutes later, Push flipped his phone closed. "Got his voice mail," he said. "He was busy doing a show at a children's hospital, but I left a message for him to call me back."

"So, what are we going to do now?"

"Get back in the Pussy Wagon and drive around," Push said, reaching for his coat. "Who knows? We may get lucky. It beats sitting up here on our asses, anyway."

Push called downstairs so that the valet would have the truck waiting for them. Before leaving the lobby, he remembered to pick up the receptionist's phone number for Scratch, who pocketed it graciously. Outside, an eight-year-old boy stood beside the front doors of the hotel, watching them climb into the truck.

"Nice wheels!" he called out, grinning.

"Thanks," Push said, not looking around.

"Stay in school, kid," Scratch added before shutting his door.

Push was laughing as they drove away. "Stay in school? Is that the best you could come up with?"

"Who knows?" Scratch replied, laughing himself. "Maybe he'll have a Pussy Wagon of his own someday."

"Along with a nasty case of crabs."

It was a slow crawl around the city. They weren't running the strobe lights this time around. The Cabinet had gotten them authorization to use them, but Push suspected that had been just for getting there. Still, if he needed them, he and Scratch could always apologize for the misunderstanding later. For the moment, they hadn't found a trace of their missing fugitive.

"He's probably avoiding the more populated areas," Scratch reasoned.

"Yeah," Push agreed. "But I still want to get the local hot spots out of the way. At the very least, we can mark them off first."

Across the pedestrian Blue Bridge, Push noticed a young woman carrying a small plastic bag being approached by a young man in a hoodie. Slowing the truck to a crawl, he ignored the angry honks from behind and watched closely. Sure enough, the thug made his move a minute later and snatched the bag out of the woman's hand.

"Purse snatcher," he said, pointing. "Or bag snatcher, anyway."

"No cops around," Scratch said, sweeping the area with his gaze. "Should we take it?"

"Might as well!"

Push floored it, hitting the strobes as he spun the wheel and raced off after the punk, who was on foot. When they were a few feet behind, separated by the asphalt, the snatcher noticed the truck following and cut across the street toward an alley. Push, however, was not about to let someone outrace him on foot. Putting the pedal to the metal, he gunned the engine and raced diagonally through traffic, making it to the mouth of the alley right after the punk disappeared into it. Scratch already had his door open and was vaulting over the hood as Push came to a stop.

The alley, sure enough, was a dead end. Nothing lay up ahead but a solid concrete wall too steep to climb and lacking any hand grips. The punk turned around and stared at them.

"Easy way or the hard way," Push said. "But you're dropping the bag right now."

In answer, the punk drew a pistol out of the back of his jeans. "Right," Push said, rolling his eyes. "I guess fame isn't everything. You want to take this one?"

"By all means," Scratch said, gesturing forward, "you go on ahead."

Push flicked his hand as the punk squeezed the trigger. The gun went off but was already sailing far back behind them in an arc. The bullet ricocheted off the side of one of the buildings as Push concentrated. People had asked before how his powers worked. In fact, he'd been interrogated on it more than once when he'd first joined the RLSA. The truth of the matter was he didn't know. In his mind, he pictured it like a great big bubble flying through the air, only this bubble was made up of his willpower and desire for action to take place.

No one else could see it. Even Push couldn't, not exactly. He could see it in his mind, and the air almost appeared to distort a little as he thrust out his opened palm. The force bubble struck the punk and knocked him backward on his ass. When he landed, there was an unexpectedly loud crunch sound that filled the alley.

"At times like this," he said softly while Scratch stepped forward, "I wish I had a catch phrase."

"I hope whatever he stole was worth it," Scratch mused, picking up the plastic bag. A second later, he dropped it and cringed. "It's dirty diapers."

"What?"

Push marched over to where Scratch was standing. The bag had fallen open when his partner dropped it, exposing the rank contents. Push turned away, feeling sick to his stomach at the sight.

"Terrific," he muttered, keeping his nose turned up and away. "Should we even bother calling it in?"

"You know the drill," Scratch reminded.

"Right."

Push made the mistake of looking down at the bag once more. The punk was coming to, so Push sent the bag toward him with a telekinetic shove before walking back to the Pussy Wagon. It took the cops thirty whole minutes to show up. By that point, Scratch had taken to sitting on the boy so he didn't try running away again.

"They didn't look happy," Scratch grumbled as they drove off, leaving the cops to handle the rest. "Also, that felt like a waste of time. I want to wash my hands soon."

"It's a slap on the wrist at worst," Push pointed out, turning into a gas station so Scratch could clean up. "We just gave their department more paperwork to fill out. Pick me up a chocolate bar while you're in there, once your hands are clean."

Scratch wasn't gone for very long. When he came back, there was a Nutella bar stuffed into the front pocket of his long coat, which he handed to Push without a word. Push accepted it graciously as he steered the Pussy Wagon back into the congested Grand Rapids traffic.

The next few hours were not pleasant ones for either of them. Twice, Push thought he saw someone who might have been their target. The first one turned out to be a guitar player strumming for spare change on a park bench. Push spotted him moments before the musician sat down. The second one was just a random goth kid arguing with a police officer about a parking ticket. Given their luck with the cops thus far, Push decided not to intervene. Besides that, the youth wasn't doing anything other than shouting angrily, and if the meter maid couldn't handle that, she was in the wrong career.

Further impeding their search were a number of recurring incidents. An old lady flagged them down as they were rounding a corner for help with her car, which had a flat tire. Push had to wonder what sort of elderly woman was willing to hail a truck called the Pussy Wagon for assistance, even if she did somehow spot them through the tinted windows. The answer to that question came as she was climbing back into her vehicle.

"By the way, boys!" she called out cheerfully. "I love cats too!"

"Don't tell her," Scratch said, holding out his grease-stained hands as he walked back to the truck. "It wouldn't be worth it. Also, can we stop so I can wash my hands again?"

At their second pit stop, Push got out to go to the bathroom. As they emerged from the restroom together, a man wearing a hood over his head pointed a gun in their direction from in front of the counter.

"Don't move!" he shouted, before flinching at the sight of them.

"Do you want this one?" Push asked calmly.

"Sure," Scratch said. "You took the last one, so I guess that's only fair."

"I said, don't move!" the gunman yelled as Scratch approached him.

"Fine," said Scratch as he fiddled with something in his jacket. "Oh, crap...."

A yellow billiard ball fell out of one of the inner pockets. The gun-toting thug glanced down just as the ball reached Scratch's boot. In the blink of an eye, Scratch kicked it forward. The ball grazed the gunman and struck the edge of the counter, breaking off a piece of it as it shot up toward the roof, striking the edge of a plastic sign hanging down and putting a large dent in it.

The punk with the gun was just turning to see what had happened as the ball arched back down toward Scratch, who was whipping out the two halves of his cue stick. With a practiced spin, he tightened the two halves together and raised the tip as the ball came down at his face. With a quick jab of the cue stick, he sent the ball through the air again, this time in a straight line for the gunman's head. The yellow billiard ball struck him right between the eyes as he turned back around, cracking the upper bridge of his nose in the process.

"Snookered," Scratch punned. "Why don't you call this one in, Push?"

The squad of cops that showed up for this one looked even less happy. It amazed Push sometimes how quickly word got around. No one needed to speak with them since the security cameras caught everything, so they left before the mood worsened.

"At least I didn't have to wash my hands this time," Scratch pointed out.

Following that, the duo managed to make it several miles down the road before being flagged over yet again. Some poor kid's cat had gotten stuck up in a tree.

"Of all the..." Push grumbled. "Does this kind of stuff really happen, or is it only when we're around?"

"Probably the latter," Scratch said. "You take this one, though. I'm not much of a tree-climber, and you're the one who was raised out in the country."

"Not every part of Alabama is rolling countryside," Push countered, even as he made his way up to the tree. "I don't even like cats."

The feline in question felt the same sentiment about Push, apparently. When the superhero finally came back down with the growling cat in his arms, he was covered in scratches.

"Thanks, mister," the girl said, taking the cat in her arms. "I thought you'd be happy to help because of your truck. Is that why you call it the Pussy Wagon?"

Push's mouth fell open. "Yes!" both he and Scratch answered before turning around quickly and leaving.

As Push shifted the truck into gear, he felt his cell phone vibrate. "I just got an emergency message from the Chicago headquarters," he told Scratch, slipping the phone back into his jacket pocket. "They're telling us to head back to the room immediately."

"Now?" Scratch frowned. "Um, but we haven't found our escaped convict yet."

"I know," said Push pointedly as they hit a red light. "Goddammit! Why do we always land on these things?"

"Maybe there's a message for us on the computer," Scratch theorized while they waited. Push glared at the light impatiently, trying to will it to change. His powers, of course, didn't work that way, but he'd always dreamed of one day having that ability and never stopping for traffic again.

"They could message either of us through our phones," Push pointed out as the light changed to green. "Or send it through the onboard computer in the truck. Why make us go back to the hotel room?"

"Any number of reasons," Scratch replied. "The first thing that comes to mind is them wanting to dick around with us."

"Yeah, really."

The Pussy Wagon had a much more difficult time getting back to the hotel. By the time they pulled up, Push was in a foul mood. Passing the keys to the valet without a word, he noted that the young boy from before wasn't around before passing through the doors. Scratch gave a brief nod to the receptionist, who responded by smiling. Push noticed her watching him after Scratch turned away, however.

As they departed the elevator into their floor, Push almost got run over by a room service waiter pushing a metal cart. It dawned on him that the man had been coming from the direction of their hotel room. That shouldn't have been enough to make him worry, but then he saw their room door up ahead hanging open. As Push ran forward, the door slammed shut. Dragging out his key, he shoved the card into the slot, then waited for Scratch to catch up. Together, the two flung it open and stepped in with their weighted cue stick and bo staff drawn.

Inside the room, a round-faced man roughly the same age as Push looked up from the steak laid out in front of him on the table. His black hair was drawn back in a makeshift ponytail. A knife and fork were in his hands, with a piece of steak cut off and speared through the fork's prongs. Snickering, he calmly went back to his meal as Push and Scratch lowered their weapons. Wrath, the man they'd been searching for, was eating steak in their room.

Wearing a pair of Push's boxers.

CHAPTER
TWO

THERE was a basket on the table just beyond Wrath's plate. It was loaded down with buffalo wings, each one saturated with hot sauce. To the left of it was a smaller basket full of buttered rolls, and on the right was an opened bottle of Pinot Noir. Wrath's wine glass was half-empty, and it looked as though the bottle was on its way to the recycling bin.

Push took in the spread. "You ordered room service?"

Wrath nodded as he stuck the bite of steak on his fork into his mouth. "The Association told me to order whatever I wanted and put it on the hotel's tab. I was hungry."

"No kidding," Scratch said.

"Wait, you've heard from the Association?" Push placed his hands on his hips and glared at Wrath skeptically. "Since when?"

"Since I called them," he said before swallowing. "They told me what hotel room you guys were staying in and that I should make myself comfortable."

"In Push's boxers," Scratch noted.

Wrath shrugged. "There was nothing for me to wear but the prison uniform, and it was a mess after the transport van crashed. The Association said they would be sending me some clothes soon."

"So the van was attacked?" Push asked, sitting down across from him.

"Just outside of town," Wrath said, gesturing out the window as he went back to his meal. "I was riding in back when something hit us."

Wrath finished off his steak and began reaching into the basket for the wings. "What happened after the van was attacked?" Push asked. The man was being awfully calm. He found it highly annoying.

"The van flipped over," Wrath said between bites of spicy chicken. "When I came to, someone was tearing the doors off their hinges. The guards were screaming, so I burned the chains off me and blasted the doors open."

"Why?" Scratch wondered.

Wrath gave him a look. "Whoever ran the van off the road wanted me dead. I wasn't thrilled with the idea of sitting around waiting for them to take me out."

"What made you think they had come to kill you?" Push asked insistently. "They could have been coming to spring you."

"I was already being released," Wrath said pointedly, not looking up. "Why would someone want to break out a free man? Besides, people were trying to kill me all the time when I was locked up. You start to recognize the signs after a while."

"Like people running a prison transport van off the road?" Scratch asked jokingly.

"Exactly," Wrath replied in a dry tone. "There are plenty of people in New Orleans with enough clout to try to have me killed. I figured one of them wanted to take a stab at it, so I took off into the woods, then looped back toward town and went looking for a phone."

Push exchanged looks with his partner. "What about the van?" he asked. "Were you the one who set it on fire?"

Wrath frowned over a chicken wing. "The van was fine when I escaped," he answered. "Aside from it being upside down, I mean. If someone set fire to it, that happened after I got away."

"And the tracer?"

Wrath turned to Scratch. "What tracer?"

"Must have been destroyed when the van crashed," Push mused, not taking his eyes off Wrath. "He could have lost it in the woods, though."

Wrath sighed. "I'm getting sloppy," he muttered, putting the half-eaten chicken wing down. "It's getting to where I don't realize it when someone has tagged me."

Scratch actually smiled.

"Are we done with the interrogation?" Wrath asked, reaching for his wine glass. "I'd like to take a shower."

"Go ahead," Scratch said. "I think I'll grab one when you're done."

Push kept a close eye on Wrath as the man crossed the suite, waiting until the bathroom door shut before speaking again. "You're being awfully friendly," he noted, giving his partner a hard stare. "Especially considering we spent all afternoon running around town looking for him."

"Um, well," Scratch replied helplessly as he reached for one of the rolls. "He's going to be working with us for a while. The Cape Cabinet wanted us to show him the ropes, so we might as well try to start off on the right foot."

Push groaned. "I had completely forgotten about that," he muttered, burying his face in his hands. "Do they honestly believe this guy can be rehabilitated?"

"It's the Cape Cabinet," Scratch pointed out, munching happily on his roll. "They'll believe anything if it gets them what they want."

"Why didn't he run?" Push wondered, after a moment. "I can't figure it out. I thought for sure he would have made tracks for New Orleans, or tried to find one of his teammates."

"Um, I'm actually more curious about the van," Scratch said, wiping his hands on a napkin. "The van looked like it had been set on fire, and there were scorch marks on the surface of the road. That whole area looked like a small war had erupted. Why do you think he lied about running off into the woods?"

"No clue," said Push, eying one of the wings hungrily. "Maybe he was worried about going back to prison?"

Scratch thought on that for a moment. "You could be right," he said, shrugging. "Anyway, it's really not our problem. Stuff like that is for the Cape Cabinet to decide."

Push hadn't taken his eyes off the basket of hot wings the whole time. "I'm pretty sure they aren't poisoned," Scratch told him. "He wouldn't have eaten one of them first if that were the case."

"No thanks," said Push, looking away. "I think I'll order something else."

WRATH came out of the bathroom wearing nothing but a towel. Push hated to admit it, but the man was in terrific shape. Apparently, Wrath had spent a great deal of time while in prison maintaining his physique. The firm pecs and eight-pack abs were marred only slightly by a light dusting of dark hair. The long strands hanging past his shoulders framed the man's face perfectly. Push caught himself staring and quickly looked away. The last thing he needed was to start lusting after a convicted criminal, even if the man did resemble something like sex on two legs. As Scratch got up to use the shower next, Push caught himself trying to remember if there was anything about Wrath's sexuality in his profile.

It took Push by surprise that he could watch his best friend head for the bathroom without picturing him naked anymore. It didn't stop his cock from stiffening slightly, but Push could at long last rein in his feelings. He and Scratch had been partners for years. After all this time, he could finally sleep semi-comfortably in the same room with the man without lusting after him like a horny yard dog. It would be a bad idea to start drooling over the convict now, even if the droplets of water cascading down Wrath's stomach as he walked made Push want to reach over and lick them away with his tongue.

Push realized with a humiliated blush just how far his thoughts had traveled. Clearly, it was past time for him to get laid. Instead of a collectable figure, he should probably have Scratch pose as bait to lure in a quick fuck for himself this time around.

A knock at the door shook Push out of his thoughts. Wrath was watching him closely, as if waiting for something. When Push didn't move, he stood up out of the chair, but Push quickly rose and made for the door. A hotel staff member greeted him, holding up a neatly-pressed suit inside plastic covering for him to sign for.

Push gave his signature and took the suit without tipping the guy. Once he was gone, Wrath came forward to look over his new clothes.

"A monkey suit," he mused sardonically. "I shouldn't be surprised."

"It's probably for when you stand in front of the Cape Cabinet," Push informed him, handing it over to the man, hoping he would change quickly. "They'll want to speak with us as soon as we get back."

Wrath just stood there quietly, looking neither pleased nor put out by his outfit.

"You wanna go ahead and get changed?" Push asked.

"Sure."

Without another word, Wrath threw the suit onto the bed and let his towel drop to the floor. Push's eyes widened as he caught a glimpse of the man in all his natural glory. Wrath didn't seem to notice Push's reaction as he quietly slipped into his clothes. When he was nearly finished, Scratch came out of the bathroom wearing a towel of his own, his costume tossed casually over one shoulder. Two years worth of conditioning came crashing down around Push as his best friend walked past half-naked while a raging hard-on threatened the integrity of Push's custom-made tights.

Push could not wait to leave.

Any hope of that was crushed a moment later. The laptop was still on, apparently. Wrath had moved it over to Push's bed, most likely when his food had arrived. The laptop gave a loud ping, signifying an e-mail message. When Push brought it up on screen, he nearly sent the machine flying with a telekinetic burst by accident.

"I don't believe this," he snarled, much louder than intended. "They want us to stay here!"

"What?" Scratch asked, looking up as he pulled the shirt down over his head. Thankfully, Scratch had been kind enough to put on underwear before losing his towel. Push forced the thought away and made himself focus on the task at hand.

"We just got a message from the Association," he explained, turning the laptop around so Scratch could see for himself. "They want us to stay here in Grand Rapids. There's been a string of bank robberies lately, and the police chief contacted them, wanting us to investigate."

"Um, what about…?" Scratch froze midsentence and glanced toward the edge of his bed where Wrath was lacing up his shoes as though neither of them were there.

In answer, Push turned the laptop back around to face him. "It says he's been given the same assignment as us," Push answered, his voice cold. "The three of us are working together on the same case."

Push noticed something at the bottom of the e-mail. "Oh, but here's some good news," he added sarcastically. "We've been given permission to order whatever we want from room service."

"Don't order the steak," Wrath warned them, getting to his feet. "They cooked it way too long."

Push looked back down at the screen. "We're supposed to meet with someone from the police department in a little over an hour. They're bringing all the information the cops have so far."

"Great," said Scratch. "We've got just enough time to order something for ourselves, then."

Wrath sat in a corner watching an old rerun of *Iron Chef America* while Push and Scratch phoned downstairs. Much as Push hated admitting it, he avoided the steak as Wrath suggested and went with a chicken sandwich instead. Scratch got a small plate of hot wings to go with his hamburger. When they were done ordering, Wrath stood up and took the hotel phone with him into the bathroom. Push was tempted to listen at the door, but Wrath came out a moment later with it in hand just as the commercial break finished running on TV, placed the phone back on the receiver, and sat down without saying a word.

It was awkward having him in the room, to say the least. Push was sorely tempted to send Wrath out, but he and Scratch were Wrath's babysitters. Keeping an eye on the man was part of their job now. None of that meant he had to like it, though.

Push and Scratch were busy chewing their food when there came a knock at the door. Without hesitating this time, Wrath stood up to answer it.

"It's a cop," he said calmly, turning around. "She's carrying a briefcase with her."

"She's early," Scratch said. "But go ahead and let her in."

The officer, a short but smartly dressed woman with dark curls, recoiled slightly at the sight of Wrath as she came through the door, but quickly recovered. Wrath didn't seem to notice and waited patiently until she was all the way in before letting the door slam shut.

"Detective Barbara Sawyer," the officer said, introducing herself. "They sent me to brief you on the bank robberies."

The briefcase she was carrying landed on the table, shaking it. "There have been four reported so far," she continued, opening it up. "The first happened after a malfunction in the security system of the People's Republic Bank. The sprinkler system went off on all three floors, flooding the place. At first, the manager thought it was just a malfunction, and when the sprinklers wouldn't shut off, he called the water department. They sent some people down to turn off the bank's water supply, but the men went in and never came out. After forty minutes of waiting, the manager called the police. We think over two hundred and fifty thousand dollars were stolen."

Wrath kept his distance as Push and Scratch looked over the photographs that Detective Sawyer handed to them.

"So the robbers were disguised as men working for the water department," Scratch summarized. "You still don't know how much they stole exactly?"

"It's hard to say," Detective Sawyer said, letting out a long sigh. "What money they didn't take was burned. Forensics says some type of chemical was sprayed all over the cash so that it would go up in seconds despite being wet."

"And the men?" Push asked, thinking hard.

"One blond, two redheads, and a skinhead with dark eyes," she rattled off. "All with fake identification. A traffic light camera got a profile of one, but his face doesn't match anything in our records. Either they're very good, or this was their first big robbery."

"It's too well-planned to be their first," Push insisted, moving his plate away. "Tell us about the second bank robbery."

"Stink bomb," she said, pulling a different file out of the briefcase. "Or rather, stink bombs, at the First National Bank of Grand Rapids. Same as before, on both floors. Both were piped through the ventilation system. The manager had been receiving threats from what he said was a terrorist group blaming him for the string of layoffs they've had in the last two years. He thought it was just a disgruntled employee playing a prank, but then the stink bombs went off."

"So everyone thought they were being gassed?" Scratch asked.

"That was the first assumption," Detective Sawyer said, eying one of his hot wings.

"Help yourself," Scratch told her, holding up his plate.

"Thanks," she said appreciatively, biting into it. "I had to skip lunch. Anyway, the manager panicked, pulled the fire alarm, then reported the bomb as a gas attack. SWAT shows up less than two minutes later, armed for bear, and goes inside."

"No one came out," Push guessed.

"The real surprise was when the *second* SWAT team showed up," she informed, after swallowing. "The manager figured out real fast that something was wrong. The crooks got away with at least five hundred thousand. The rest was hosed down with a bleach compound that bled the ink right off the paper."

Sawyer wiped her hands with a napkin before pulling out yet another file. "Number three happened at Citizen's District Bank. Someone delivered a twelve-layer cake to the lobby. Nobody thought anything strange about it until one of the customers noticed it was ticking."

"A gigantic cake gets delivered and no one finds that unusual?" Push wondered. "What sort of bank is that? Was the cake made entirely out of chocolate or something?"

"It was the bank president's birthday," she explained. "Most said that they thought one of the higher-ups was playing ass-kisser at first, until someone pointed out that cakes normally don't tick. So the bank gets evacuated, and pretty soon the bomb squad shows up."

"They go in and never come out?" Scratch offered.

Detective Sawyer shook her head sadly. "Actually, a second team showed up right after them along with a squad of cops. They claimed to be the real bomb squad, and by this point, the stories had started circulating. In all honesty, the manager really couldn't be blamed for what happened. There were cops with the second bomb team to validate their story, so when they said they were going in, no one stopped them."

Push frowned. "They were the bank robbers?"

"Yup," said Sawyer. "They used tranquilizer darts to subdue the real bomb squad. Pretty smart, really, since those things can be fired with an air pistol and won't be overheard. An estimated seven hundred and fifty thousand was missing. The rest was loaded into the vault, where the real bomb was placed."

"And bank number four?"

The last file folder was the heaviest. "The Bank of Illinois," Sawyer declared. "The biggest heist yet. Nearly a million dollars missing, the rest blanketed with some sort of glue. Completely unusable now."

"How did this one happen?" asked Scratch, flipping through some of the photos.

"This one," Sawyer began, rubbing her forehead wearily. "Somehow, a swarm of insects was released inside the bank. We still haven't figured out how that happened, but it started a panic. Customers were running out screaming before the alarm even sounded. By this point, the department knew to keep an ear out for any calls about weird things happening at banks, so we got there fast. We made sure the exterminators were who they said they were, and nobody went in or out afterward who wasn't supposed to."

"And?" Push asked, setting the photos down.

"That was it," she replied. "It was weird. Nothing was stolen and the money was untouched, so we thought maybe it was just a false alarm. Either that, or somebody else was having a go at pranking a bank. Next day, we get a call about the vault being covered in glue."

Push thought hard for a moment. "They needed to get everyone out of the bank," he said, running over the facts. "The police were getting wise to how the crimes were being committed, and wouldn't keep falling for the same trick."

"They must have sneaked in somehow during the panic, and hid somewhere," Scratch added, his brow wrinkled in concentration. "Um, how did the crooks get out of each bank? You never said."

"We don't know," said Sawyer, throwing her arms up in surrender. "No one can figure it out. We thought it might be an inside man. That's still a possibility, but from the looks of things, these guys aren't going to stop. I can't picture one gang having that many inside men for different banks. It doesn't quite add up."

"Are the banks owned by the same company?" Push wondered, still deep in thought.

"The same man," Sawyer corrected. "Dr. Arthur Stephens owns all four banks. We think he's the reason they were targeted."

"Someone has an agenda."

It had been so long since Wrath had last spoken that the sound almost made Push jump. Ever since the arrival of the detective, he'd been standing quietly off to the side.

Sawyer looked back to Push. "Who's he?"

Push opened his mouth, but Wrath beat him to it. "Wrath," he told her, pushing away from the wall. "Just Wrath. Former member of the Deadly Seven and, until today, Prisoner number 441822 of the East Arlenton Correctional Facility."

Wrath stopped in front of Detective Sawyer. When she didn't move away, he very carefully took her by the hand and raised the back of it up to his lips. "May I?" he asked politely.

The detective said nothing, but didn't jerk her hand away. Taking this as permission, Wrath placed the barest of kisses there before letting her go. Detective Sawyer rubbed the back of her hand like she'd been scalded.

Scratch watched the scene unfold with a cocked eyebrow. "I didn't know you knew anything about bank robberies."

"I was a criminal," Wrath reminded him, backing away slightly. "You'd be surprised the kind of things you can pick up on, even if you never participate."

"I'm sure," Push muttered.

Wrath glanced down at him. "Whoever is robbing the banks has a grudge against this Dr. Arthur Stephens," he explained. "But they aren't the ones pulling the strings."

"How do you figure?" Sawyer wondered, keeping her eyes on him.

"These robberies feel more like attacks to me," Wrath said, pointing to one of the photos on the table. "The banks aren't just being robbed. Their reputations are being ruined. The money that isn't stolen is destroyed in some way. This makes tracking the stolen money much more difficult, but it also means the banks are essentially without funds until the insurance companies can replace what was destroyed. Also, the attacks seem to come during the busiest hours of the day. These guys want people to talk about what happened. Money is stolen, the rest is ruined, and the bank's reputation takes a hard blow. This smells like retribution to me."

"They don't want to hurt Dr. Arthur Stephens financially," Sawyer said, coming on board Wrath's train of thought. "They want to ruin his reputation."

"But they aren't the ones behind it," Wrath finished confidently.

"How'd you figure that?" Scratch wondered.

"Yes, tell us," said Push, turning his chair around. "I'm curious to know."

"This takes time," Wrath explained, looking at Push specifically now. "Planning, and an intricate knowledge of the banks, staff, and security systems. Plus, the people doing the actual robbing are pros. They aren't wasting time."

"In and out," Scratch said, looking over the evidence splashed across the table. "Like clockwork."

"Mm." Wrath nodded. "This kind of operation takes money. You'd need a lot of funding to get something like this off the ground and keep it functioning. I have a hard time buying into the idea that someone with that sort of cash already would waste time on a petty revenge scheme."

"Rich people are eccentric," Push said, earning him the barest of smiles from Scratch. "People sometimes do strange things."

"For someone with that sort of money, though," Sawyer said, frowning, "it would be easier and simpler to buy out Dr. Stephens's property. Or sabotage him in some other manner."

"I imagine the doctor is in somebody's way," Wrath mused. "But they're in a position where doing as Sawyer suggested would pose too great a risk. Either that, or this is just the first part of a much bigger scheme. In any case, they have a patsy to take the fall for them, someone who also wants to see Stephens ruined and who will be arrested in their place in the end."

"Um, did anyone talk to this Stephens guy?" Scratch asked Sawyer. "Does he have any enemies?"

Sawyer laughed. "Does he ever!" she said. "We wanted to know the same thing. The next day, his secretary faxes an eighty-page list of people who could conceivably be holding a grudge against Stephens at the moment."

"Not a very popular guy, huh?"

Detective Sawyer gave Push a level gaze. "He's a very rich man. You don't get as much money as he has by being nice. Ten percent of Grand Rapids is owned by him personally. He has holding shares in another fifteen at least. This town practically runs on his blood."

"Ah," said Scratch, realizing something. "He was the one who told the police chief to contact the Association, wasn't he?"

Detective Sawyer froze.

"It's all right," Push told her quickly, giving Scratch a look. "We're used to that sort of thing by this point."

Detective Sawyer left shortly thereafter, not angry, but in a less than stellar mood. The briefcase she'd brought with her was still on the table, its contents scattered everywhere. Push and Scratch finished their meal as they looked through the details of each robbery.

"Wrath," Push called out. "Come here for a minute."

Wrath had gone back to his place against the wall. At Push's request, he obediently came over to the table.

"Sit down," said Push. "Help us out with this mess."

Taking the seat in front of him, Wrath began digging through the paper trail. A half hour of searching later, he stood up to remove his jacket.

"Getting anywhere?" Scratch asked.

"Not really," he replied. "I was hot. Most of this information is superfluous."

"There could still be something," Push insisted. "Keep digging."

"The cops would have gone over it with a fine-tooth comb," Wrath insisted, though he continued to rummage through the pile in front of him. "There's no way they would've passed all of this on otherwise, especially not to an outsider, and they definitely wouldn't have left it in a room with a convicted felon."

Push threw down the papers in his hand. "What do you suggest, then?"

"We need new information," Wrath said. "If you want to learn who is really behind all of this, we have to go straight to the source."

Scratch frowned. "You know someone we can ask?"

"Not really," Wrath said. "Grand Rapids is a long way from the Crescent City, but there are always places you can go for information, so long as you're willing to pay for it."

"Such as?"

Wrath gave Scratch and Push both a once-over. "Not like that," he said, before looking down at his fancy new suit. "Not like this, either."

IT WAS a while before any of them were ready. Push begrudgingly followed Wrath's directions through Grand Rapids and left the Pussy

Wagon several blocks from the neighborhood he guided them to. The place looked like a demilitarized zone.

"Why here?" Push wondered. "And how would you know about this place? I didn't think you'd ever operated in Grand Rapids before."

"Every town has a place like this," Wrath responded, leading them down a broken sidewalk with craters big enough for grass patches to grow through. "Even if it's just a couple of buildings. The trick is knowing where to look and how to ask."

"This explains the change of clothes," Scratch mused, looking himself over.

"We couldn't come into a place like this wearing spandex," Wrath replied, turning at a corner. "The locals would have murdered us on principle, and I hate having to agree with someone who's trying to kill me."

Scratch was wearing an old white muscle T-shirt that they'd let rest on the engine of the Wagon for a few minutes. It wasn't perfect, but it added to the effect nicely all the same. He was still wearing the blue jeans from his costume, minus the arm and leg guards. Push was the one with the biggest change. Wrath had suggested he wear all black, since every other color made him stand out like a sore thumb. The glasses on his face were, Push strongly suspected, just so the former supercriminal could have a chuckle at his expense. Wrath himself was in an all-black ensemble as well, yet much classier. A solid dark overshirt clung to his body around a black tee with slacks.

All of their clothes had come cheap but worked with him, which Push hoped was the entire point. He could see now why Wrath had put up a fight about them looking the part. The area of town they were in felt dangerous. It made his skin itch. This was the sort of place that didn't welcome outsiders.

"So, um, how come you get the fancier clothes?" Scratch asked as they reached the end of an alleyway.

"Because I could probably fit into a place like this," Wrath replied calmly, pointing to a door. "Neither of you could, unless you're with me. I'm pretty sure this is the place."

The door looked like it was halfway off its hinges. It was stuck on the side of a building covered in graffiti, next to a rotten wooden fence. Unless someone was looking for this place, Push doubted they'd find it. Wrath gave the door a nudge with his foot, forcing it open. Beyond it was a flight of stairs leading down into what appeared to be utter darkness.

The metaphor was not lost on him.

"Come on," said Wrath, taking the lead again.

Push wished he was wearing his goggles right now. He stumbled on the third step and nearly fell into Scratch, who was following behind Wrath. Thankfully, Push caught himself before sending his friend down the stairs in a tumble, but the trip brought him close enough to breathe in Scratch's scent near his neck. The smell made Push dizzy, and in the dark, he had to stop to keep from falling.

The others were waiting on him when he finally made it down. By now, Push's eyes had adjusted well enough to see better. He just hoped the others couldn't tell he was blushing.

"Ready?" Wrath calmly asked.

Push nodded, then remembered they might not be able to see. "I'm ready," he said. Even his voice sounded strained. He felt like such a loser. "Let's go," he insisted.

There was noise coming from somewhere. Wrath led them down a narrow corridor stretched out beside the stairs, where another door was hidden. This one was fastened securely, and was apparently where the sounds were coming from. Wrath turned the knob and stepped through. The light that spilled out into the hallway disoriented Push for a moment, but he followed after without a word.

All three emptied out into an open room. A few tables lay scattered about here and there, all occupied by patrons drinking cheap beer as they played cards. Others stood around pool tables that had small piles of cash resting under glasses. A bar stood against the wall on the far side. In a corner, a DJ was spinning records. Everything about it reminded Push of a speakeasy from an old film noir. For a moment, it felt like he'd gone back in time.

Wrath didn't waste time. He was already moving toward the bar. Push and Scratch followed quickly. Somehow, despite the people blocking their way, Wrath was able to glide across the room like a ghost. He was already sitting on a stool with a shot glass in hand when they reached him.

"What kept you?" he asked, raising the glass to his lips.

Both Push and Scratch ignored him and signaled the bartender for a beer. He gave each of them a look before glancing toward Wrath, then complying.

"Relax," he advised once they'd sat down. "You're here with me."

Wrath's eyes were sweeping the room as he downed his second shot. He ordered a third before the bartender got around to bringing Scratch and Push their beers. Both men were watching Wrath closely as he scanned the room a moment longer before swiveling his stool around to face the bar again.

"One more," he told the bartender, who quickly poured another shot of what Push thought was vodka into his glass.

Push watched as Wrath downed the glass, then tossed his head back. He held that same pose for a moment longer.

"Was it that good?" Scratch asked jokingly.

Wrath ignored him and continued to lean back slightly on his stool, as though the alcohol had helped him achieve nirvana. Most of the other bar patrons were going about their business, but every minute that ticked past, Push could feel a different pair of eyes drilling into him. If something bad happened, they were outnumbered, and their guide was more likely to leave them to the sharks than pitch in. Push had to fight back the urge to strangle the man. His better nature was on the verge of losing when Wrath suddenly turned back toward the room.

"There," he said, his voice barely a whisper. "The one heading off to the left."

Push didn't turn in time to get a good look, but he saw the shadow of a figure disappear through what looked like another door, even though he hadn't noticed one there when they'd come in.

Without a word, Wrath jumped down off his stool and headed for the door. Scratch glanced at Push for a moment, then saw the bartender was glaring at them expectantly. By the time they were done paying for their beer and Wrath's drinks and made their way back through the maze of a room, Wrath was already waiting for them at the top of the stairs.

"You guys take forever," he muttered. "You must spend more time driving than running."

Both men gave Wrath a hard glare.

"This way," he said, ignoring them. "We've got to catch up to that little twerp who was leaving the bar in a hurry. Chances are, he knows something."

"What makes you think he knows anything?" Push asked, catching up to Wrath.

"Because he left right after we got there," Wrath pointed out. "And it was obvious to everyone in the room that we were there to look for someone. It was only a matter of time before one of them ran. Now we have to find out whether he ran because he knows something we want to know, or because he has something we could use."

"Okay," said Push, staring at Wrath's back. "One last question. Why should Scratch and I trust you?"

Without turning around, Wrath calmly answered, "Because I know this area better than either of you ever will, and you need someone who understands how this kind of territory works if you want to find the guy behind those bank heists fast. However...."

Wrath stopped then and looked behind him. "I'm not the one in charge here," he finished, giving them both a look. "You two are. I'm just the guy who's out on parole, so if either of you has a better plan that doesn't involve so much walking, I'm all ears."

Push opened his mouth. What he'd been on the verge of saying, he wasn't sure, because Wrath suddenly went rigid and whirled around toward the mouth of the alley. Without thinking, Push lowered his head slightly in a defensive crouch as bright orange flames burst to life in the supervillain's hands. Two armed men stepped into the alley and took aim. Behind them, the door to the stairs was kicked open and out stepped the bartender, carrying an assault rifle.

Push turned to the bartender first. One quick telekinetic blast from his palm and the assault rifle went flying. Wrath let out a roar and opened up with a burst of flames that might as well have come out of a jet engine. The resulting combustion made Push's ears pop. When the fire died down, he saw both men rolling to a stop out in the street with smoke rising off their bodies. His first instinct was to check and make sure they were okay, but then Scratch went for the rifle. The bartender leaped forward at the same time, forcing Push to let loose with another telekinetic force bubble. This one was strong enough to blast the man back against the wall.

The crunch he made was sickening.

Wrath strode calmly toward the big man as though nothing out of the ordinary had happened. The bartender's eyes fluttered open seconds before Wrath seized him by the shirt, slamming him into the wall. Even as he rushed to stop him, Push couldn't help but feel impressed by the action. The bartender looked to be at least three hundred pounds, and a lot of that was muscle. The act should have left Wrath winded, but his breathing barely changed as he leaned forward into the larger man's face.

The bartender's eyes darted over to where the ground was scorched. "It can't be," he whispered. "I heard you was bein' let out on parole. They said you was goin' legit!"

Something flashed in Wrath's eyes, and he let the man go. "Never," he snarled, as the big man landed on his ass. "Ever…!"

Fire licked between Wrath's fingers as he clenched them into fists. The red flames quickly flashed to blue. "Call me *'legit'*!" he screamed.

The blue flames were joined by a burst of red and orange, which flowed up from Wrath's shoes until he was little more than a column of pure fire. Push and Scratch both jumped back out of the way to avoid being burned. Scratch took aim with the assault rifle but hesitated in pulling the trigger. Push held his palm up and almost sent Wrath flying, but then the bartender shouted.

"Stop! I'll tell you whatever you wanna know!"

The fires around Wrath died slightly. "Someone sent me a message," he hissed, his voice deep and snarling now. "They wanted me to join their little operation, rob a couple of banks. I'm done with petty crime, though, and these guys are giving boys like me a bad name. Where can I find them?"

"You...." The bartender was shielding his face from the heat. "You mean the Pranksta?"

Wrath lowered his arms, and the fire surrounding him slowly went out. "Is that what he's calling himself these days?"

"Yeah," the bartender said, sweating bullets. "I think so. People 'round here, they say there's some cat in town callin' hisself the Pranksta Gayngsta. Nobody in my place'll work for him, but they say he pays pretty well. Times like this, most people will work for anybody if the cash flows regular."

Wrath shook his head. "Pranksta Gayngsta," he muttered. "What has crime come to?"

The bartender looked over toward Push for a second. Wrath noticed and lit up a fireball in one palm. "Eyes on me, big guy," he said, leaning forward. "Any idea where I can find this bozo?"

The bartender's eyes never left the ball of flame. "Nobody who does work for him will talk about the cracker," he said. "But I hear stuff. They say he's got a place set up in back of the Tin Woodman. It's out on 25th."

Wrath closed his hand in reply, and the fireball went out. Straightening, he walked over to Scratch, who was still holding the assault rifle like he might open fire. Push noticed that Wrath kept his hands visible the whole time.

"May I?" Wrath asked Scratch politely.

Scratch hesitated a moment, but eventually conceded. Wrath took the rifle out of his hands carefully, then held it up where they could see. Touching the metal in the center, he began heating it with one hand until it glowed red. The bartender watched, frowning, but not getting up. When Wrath was satisfied with his work, he turned so the bartender could see, and bent the gun in half.

"It's been a pleasure doing business with you," he said, tossing the gun aside.

Once they were out of the alley, Push sighed, then moved to check on the two men that Wrath had blasted. Neither one looked like they had moved.

"They should be fine," Wrath said. "I remembered not to give them a full blast."

Push didn't answer, and checked both of their vitals. "They're alive," he confirmed, speaking to Scratch specifically. "But they've got some nasty burns. He could have killed them."

"They were armed," Wrath reminded. "And wouldn't have hesitated."

"And if either of them were dead right now," Push said forcefully, "you'd be waiting for a police car to take you back to prison."

Wrath's eyes narrowed. "Duly noted," he said crisply. "What should we do next, sir?"

Push ignored him. "Have you ever heard of the place that guy was talking about?" he asked Scratch. "The Tin Woodman?"

"He said it was on 25th," Wrath added, earning him another glare from Push.

"Should we go there now?" Scratch asked, looking toward Wrath.

"We can tell the Association what we know so far," Push said. "But it sounds like a good idea. If nothing else, we can have a look around first and see what kind of place we're dealing with. Assuming our new charge isn't too drunk."

They were walking back to the Pussy Wagon before Wrath answered. "I'm not drunk," he informed them. "Alcohol burns out of my system real fast."

"Ha ha," Push retorted. "Let's get out of here before the locals start shooting at us."

"I don't think we have to be too worried," Scratch told him. "From the sound of things, the people around here aren't happy with this Pranksta guy."

"It's always nice to do something that will help the community," Wrath joked.

When they reached the Pussy Wagon, Scratch let Wrath climb in the back before getting in. Push was already punching something into the onboard computer.

"Calling the cops?" Scratch asked, sounding confused.

"Radioing for an ambulance," Push corrected. "We can't leave those two lying there in the street like that."

"They'll be long gone before the ambulance shows up," Wrath said.

"He's right," Scratch agreed. "If they're conscious, they've probably already left."

Push frowned, angry at himself and both of them for being right, then closed the window. "Fine," he said between his teeth. "But I'm reporting to the Association before we go any further tonight."

"Okay," Scratch said. "I don't have any objections."

"Neither do I," Wrath added.

"Nobody asked you," Push growled.

The silence that followed inside the Pussy Wagon was deafening. Push's hands gripped the steering wheel as he worked the truck through traffic over to 25th Avenue. Every few minutes, Scratch would glance at him. Push could feel his roommate's eyes on him. It was making his cock hard. He was sick of getting erections at inappropriate moments like an eighth grader. He'd thought he would be over this by now. Scratch wasn't interested in him that way, and he was fine with it.

So why wouldn't his cock go down?

Spotting a parking space, Push rolled into it, beating out a couple in a fancy sports car who blew the horn for a good fifteen seconds before moving on. Push undid his seat belt and jumped out without a word. Scratch followed, leaving Wrath behind in the backseat.

"Push," Scratch called out. "Wait up."

Wishing he were anywhere else in the world, Push slowed to a stop behind the truck and waited for his friend to catch up.

"Um, Push," Scratch said, leaning up against the back. "Is everything all right, man?"

Push sighed. "No," he admitted. "And I'm sorry."

Scratch looked taken aback by his bluntness, but quickly recovered. "Okay," he said. "Um, what's wrong?"

That was the last thing Push wanted to talk about. "I don't like him," Push said instead, not lying outright. "He gets on my nerves, and I keep wondering whether I'm going to have to put him down. I'm not used to having to worry about whether the people I'm working with are going to stab me in the back."

Scratch looked at the rear window. It was tinted, and with the sun going down, there was no way he could see through it. His eyes remained fixed on the spot where Wrath had been sitting when he'd gotten out for a moment.

"I don't think he's going to turn on us," Scratch said carefully. "He's a pretty smart guy, and stabbing us in the back will just get him sent back to jail."

"I've read his file," Push reminded. "Some of the stuff he's supposed to have done is pretty sick. I don't see how anybody could do that and move on afterward like it was no big deal."

Scratch didn't answer.

"Plus," he added, "the way they talk about him in that file, Wrath was always the one who was hard to control. The psych profile on him suggested that was how he got the name. Now, though, he's being way too calm. It's almost like he's waiting for something."

"You think he's messing with us." Scratch didn't phrase it as a question.

"I think he's got something planned," Push said. "And trying to figure out what that is has been making me nuts."

Scratch glanced behind them again. "I don't know what to say," he admitted. "But for right now, the guy's been pretty useful. He did find us this place."

"I know," Push agreed. "You've been awfully cozy with him."

Which was what really ate at Push, though he refused to acknowledge it aloud. Even under the darkening sky, it was easy for

Push to make out the row of abs the grease-stained muscle shirt clung to. Push wanted to reach out and brush his fingers over them. The sad thing was, Scratch might actually let him do it. The two had been roommates for a long time, and Scratch was never especially shy, or put off by the fact that Push was gay.

Push had never touched him. Before they'd met, Push's experiences with straight men had led him to conclude that they scared easily. In the beginning he hadn't planned on them being so close. They'd first bonded during the year of Association training. When Push had needed a place to stay after a particularly bad break-up, Scratch had offered the use of his apartment. And when the place was destroyed thanks to a battle with some gang-bangers out for revenge, the two had looked for a new place together like it was the most natural thing in the world to do.

It was not heavily advertised, but Push was a great big dork. He suspected the Cape Cabinet didn't want the world knowing their poster child was such a geek, even though the entire Association roster fit that particular description to a degree. Scratch, surprisingly, was just as bad as he was. The two collected figurines, read comics together, and sat up for hours watching cartoons when they weren't fighting bad guys. It had become something of a joke between them ever since the Association moved them both into full-time work. In so many ways, Scratch was the ideal man for Push.

But he was straight and would never feel the same way.

Just recently, Push had begun to acknowledge the fact and work toward accepting their relationship for what it was. He had worked so hard at keeping his friend at arm's length so Scratch wouldn't panic. Push knew better than to jeopardize the good thing he had. Now it felt like all his hard work was breaking apart in his hands, and though the man had done absolutely nothing to deserve it, Push was laying all the blame at Wrath's feet.

Raising up, Push rebounded off the tailgate of the truck, putting some distance between himself and Scratch in the process, and took a deep breath. Wrath wasn't to blame for what was wrong with him. That much was certain. He could handle this, if only for tonight. As soon as this assignment was over, he would ask the Cape Cabinet to reassign Wrath. Regardless of his emotional state at the moment, Push still didn't trust the man, and until he got himself under control again, Push didn't want to be around the ex-con any more than he had to.

"Sorry," he said quietly as Scratch gave him a hearty clap on the shoulder. "You didn't deserve that."

"I just figure giving him the benefit of the doubt is the lesser of two evils," Scratch explained, not put out at all. "He could always let us down, but this way, it's on his own head. Plus, I know you've got my back, so there's zero chance he'll get a chance to stick a blade there. Remember what happened to those punks who held up that liquor store?"

Push groaned. "Not one of my prouder moments," he replied. "I guess I kind of lost it when I saw you were down. It's a good thing none of them were hurt too badly."

"The one who got in the lucky shot had five broken bones," Scratch pointed out, grinning now. "You gave the other two concussions. The Cape Cabinet thought they were going to scream brutality."

"Good thing the store owner backed us up," Push said. "Come on. Let's get this over with so we can head back to Chicago. First, though, I want to grab something from the tool box."

Wrath was getting out of the truck as Push reached into the tool chest that was set in the truck bed next to the rear window. They'd stored their weapons and gear before leaving the hotel, just in case. It was the one thing Wrath hadn't argued over.

"You're changing," he noted.

"We're not going into the ghetto," Push pointed out. "And if we're going to do this, I want to be prepared, instead of getting caught with my pants down like before."

Wrath turned around and waited as Push yanked the shirt he was wearing up over his head. "Your call," he replied calmly.

Aside from one or two catcalls, Push slipped back into his costume without event. Scratch went next and, since he was already wearing half of his, dressed much faster. When they were ready, Scratch beat on the side of the truck to signal Wrath to turn around.

"I've been thinking about something," Scratch said as they worked their way down the street, keeping any eye out for the Tin Woodman.

"Wrath could use a costume. I mean, he can't fight crime in that monkey suit the Cape Cabinet sent him."

Push chuckled. "Yeah," he agreed, enjoying where this was going. "I mean, the way he's dressed right now is fine, I guess, but he really does need some type of outfit."

"One that strikes fear in the hearts of criminals everywhere?" Wrath inquired. "What would the two of you suggest?"

"I think you have the 'fear-striking' bit down, dude," Scratch said, glancing back at Wrath. "I thought the bartender was going to shit himself. I'm very impressed with your acting skills. Were you in some kind of prison theater program?"

"Ah, that," Wrath said, smiling. "No, I'm afraid the warden for East Arlenton was not a patron of the theatrical arts."

"Too bad," Push mused.

"However," Wrath added, his voice dropping an octave or two. "What made either of you think I was acting?"

Push and Scratch stopped in their tracks. Wrath was standing behind them a couple of feet away, as if he'd anticipated their move. "Because I was ready to blast you back," Push said, holding his hand up. "And Scratch had a gun trained on you."

"Wouldn't have been the first time," said Wrath, never losing his smile. "Incidentally, I think I may have located our Tin Woodman up ahead."

Push frowned, but looked around at where Wrath was gesturing. On the opposite side of the street at a corner up ahead of them, a bar sat with two statues of tin men carrying chopping axes. The statues were facing one another on either side of the front door, as though standing guard. Up above them, a bright rainbow-colored flag waved proudly in the evening breeze.

"The Tin Woodman," Wrath said, walking up between them. "One of the friends of Dorothy when she traveled through Oz to visit the Wizard. It's not the subtlest metaphor I've ever seen, but I kind of like it nonetheless."

Scratch was too busy laughing to comment.

"Is he going to be okay?" Wrath wondered as they made their way across the street.

Scratch snorted. "I'll be fine," he assured. "There's nothing in there that I haven't seen before. Push and I used to go to gay clubs all the time."

Wrath's eyes widened in response.

"It's true," Push affirmed. "Back when we first started working with each other, Scratch and I were hanging out with some of my gay buddies at the time, and they all wanted to go to this big dance club on the east side. Scratch never said a word. He just sat at the bar and drank cocktails the whole time. He's more comfortable in a gay bar than I am."

"So what about you?" Scratch asked. "You're not going to panic on us, are you?"

"I grew up in New Orleans," Wrath reminded them. "It's one of the gayest cities in the world. There are more rainbow flags flying in the French Quarter than red, white, and blue ones."

That statement managed to get Push to crack a smile.

"Did you honestly believe I had never been in a gay bar before now?" Wrath asked as they reached the front doors.

Scratch saluted the tin statue on the left. "At ease, soldier," he said, before turning back to Wrath. "Actually, I don't know much about you aside from the fact that you've been in prison. Push spent more time in your file than I did."

"Really?" Wrath gave Push a look. "That's interesting."

"He was preparing himself in case you go nuts and start killing everyone," Scratch added.

Wrath didn't look offended. "Always nice to be prepared," he said, reaching for the door handle.

The interior of the bar was pretty standard, though much nicer than the underground one from earlier that day. There was a box for the DJ off to the side. The bar itself sat in the middle of the room with seats all around. Tables and chairs hugged the walls near the windows, and a region in the back had been reserved for dancing and playing pool.

The only thing that stood out was the men dancing on top of the bar in their underwear.

"Ah," said Wrath, looking around. "So it's *that* sort of bar."

A number of the barflies were clutching dollar bills. Each time one of the young men danced their way, they would stop so the patrons could make a deposit. Push noticed that, in spite of the entertainment, several people were staring.

"You know," Wrath said thoughtfully. "We had a place like this back in New Orleans, just off Bourbon Street. I wonder if whoever owns this place got the idea from there?"

Push didn't respond. The bar patrons had gone back to ignoring them in favor of the dancers, so he took the opportunity to grab a nearby seat at a corner that was empty. Wrath and Scratch joined him just in time for a boy no older than twenty to dance by wearing boxer briefs that were two sizes too small.

"Anyone got a dollar?" Wrath asked.

The boy overheard this and proceeded to dance his way farther down the bar toward an eager-looking elderly man clutching a roll of what might have been twenties. Curious, Push touched the dial on his goggles and zeroed in on the wad of cash. Sure enough, there were twenties in his grip, along with quite a few fives and tens.

"Someone's getting lucky tonight," Scratch noted.

"These guys probably pay their rent with what they make in tips," Wrath said. "So they go wherever the money is."

"Can't say I blame them," Push muttered. "I'm glad I never had to dance my way through college, though. It would have been humiliating."

Wrath gave Push a once-over. "I don't see why. You're built better than any of the dancers in this place."

"Back then, I wasn't," Push replied, before remembering who he was talking to.

Scratch jumped on board, though, and ran with it before he could clam up. "Were you really born in New Orleans?" he asked Wrath.

"I never said that I was born there," Wrath replied. "Only that I grew up there. I spent a good portion of my time working my way through the French Quarter after I got recruited."

"What about before?" Scratch pressed. "Where were you born?"

Wrath turned to Push in response. "Didn't the file tell you that?"

"There was nothing about where you were born," Push said absentmindedly. "No one knows anything about where you were before New Orleans."

"Where was it?" Scratch asked again.

"Somewhere very far from New Orleans," Wrath replied evasively. "Though, I think of New Orleans as my adopted hometown. There was more to do in that city than anywhere else in the world. I could have stayed there forever."

Another dancer came by, this one a couple of years older and covered in tattoos. Without a word, Scratch reached into his coat pocket and pulled out a couple of ones, then offered them to Push. Push was too preoccupied with staring out the window, however. Seeing this, Wrath intercepted them and stood up. Push looked back just in time to catch Wrath eye-level with the dancer's crotch, running the dollar bill up and down the cleft of his abs before stuffing the bill into the front of his tighty-whities. The dancer gave Wrath an appreciative nod before moving on.

Push stared at Wrath like he'd just sprouted two extra heads. "We're supposed to be checking the place out," Wrath said pointedly. "Unless I got it wrong."

"Do you think the answer was in that guy's underwear?" Scratch asked, fighting back a laugh.

"It might be," Wrath said seriously. "If anyone would know about something fishy, it would be these guys. Think about it. They spend every night here, usually flirting with drunk people. If anyone in this place works for the guy we're looking for, they've probably let it slip while one of the dancers was grinding into their crotch. After having one too many drinks, people will talk to anyone willing to listen."

"I don't know," Scratch said skeptically. "None of these guys look bright enough to change a light bulb."

"They aren't supposed to," Wrath said, folding his arms. "I had a friend who worked as a waitress, and she hated her job because if you want big tips, you have to act like you don't have a brain between your ears."

"It sounds like she worked at Hooters," said Push as he took one of the bills in Wrath's hand to pass along to another dancer.

"Nope," Wrath replied. "Pat O's. She was a physics major."

A moment passed, along with several more dancers, all of whom were indistinguishable from one another in Push's eyes. "So, what's the plan?" Wrath asked. "Do we just sit here and alleviate the economic strife of the American go-go dancer?"

"If any of these guys knows something like you say," said Scratch, leaning past Wrath to speak to Push, "we should probably speak with them in private."

"If we can pull one of them away," Push pointed out, moving his arms so another dancer could get by. "No one will speak with us. People think of us too much like cops nowadays."

"We don't have to," Wrath said. "Just ask one of them for a private dance."

"I don't think either of us has that kind of cash," said Scratch, backing up slightly as Push glared.

"You don't need it," Wrath insisted, pointing to a cash machine near one of the pool tables in the back. "That, or just see if the bartender will ring it up for you on the credit machine. Most places these days accept credit cards, and the Association probably has an expense account for things like this, just like back at the hotel."

Push went rigid. As it happened, there was a credit card in his wallet for Association business. The odds were that Wrath didn't know about that specifically, and was just harboring a wild guess. Scratch, on the other hand, knew perfectly well, and was even staring at the pocket where Push usually stored his wallet away.

"No," he told his friend flatly. "I am not getting a lap dance."

"That has to be the first time I've ever heard anyone say those words with a straight face," Wrath noted.

Scratch snickered. "Push had a bad experience with a stripper once back when he joined a fraternity. He's a little uncomfortable with the idea these days."

Wrath seemed to find this very amusing. "And here I thought that being a hero meant making sacrifices," he said dramatically, and a little louder than Push was comfortable with. "You should be ashamed of yourself, sir! Your Association, your country needs you to do this. You must go out there and allow one of these fine young men to grind their asses into your crotch. It is your duty!"

One of the dancers, the one with the tattoos from before, spun back their way just as Wrath was finishing his inspirational speech. The moment Push looked up, the boy in question began to laugh and even flashed Push a glimpse of his junk.

"He seems okay with the idea," Scratch noted. "How about you?"

Push turned around in his chair and stared daggers at Wrath. "I don't think I made this clear before," he said softly. "But I really do hate your guts. If you think one of these go-go boys knows something, why don't you let them bounce up and down in your lap for an hour?"

"Because I can't afford one," Wrath answered at once.

In response to that, Push reached into his wallet and yanked out the Association credit card. "Here," he said, flipping it at Wrath, who caught the plastic strip a second before it would have smacked him across the eye. "Have fun."

Scratch frowned at this. Wrath, however, looked the card over as though unsure of its validity. A moment later, he was grinning from ear to ear as if Christmas had come early.

"Thanks!" he said earnestly. "I wish everyone hated me this much."

Wrath was gone in the blink of an eye, all but skipping over to the bartender at the register with the card in full view.

"Somehow," Scratch said, moving into Wrath's seat so Push could hear him better, "I get the impression that this wasn't how you expected things to go."

Push was staring with his jaw hanging open. "Where exactly did my plan of handing over a credit card with a five-thousand dollar limit to a supervillain go wrong?"

Wrath, meanwhile, was talking animatedly with the bartender, who plucked the card out of his hand gleefully and swiped it. A moment later, after the card had cleared and Wrath had given his signature, the bartender flagged down two of the dancers from the bar. Push's eyes were practically bulging out of their sockets as Wrath snaked an arm around each man before heading for a set of stairs leading up, stopping only to deposit some quarters into the jukebox.

"Um, I gotta say," said Scratch, watching them disappear. "The man knows how to live!"

CHAPTER
THREE

PUSH gritted his teeth and kept his eyes tightly closed as the young man's hand pressed into the crotch of his tights. He was doing his damnedest to remain soft, but the brain in his pants was having none of it. Not even the mental image of Divine eating feces could hold his erection back.

Taking a different tactic, he tried focusing on the talented boy straddling his lap. There had to be some flaw he could zero in on. They were about the same height, something Push had forgotten could matter during instances like this. Being short, Push easily forgot how intimate looking someone in the eye could be. He hadn't asked for the dancer's name. The amount of alcohol in his system, combined with the go-go dancer's stubborn refusal to keep his hands to himself, had made Push forget his manners. He was supposed to be pumping the kid for information, not the other way around.

The dancer had his cock free of the stretchy fabric now, and was moving his hand up and down in a way that made Push think he did this sort of thing professionally. For the moment, Push was too drunk to care that his junk was flashing the room. They were off to the side near one of the pool tables. After Wrath went upstairs, Push had ordered a Jägerbomb and two tequila shots. When that amount of liquid courage proved inadequate, he'd gone to piss, come back, and ordered another Jägerbomb before snagging the first dancer to come down from the bar. Push loathed the thought of leaving the work up to the ex-con, but things had gotten off track somehow.

Usually, he was embarrassed about having someone see his package in the light. Overall, he was nervous about being naked in general. Annette had convinced him to do the photo shoot only after swearing up and down that no nude photographs would be allowed. Push had always been insecure about his body. Even as a kid, he'd been small.

Not that his dick was small, mind you, but it was far too thick, and not very long. Unless he was fully erect, Push's cock seemed average. Of course, that wasn't the case right now. The young man in his lap was doing a very good job. Between him and the booze he'd foolishly downed all at once, Push was having trouble thinking, period.

It was the jerking in his balls that finally got his attention. "Stop, or I'll go," Push warned, between heavy gasps.

"So go," the kid encouraged, sliding down off Push's lap. "I've always wanted to make a superhero cum!"

Before Push could stop him, the kid was sucking the head of his cock into his mouth. Flicking it with his tongue, the dancer played with the piss slit there, encouraging pre-cum out from the crevice. Push grabbed the back of the kid's head before he could stop himself, and forced his thick dick all the way in. The dancer gagged but didn't protest. Instead, his slurping and moans could be heard even over the noisy thumping that passed for music. Push realized he was matching the movement of his forceful thrusts to the rhythm of the beat. The bass was loud enough that it echoed through him, and with everything else that had happened, Push felt himself go in seconds.

The orgasm that rocked his body caused Push to convulse. Everything swam around him. He couldn't remember the last time he'd let himself feel this much. As a second wave struck, a strange pressure grew in his right forearm. With a jolt, Push realized what it was and tried to regain control. The dancer was still slurping down his cum like it was mother's milk, urging more out by fondling Push's balls. This caused another jolt to rock Push's body, and before he could stop it, a telekinetic blast exploded out of his hand.

The force bubble sent a nearby table flying. Thankfully, it was empty, and merely clattered against the wall a few short feet away. Another blast, however, rocketed out as the dancer gripped his nut sack tightly. This one struck the jukebox, shaking several CDs inside of it loose. A heavy metal number Push didn't recognize blared out, competing with the techno-mix echoing through the club.

Fed up, Push grabbed the dancer by the back of the hair and yanked him away. This turned out to be a poor choice, for the dancer assumed Push was trying to play rough, and yanked on Push's balls, *hard*! The result sent a final rope of cum flying right into the kid's face. At the same time, another small orgasm went through Push. His right palm was pointed down this time, and the force bubble that was released blasted Push straight up into the air.

At least the dancer had thought to let go beforehand. The shock wave sent the kid sprawling to the floor. Push came back down onto the chair hard, just in time to notice Wrath was standing off to the side by himself, watching the scene unfold.

Without a word, the dancer jumped up off the floor and ran for the back of the club. Push watched him leave, feeling very miserable all of a sudden, with the sober realization that the mess left on his cock and balls would most likely leave a stain on his pants for all the world to see.

Push's eyes settled on Wrath, who was still observing him, wearing a strange, thoughtful expression. When he moved, it was so sudden that Push had to blink. Looking around, he spotted Wrath at the bar, asking the bartender for something around a pair of nicely-muscled legs. The bartender nodded, then reached under for a roll of paper towels. Wrath appeared to thank the man, and handed the card to him again before walking off.

Push felt himself tense up as Wrath approached. "Here," said the supervillain, offering him the paper towel roll. "You can clean up with these. The bathroom is over there."

Wrath pointed to where the bathroom was. Confused now, and more than a little humiliated, Push hopped up out of his chair, then marched past Wrath without saying thank you.

It took longer than Push would have liked to clean up. He'd made quite a mess, and despite the dancer's best efforts, not all of his cum had gone down the kid's throat. In addition to making sure he didn't stain his outfit, Push also wanted to dry himself off properly. Tucking his cock and balls back into his tights while they were still wet would have defeated the whole purpose. Finally satisfied, Push exited back into the club and swept the area for any sign of Scratch.

His best friend was still sitting in the same place, talking with Wrath, who rose as Push moved around the bar toward them.

"How did it go?" Wrath asked.

Push very nearly called Wrath something that would have made his mother's ears burn before he realized what the man meant.

"Nothing," he said instead, feeling himself blush.

Wrath considered Push for a moment. "I found out something," he said innocently. "Would you like to hear?"

"Sure," Push muttered, wishing now that he'd had another drink.

"The entrance to the Pranksta Gayngsta's lair is in back of this place," Wrath said, pointing to where the dancer had exited in a rush earlier. "Apparently, this area of the city is old, and there's a connecting door between it and the building that used to be a supermarket next door. Some of the dancers have heard weird noises during the day before things pick up. The manager keeps telling them to ignore it."

"Weird noises?" Push asked skeptically.

"People screaming," Wrath elaborated. "And heavy machinery being worked on. The building was abandoned years ago for safety reasons. No one should be inside."

"Very suspicious," Scratch admitted.

"A few of the other dancers have taken an extra job running 'errands' for the manager," Wrath continued. "They come and go through that connecting door all the time. Sometimes they're gone for hours. A few of them won't show up for work, but the manager does nothing. Then, suddenly, they march out from the back like nothing's wrong. There's no employee entrance to this bar. You're supposed to come in through the front, so these guys are getting in some other way."

Push glanced past Wrath to where Scratch sat watching him. "It sounds fishy," he readily agreed. "But we have no solid proof."

"Why not have a look around?" Wrath wondered.

"There's still a procedure we follow," Scratch explained. "In situations like this, it's best that we work with the cooperation of the local authorities."

"They tend to get riled if we take all the credit," Push added.

"Wonderful," Wrath mused. "What does this 'procedure' have to say about our current situation? Do we sit here and wait for something convenient to happen?"

"Nah," Scratch said. "That only happens in comic books."

Someone that Push thought looked like a manager was over by the jukebox now, along with several spare dancers, looking it over.

"Let's go check it out," he said abruptly, getting to his feet.

Push had hoped the telekinetic outburst would have burned off the alcohol in his system. Apparently, he'd overdone things and was still a little tipsy. Nothing shook when he stood up, however, which was a good sign. Wrath climbed down immediately after, looking ready to go.

Scratch hesitated. "We need proof," Push pointed out to him. "And we're just going to have a look around. We've done that sort of thing before."

The hesitant expression on Scratch's face didn't completely fade away, even as he jumped down to the floor beside them. As Push made for the door, Scratch came up behind him. His friend leaned so far into him that Push almost felt the stubble of facial hair touch his neck.

"Um, are you sure you're okay?"

Push frowned, but kept going when Wrath reached the door first. "I'm cool," he assured Scratch, paying more attention than he would have liked to keeping his steps in rhythm.

The air outside helped clear his head. Wrath had taken the lead, and Push allowed it, anxious now to see what the former criminal could do. The building they were going to investigate stretched all the way down the street to an area that was hardly lit at all. 25th Avenue, where they'd just come from, shone like a beacon. This part of the city might as well have been on the other side of town. Push stepped on a crack and almost fell forward into Wrath as the man stopped short.

"I sense something," he said quietly.

"What?" Push asked, straightening himself up.

"Nothing," the man replied very quickly. "I think we might be close to an entrance."

"What makes you say that?" Scratch asked.

Push could hear the skepticism in his friend's voice. "Let's wait and see what he does," Push whispered quietly. "I'm interested in seeing him work now."

"You sure?"

Push nodded, even though Scratch was probably as blind as he was. Thinking this made him remember the night vision on his goggles, and he mentally slapped himself for being so stupid.

And drunk.

Wrath, meanwhile, had moved on ahead slightly in the darkness. "We know he's hiding something," Push said, switching his night vision on. "Maybe this way, we'll figure out what it is. And if not, they say it takes a thief to catch one."

With his night vision on now, Push could make Wrath out in the distance. The man was searching along the side of the building, touching it with the tips of his fingers as if reading Braille. Push kept a close watch the whole time, anxious for signs that Wrath was up to no good. A moment later, the man stepped back. His face was scrunched up, as if considering something.

"There's definitely people inside that building," he said after rejoining them. "At least fifty, if not more."

"What if they're homeless?" Scratch suggested. "Buildings like these are known for having squatters."

"Squatters would try to stay quiet," Wrath argued, keeping both eyes fixed on the building's upper windows. "Whoever is inside doesn't care about being overheard. I think they're getting ready to move to a new location."

"Explain," Push insisted flatly.

Wrath smiled, amused. "The whole idea behind a secret hideout is for it to stay secret. A criminal worth half his salt wouldn't roll such heavy machinery nonstop unless he was planning something big. For my money, he's either getting ready to move or preparing for another heist."

"It doesn't really matter, then," Scratch stated, giving Push a glance. "We need to find out who's inside before we call the cops in."

"I know," said Push, though he sounded less than happy about it, even to himself. "If we could get up to the roof…."

"Gotcha."

Scratch reached into his coat pocket and pulled out the two halves of a different cue stick. Push knew of three that his friend carried. All of them had triangle designs patterned across the length in various places and were color-coded. The black one was weighted with iron so Scratch could wield it like a battering ram. The red one fired a rescue flare to signal for help. This one was green, which made Push's stomach queasy.

"The last time you used this, I wound up trapped in a Dumpster," he reminded Scratch flatly. "You said you were never going to bring that one with you again."

"Professor Trixter gave me some pointers," Scratch insisted as he twisted the two halves together. "He suggested I use a tensile steel combination with titanium wired in between for better torque. The only thing we should have to worry about now is whatever part of the roof the anchor attaches to coming loose."

"So long as that's the only thing we need to worry about," Wrath teased.

"I still think it's a bad idea," Push insisted, ignoring Wrath. "But we need a way to get up to the roof. The sooner we wrap this case up, the sooner we can leave."

"The metal cord should hold all our weight," Scratch encouraged, before looking to Wrath. "How much do you weigh, incidentally?"

"Enough," Wrath replied. "But if it will make you feel better, I volunteer to be the first victim. That way, if something goes wrong, it won't be either of you who gets hurt."

Push and Scratch both frowned. "Unless you don't trust me with your equipment," Wrath added.

A moment later, with the cue stick in hand, Wrath was taking aim at the far end of the building inside the mouth of a dark alley.

"Just turn the bottom part slightly," Scratch instructed. "Make sure you take aim with it first, though."

"Right," Wrath retorted. "Going up."

The cue stick gun made no noise at all as the tip burst forth from the extended lower half and shot straight up in the air.

"Remember to toss it back down once you're secure," Scratch added as the anchor spread apart into four hooks and took hold of the building's edge.

"I'll aim for one of your heads," he promised before engaging the tiny built-in engine to wind the cord back up. "Next stop, lotions, notions, motions, commotions, ladies' lingerie, and men's shoes!"

Push watched Wrath scale the side of the building. Soon, he had vanished over the side.

"Double or nothing he decides to run for it," he heard himself mutter.

"He wouldn't get far," Scratch replied. "This guy doesn't strike me as the stupid type. Now that we're alone, though, maybe you should sit this one out. I'll be fine keeping an eye on him."

"Why?" Push demanded, and even to him, it sounded like an accusation.

"Because you're sort of drunk," Scratch stated bluntly. "I can't remember the last time I saw you drink on a mission, much less get drunk off your ass on one. What the hell is your problem tonight?"

Push opened his mouth to answer, despite not knowing what to say, but was spared from making an even bigger ass of himself when the cue stick smacked him squarely atop his head.

"I'm going up," he grumbled, snatching the stick off the ground before Scratch could get to it. "See you when you get up there."

All in all, scaling the side of the building in his condition wasn't as hard as Push expected. He and Scratch had gone wall-rappelling before, and the principle felt more or less the same, minus a safety net and footholds. Still, he managed to make it up to the roof without incident and tossed the cue stick back down. A few minutes later, Scratch joined him.

"He's not here," said Push flatly as Scratch hauled himself over the side.

"What?" his best friend asked, standing up.

"Wrath," Push elaborated. "He's gone."

There was no one else on the roof. A skylight was centered in the middle. With his night vision still on, Push could see there was no one hiding behind it. Just to be on the safe side, he switched over to the thermal scanner and read the same thing.

Scratch looked around unhappily. "We'll find him later," he said finally. "Right now, we should do what we came here to do, and call the cops."

"I'm right there with you," Push said. "But first, I need to take a piss. I think the tequila I had earlier is coming back to haunt me."

Not wanting his friend to watch him with a hard-on sticking out, Push wandered over to the building's far edge. A low groan escaped through his lips as he emptied his bladder over the side.

"Do you always do this sort of thing?"

Push nearly jumped and came close to spraying Wrath with his urine. "Where the hell did you come from?" he shouted.

"You might want to be quieter," Wrath warned, giving him a hard glare. "There are quite a few angry people below us."

"Be happy I don't spray acid," Push retorted, aiming over the side again.

Wrath blinked in the darkness. "I'm sure that's supposed to mean something," he muttered under his breath.

"Where were you?" Push demanded, turning farther away when Wrath didn't avert his gaze. "When I got up here, you'd vanished. Have you got some type of invisibility power?"

"I was down there," Wrath said, pointing.

Push turned, moving one hand away from his dick so he could adjust the goggles back to night vision mode again. There, just past the building's ledge on the far side, a slanted roof led down to a much smaller building.

"I noticed it as I was casing the rooftop," Wrath explained. "So I thought I'd check things out while you guys were on your way up. I didn't think it would take as long as it did."

"Please tell me you at least found something interesting," Push grumbled, tucking himself back into his tights.

"I did," said Wrath. "They have a security system, and I'm fairly sure it extends to the roof. The guys they had watching the monitors were making a lot of noise when I spotted them. It looks like there are motion sensors and hidden cameras all over this place."

"That means we've got company," Push said, whirling around.

"That," Wrath added, "and someone most likely captured footage of you taking a whiz off the side of the warehouse."

Push ran back to Scratch, who was leaning against the opposite side of the skylight. "You found him," Scratch stated.

"Company's coming," Push warned, whipping out his bo staff. "According to him, whatever is going on here, they've got security everywhere. We've been spotted."

"What do we do?" Scratch asked, reaching into his coat pocket for the black cue stick. "Fight our way out?"

"Negative," he replied, getting his phone out next. "I'm sending an emergency code to the Association hotline. They'll have the cops out here soon. In the meantime, we get off the roof."

"Too late," Wrath said.

His words were punctuated with the sound of a door being forced open. A hatch, invisible in the dark even with Push's goggles, swung outward. A swarm of goons spilled out onto the roof, armed to the teeth. The moment they spotted Push and the others, the goons took aim.

"I might ought to have mentioned the hatch before," Wrath said. "Sorry about that. It slipped my mind."

Push lashed out with his telekinetic blasts in response, knocking three of the attackers backward. "Forget about it," he yelled. "Take them down before they pump us full of lead."

Flames burst out of Wrath's hands as he held them high over his head. "I can do that," he said cheekily.

Scratch tossed two blue cue balls into the air, then sent each one flying with a jab from his cue stick. The first one tapped the edge of the skylight, rattling it slightly, before catching one goon in the chest. The striped blue ball exploded on contact, covering the man's chest in a thick, sticky fluid. The blow caused him to stagger, and he wound up flat on his face, stuck to the surface of the roof. The glue was quick-acting, binding him there in seconds.

The second ball hit another man right across the face. There was no preamble to this one. The blow created a whiplash effect, and he was thrown back onto his ass, but wasn't glued down. This problem remedied itself a second later, however, when a different goon tripped over an extended leg that was stuck out at an odd angle. The result was that one's face was stuck to the groin of the other's pants. It would have been funny, but Push had no time to admire the humor in the situation.

The others had begun opening fire. A few short telekinetic bursts knocked their guns away, but the ones he'd blown back before were getting to their feet. Wrath stepped forward as the gunfire died down. A halo of fire encircled his head like a reef. The man was leering the whole while, as if he were having the time of his life. With one smooth gesture, part of the roof exploded. Fire burst from Wrath's hands as he brought them down, smacking the goon squad around like they were rag dolls. Wrath's hands moved as if he were the conductor leading an orchestra. With each flick of his wrist, flames rose high into the air.

There were bodies lying all around now. Some of the goons looked badly injured, while others got to their feet slowly. Push charged forward, hoping to finish this before Wrath killed anyone and counting on Scratch to put their firebug out of commission if he tried anything. His telescopic bo staff extended as Push came to a stop between two men covered in soot and light burns. One's pants leg was smoldering. Push knocked the guy's legs out from under him and used a quick telekinetic burst to snuff out the fire. The other fell after a succession of blows to the head. Push spun his staff expertly, taking out a third, and then a fourth. Drunk or not, he was in his element now, and he had the benefit of being able to see in the dark with his goggles.

It wasn't until after they were all down for the count that he took notice of their attire. "They're dressed like clowns."

Even saying it out loud wasn't enough. Push stared down at the men he'd just helped clobber. "Please tell me we did not just attack a homeless troop of circus performers," he groaned.

"They were shooting at us," Scratch reminded him, coming up behind him. "But you're right. They're wearing clown makeup."

"I always thought stuff like this was copyrighted," Wrath said, looking around at the bodies lying awkwardly at their feet.

"Never mind that," Push said, backing up slightly into one of the goons Scratch had glued to the roof. "We still need to get out of here."

Something sailed through the air in an arc toward them. Wrath moved to blast it, but then paused as the object hit the ground and bounced. It was a squeaking rubber purple dinosaur, and it stopped a foot or so away from Scratch's boot. A second toy, this an orange bear wearing a red shirt, rolled to a stop inches from Wrath.

None of them moved. "Um, was that supposed to be somebody's idea of a joke?"

All three whirled around at the same time as a strange sound filled the air. A few steps back, coming toward them from the skylight, was a cymbal-banging monkey in a tall hat. It stopped before all three of them and chattered.

"We're being surrounded," Wrath stated sardonically. "Whatever shall we all do?"

Simultaneously, all three toys let out a noisy pop. A green cloud filled the air around them, cutting them off. Scratch tried to cover his and Push's mouths, but the gas was fast-acting.

Its effect was instantaneous. "I cannot believe," Push heard Wrath say as unconsciousness flowed over him, "I fell for that."

"Me either," he grunted, before the light faded completely.

SOMETHING struck him across the face, hard enough that the jolt should have hurt. Knowing this helped clear Push's head enough to realize something was wrong. Against his better judgment, he forced himself awake the rest of the way. The room swam for a moment. A number of indistinct figures were standing in front of him. After a couple of quick, deep breaths, the fog clouding his brain cleared up enough for Push to realize he was tied to a chair.

They were in a warehouse—*the* warehouse, Push assumed. The lights were dim, but clear enough that Push could take in his surroundings. Boxes littered the entire space. Some of them were open, with the contents spilled out over the side. If just what Push saw was any indication, this place was loaded with enough ammo to start a war.

Wrath was standing among the troupe of clowns in front of him, arms folded and staring at Push with a look of utmost loathing.

"Wakey-wakey," the one in the center jeered.

Push blinked and focused on him. The guy was tall, and it didn't appear to be solely due to the platform boots he wore. Push had to blink again several more times to make sure he wasn't seeing things. The man's outfit was like a mish-mashed cross between a drag queen and a corporate rapper. It might have been the gas he was dosed with, but for a moment, Push thought he was being leered at by Joel Grey from *Cabaret* dressed like Snoop Dogg.

Push had never seen anything so horrifying, and simultaneously ludicrous, in his entire life. The guy's costume resembled something a fashion parade might have run down, then backed over.

Without a doubt, he was standing in front of the Pranksta Gayngsta.

"Nice of you to join us," the Pranksta said in a nail-biting falsetto tone. "While you're still alive, anyway!"

"That explains the gas. You wanted him on your side," Push said, his eyes darting over to where Wrath stood. "It sure as hell didn't take you long to sell us out."

Wrath said nothing.

"Where's Scratch?"

"See?" Wrath said to the Pranksta in response. "I told you. Keep the other one alive, and he'll give us anything."

The Pranksta smiled for a second, then glared sharply at Wrath. "I'm not convinced yet," he snapped.

"You should be," Wrath responded. "Our guest is in love."

The other clowns laughed, made kissy noises, then hosed Push down with string spray. "Finally," the Pranksta cheered. "I have a chance to try out my new heart-shaped Valentine bomb. Custom-made with C4, for an explosive treat in every bite."

The clowns laughed again, as if on cue.

"Before I kill him, we should allow the lovebirds one last chance to be together. Maybe a nice, romantic candlelit dinner for two? Or," the Pranksta growled sharply. "I could just blow them both to kingdom come at the same time. A one-way honeymoon to the afterlife!"

None of the clowns so much as moved. "Well?" the Pranksta said, looking around. "Laugh!"

Wrath shook his head as the clowns surrounding him doubled over with false hysterics.

"You make me sick," Push screamed. "Scratch was willing to give you the benefit of the doubt. I never wanted to take my eyes off you, but he was convinced you at least deserved one chance to prove everyone wrong. I wish I'd listened to my instincts the first time and blown you back to the slammer."

Wrath stepped forward and knelt down in front of Push's chair. Their eyes met for a moment, and something deep inside them made Push's words catch in his throat.

"You are really, really bad at this," Wrath stated, flicking his wrist. "Did you know that already?"

Push looked down and saw the ropes binding his feet together were burning. "Fuck!" Push screamed, rocking the chair in an attempt to free himself.

Surprisingly, the ropes snapped clean in two. Wrath was already moving again, igniting the bindings holding his arms down. Those came apart next, and by that time, the pyrokinetic was already standing behind him, working on the ones around his wrists.

"Here's your staff and goggles," Wrath said, placing them in his hands. "I palmed them when no one was watching. Scratch is in the other room in the far back. The last time I saw him, he was fine."

Everyone was staring at Wrath in shock. "What are you doing?" the Pranksta Gayngsta demanded, shrieking louder than ever.

"Your voice was getting on my nerves," Wrath said calmly as Push stood up. "And I was tired of listening to him whine, so I'm switching back over."

"I don't whine," Push insisted.

"You were whining," Wrath stated. "Loudly. Scratch could probably hear you in the room they've got him chained up in."

"You are supposed to be on my side!" the Pranksta ranted. "Everyone… shoot them a lot!"

"May I?" Wrath asked Push, raising both arms. "I promise I'll try not to…."

"Do it!" Push screamed as the clowns raised their guns.

Wrath let loose with a stream of fire that swept down the row of clowns. Most dropped their guns and screamed as the flames licked at their bodies. Push started from the opposite end and blasted the ones still upright back into the pile of crates they'd been posing in front of. Without even speaking aloud, both men thought of the same plan and worked their way toward the middle. The Pranksta Gayngsta had already ducked and was rolling out of the line of fire. Push saw him reach into his coat pocket and pull out a stuffed animal.

"Bomb," he said calmly, pointing.

"I got it," Wrath replied.

The Pranksta gave the droopy-eyed dog plushie a quick squeeze before tossing it into the air. Wrath pointed his finger and sent out a jet blast of fire that knocked the innocent-looking device back. The thing was still burning as it arched through the air away from them before exploding in a puff of blue smoke.

"He's running," Wrath said.

"I've got him," Push replied, giving chase. "You go get Scratch."

The Pranksta Gayngsta was digging something out of one of the nearby crates. As Push drew near, the head clown rose up carrying some kind of gun in his hand. The mystery behind that was solved when the Pranksta fired it and a small spear with a "Bang" flag attached embedded itself into a support beam inches from Push's head.

"Oops!" the clown cried out while reloading his gun. "Guess I'm all thumbs today."

Push lashed out with a telekinetic blast, but the Pranksta was ready and dodged out of the way, firing the spear gun again as he rolled to the side. The blast caused a crate to break open, sending grenades flying. Several rolled out onto the concrete floor as Push spotted Wrath burning a path through a mob of the Pranksta's goons. Most of them were on the run, having been disarmed or heavily injured. Between attacks, Wrath would send a blast of fire up into the rafters.

Push watched for a second before shouting. "Wrath! Scratch, remember?"

Wrath leveled his eyes at Push, but nodded and broke into a run. When Push looked back around, the Pranksta was fitting one of the grenades onto a spear.

"Try pushing this away," the clown jeered.

"No thanks," replied Push confidently.

Push swung his arm up in a backhand gesture as the Pranksta fired. The spear was thrown wildly off course up to the ceiling as a result. There was a moment's pause as the Pranksta stared up toward the roof in shock. Push, meanwhile, dove toward the man as the grenade detonated above them. There was just enough time to tackle the crook out of the way before part of the ceiling came crashing down.

Both rolled to a stop next to what looked like a military-issue jeep. "Make one wrong move and I will turn you over to the guy who likes to burn things," Push warned, before getting up.

As he stood, sirens echoed in the distance. The police were on their way, and Push spotted Wrath helping Scratch along. A smile broke over his face before he could stop himself, and for once, Push couldn't have cared less. It felt great to be alive and to see his best friend all right. Push placed a boot down onto the Pranksta Gayngsta's chest to ensure he didn't try to escape.

"Were you really going to sell us out to this guy?" he asked after Wrath had deposited Scratch onto a crate.

"Do you really think I would've taken orders from someone dressed like that?" Wrath responded, searching the ceiling.

Push stared down at the Pranksta. "It's better than nothing, I suppose."

"What are you doing?" Scratch wondered, watching Wrath closely.

In answer, Wrath walked over to the Pranksta and yanked something out of the man's ear. "He was listening to someone the whole time," Wrath explained, holding the Bluetooth up so they could both see it clearly. "I couldn't hear anything, but it felt to me like this dumbass was taking orders from somebody else."

"Adding credence to your theory," Scratch said thoughtfully. Push looked his friend over and gave a nod of relief. It didn't look as though Scratch was hurt badly.

"I thought I saw someone moving around in the rafters earlier," Wrath went on. "It could have been whoever he was talking to."

"Or just another goon," Push pointed out, feeling very tired all of a sudden.

"Why would he have a goon hiding in the rafters?"

Neither of them had an answer.

"Could I perhaps ask you something, gentlemen?"

All three stared down at the Pranksta, whose voice had undergone a severe change all of a sudden. Though it was nothing close to a bass, the shrieking falsetto was gone now.

"Could you maybe take your boot off my chest?" he asked in a very polite tone. "I have this asthma problem, see?"

"Want me to hurt him?" Wrath asked calmly.

Before Push could answer, an explosion echoed through the warehouse. All of them turned as a side door was blown clear off its hinges. A second later, SWAT members poured into the building with rifles aimed at the ready.

"Freeze!" a woman's voice yelled. "Police!"

CHAPTER
FOUR

IT WAS a long time before things got straightened out. Thankfully, having clout with the Association helped. It also helped that the Grand Rapids police department had asked for their help in the first place, so anyone complaining about the fact would have to do so in private. Scratch, as it turned out, was fine save for a few bruises that were laughable compared to other injuries he'd shrugged off before. Since his friend wasn't feeling any pain, Push let him handle things with the cops. There were forms to sign, testimonies to give, but thanks to some prodding from the RLSA higher-ups, all three were let go relatively soon. They could have spent another night at the hotel, but Push was longing for his soft bed and pillow back at the apartment. Scratch agreed to drive back. Once they'd gathered what little was in the room, the Pussy Wagon was making its way back to Chicago.

During the drive, Push dozed in the passenger seat. During one of his more lucid states, he heard Scratch call out to Wrath.

"I just wanted you to know," Scratch said, once he'd commanded Wrath's attention. "You did pretty good today."

At first, Push didn't think Wrath was going to respond. "Sure," the pyrokinetic said after a moment. "Who do you think the Pranksta Gayngsta was working for?"

"Who knows?" Scratch replied, sighing. "At this point, it's really more of a job for the police. They'll have a bitch of a time tracking down all the men working for that crackpot. I don't envy whoever gets stuck doing cleanup."

"Maybe they'll find him," Wrath said quietly.

"Who?" Push muttered, stretching uncomfortably in his seat. He hated falling asleep sitting up. It always made him stiff.

"Nothing," Wrath said quickly.

"The guy that Pranksta character was taking orders from," Scratch explained. "Wrath was, um, wondering who he was."

"Oh."

Push was too tired to think on the subject any more. Soon, they were on the outskirts of Chicago. The city was lit up like a Christmas tree as their truck rolled back into town. The view brought a stillness to Push's soul as he gazed across the row of skyscrapers.

"Shit!" Scratch cursed all of a sudden.

"What?"

Scratch turned away from the road to stare at Push. Even in his tired state, it made his toes curl just a little. "We never did find out where Wrath was supposed to stay. Call the office right quick and find out for me. I'd rather not have to work my way through Chicago traffic at this time of night if I don't have to."

Push did as his friend asked, ignoring the butterflies that were beginning to swoop in his stomach now, and punched in the number for Margaret Liu's office. She answered on the third ring, sounding harassed. The woman often worked late hours.

"Margaret," he said, stifling a yawn. "Sorry to interrupt, but no one's told us what to do about Wrath, the guy from the attacked prison transport? Yeah, we're on our way back into Chicago now. Did they ever set up a hotel room for him?"

After a moment, Push nodded. "Yeah, it won't be a problem. If it's just for one night, I guess that'll be fine. Anyway, the Cape Cabinet was wanting to talk with him, and it'll save us the trouble of having to pick him up in the morning."

"Problems?" Scratch asked as Push hung up the phone.

"No one's told her anything," he said. "She thinks it would be best if he spent the night with us. She'll get someone working on it tomorrow."

Wrath's voice startled both of them. "Sorry to impose," he said in the same quiet tone he'd been using since the ride began.

Scratch looked into the rearview mirror. "You can have my room," he offered. "I can crash on the couch for one night."

"You're sure?" Push asked.

"He helped me out of those chains," Scratch reminded him. "I didn't have time to tell you before, but they'd chained me up to a chair in back and left me alone with three guys in drag who were packing semi-automatics. Um, I'd prefer not going into any details about what they were planning to do, but it was a relief when Wrath blew the door down."

"Gotcha."

For Push, it was a relief to finally get home. The Pussy Wagon stayed parked outside in front of their building. Neither felt like returning it now, and it would be better to wait anyway since they would be reporting in to headquarters first thing tomorrow morning. Wrath followed behind the two as they climbed the metal and concrete stairs up to the third floor. Push unlocked the door and felt the glorious sense of being home wash over him.

Wrath was the last one to enter. After having a look around, he walked over to the couch and sat down.

"Make yourself at...."

Push stopped midsentence as Wrath stretched out lazily across the sofa, tucked a pillow underneath his head, and promptly fell asleep.

"I guess you'll get your bed after all," Push said as Scratch looked on beside him.

"Oh well," Scratch replied, heading for his room. "I wasn't wild about giving the bed to him anyway. That couch is lumpy as fuck!"

As IT turned out, Push did not rest as easy as he expected to. Vivid dreams clouded his mind, waking him up more than once. Each time he awakened, they vanished like smoke. It was like trying to cup water in his hands. Any attempts left him feeling frustrated, since at that moment, they'd seemed terribly important. When the alarm finally went off the next morning, it was a relief, despite how tired he still felt.

The hot shower made the prospect of facing the day much easier. There was only one bathroom, a spacious one that contained a shower stall, circular tub, and toilet. It connected the gap between his and Scratch's rooms. Each of them had an alcove that held a lavatory, sink, and space to hold personal effects. It was a set-up rather reminiscent of college, though Push only knew of one or two other residents who attended classes.

As Push secured the towel around his waist, he noticed the smell of coffee drifting into his room from the crack at the bottom of his door. Scratch, it seemed, had gotten up early and brought breakfast back. It was a routine of theirs that they splurged on from time to time. Since Scratch had done it, that meant it would be Push's turn soon. Thinking this, Push stepped out of his room still wearing the towel.

And received quite probably the biggest shock of his life.

Wrath was standing in their kitchen cooking breakfast.

Wearing a white apron.

And not wearing a shirt underneath.

The effect was somehow arousing. Push felt his emotions seesaw back and forth between randy and irritated as Wrath dumped something that looked like ramen noodles out of a strainer and into a frying pan. Half the contents of a spice rack were laid out on the island behind him. Whatever he was doing over there, it smelled incredible.

From this vantage point, Push noticed something that had escaped him last time. Two different tattoos marked Wrath's back. On each shoulder blade, there were circles with different symbols inside. The one on the left was a strange marking that might have been a tribal design meant to look like antlers. Surrounding it were flames, which reminded Push of a sun. The second held some sort of cup that overflowed down the sides. Its outline was marked by three crescent moons, one on the top and two on the lower opposite sides. They almost felt religious somehow.

Push might have had an easier time figuring it out if he weren't getting distracted by the way the muscles underneath Wrath's skin shifted each time he moved even the slightest bit. Looking away, hoping to find something else to stare at, Push's eyes fell to the breakfast table not far away. Two plates were already set and loaded down with food.

Some sort of omelet with ramen noodles spilling out of the folded halves covered a big portion of the plate, but there was also seasoned rice with peppers and tomato bits, strips of turkey bacon, and buttered toast. It was a regular early-morning feast.

And in the center of the table was a poison test kit.

Behind him, Push heard Scratch's bedroom door open, but didn't turn around. "Something smells great," his best friend muttered. "Did you go out for breakfast this time?"

Push simply pointed to the table. Scratch paused, standing at his side, and looked over the spread. Then his eyes settled on the kit decorating the table.

"When did we buy that?" he wondered.

"It was a gift, remember?" Push said. "After Flashpoint almost died trying to solve that case where all those restaurant chefs kept getting poisoned, he started passing them around at the office party."

"Um, right," Scratch replied, still not taking his eyes off the table. "I'd forgotten about that."

"Flashpoint keeps insisting we use it," Push reminded.

"Yeah." Scratch's eyes darted to where Wrath was finishing up. "I think that might be kinda rude, though."

In the end, they both decided to risk it. If Wrath was playing some sort of sick, manipulative psychological game, Push could always kick himself over it later. Both of them dug in after a moment's hesitation while Wrath continued to piddle around in the kitchen, cleaning up the mess without so much as a word. Once he was finished and the dishwasher was churning away quietly, he pulled out a plate of his own that had been keeping warm in the oven and ate quietly at the far side of the island.

"You can come and sit down," Scratch told him, pointing to the empty seat. "We'll allow it."

Wrath waited a moment, as if thinking it over. "It's the least we could do," Push added, half joking. "Considering you went to all this trouble."

"No trouble," Wrath said quietly, taking his plate with him as he walked over to where they sat. "I was bored."

"What time did you wake up?" Scratch wondered, before taking a big bite of rice.

"A few hours ago," Wrath replied. "I had to go to the bathroom, but your doors were locked."

"What did you do?" Scratch wondered, chuckling. "Piss off the side of the balcony?"

"It was that or use the kitchen sink," Wrath answered in a nonchalant tone, picking up a slab of toast. "I saw it as the lesser of the two evils."

Push promptly burst out laughing, and Scratch quickly joined in. "Mind Bender," Push explained, choking on a bit of toast. "Remember, Scratch? He got drunk after we'd already gone to bed and didn't want to wake us up."

"Someone actually called the cops on him," Scratch said to Wrath. "One thirty in the morning, and they come pounding on our door with a complaint about indecent exposure. By that point, Mind Bender was already unconscious on the couch."

"What happened?" Wrath asked, intrigued by this bit of information.

"Not a damn thing," Scratch replied. "The cops backed off once they found out who we were, and what the problem was. They just, um, turned around and left."

"That was back before Mind Bender stopped drinking," Push added. "I think having to explain the situation to the Cape Cabinet rattled him."

"Speaking of which," Scratch reminded him gravely, "we've still got to report to them. How much time do we have before we're supposed to be there?"

"Another hour or so," Push said, tackling his food with a vengeance now. "We'd better get moving."

When all three were finished, Push gathered up their plates, even Wrath's, and placed them in the sink for later. Wrath was on his feet now, removing the apron he'd cooked in.

"Why the porn star approach?" Push wondered before he could stop himself.

Wrath looked up at him. "Sorry?"

"He means, you're not wearing a shirt on under that thing," Scratch elaborated. "You're wearing it like some kind of porn star would."

Wrath looked at the apron in his hand. "I only have the one shirt," he reminded them, pointing to where it lay neatly folded on the arm of the couch. "I didn't want to stain it."

Neither could think of anything to say, so they quickly ducked into their rooms. Push pulled out one of his spare costumes and changed quickly, then let Wrath in so he could shower and shave. It dawned on him then that the man didn't even have a razor, so Push begrudgingly loaned him his Norelco.

The drive to the Association building was uneventful, save for Push's constant swearing. "You don't like to drive much, do you?" Wrath noted as Push came close to sideswiping someone.

"I don't mind driving at all," Push retorted. "I just hate everyone else who's doing it."

Iron Mechanic was waiting for them in the garage as soon as Push parked in an available space. "You made it back," the big black man noted. "How'd she handle?"

"Pretty good," Push admitted.

"Word came down this morning," Iron Mechanic told him as Scratch and Wrath climbed out. "They want some modifications added to it by noon today. Apparently, it's gotta roll out on some new gig, so the Capes have me dropping everything so I can get her ready."

"Good luck with that," Push replied.

Iron Mechanic shook his head, then went rigid as his eyes landed on Wrath, who had just come around the front of the truck, admiring it.

"New guy?" Iron Mechanic asked.

"Something like that," Push replied. "You don't recognize him?"

Iron Mechanic squinted at Wrath for a moment, thinking hard. Wrath watched the man watching him, standing perfectly still as if anticipating an attack. After a moment, Iron Mechanic looked away and walked off without a word.

"That went really well," Scratch noted sardonically.

"I am about to march with head held high into a building full of superheroes," Wrath pointed out, coming over to stand beside them. "Unarmed, I might add. A number of people died during the New Orleans Super Brawl, as the press called it. Taking this into consideration, it actually did go quite well."

Scratch frowned hard. "I really hadn't thought of that before now."

"No one's going to try and kill you," Push insisted, though he didn't quite feel the same way inside.

Wrath leveled his gaze at Push in reply. "It took zero convincing on my part for you to believe I'd sold you both out to a man who called himself the Pranksta Gayngsta, and who dressed in a manner that Anna Nicole Smith would've been ashamed of."

Push actually felt bad about that, very briefly.

"If I don't die before the day is halfway over, it will be a miracle. Your Cape Cabinet has to know that. I'm pretty sure they want to see how well I handle the pressure."

Scratch nodded. "That actually sounds like the kind of stunt they'd pull."

Push hated to admit it, but the man was right. "I'd rather not spend the day fighting off a bunch of people I'm supposed to be on the same side of. Does anyone have any ideas?"

"Flank," Scratch said simply. "You take point, and I'll come up from behind. If anyone wants to take him out, they'll have to go through one of us first."

Push frowned, but agreed.

No one bothered them on their way through the building. A few people waved, but as far as Wrath's presence went, he might as well have been just another visitor or a newbie they were showing around. He suspected that it had a lot to do with the way Wrath was dressed. He was still wearing the suit that had arrived at the hotel yesterday. Dressed like an average businessman who'd just come from work, there was really no way of telling Wrath from anyone else.

Well, that wasn't entirely accurate. Push could feel Wrath watching him the whole time they stood in the elevator together. It was like standing next to a hot poker. Even when Wrath wasn't tossing fireballs, something about his presence made the temperature rise. It made Push's skin crawl, yet at the same time, he felt drawn to it like a magnet. It didn't help that the elevator was crowded. At this time of the morning, there was no way they could have found one that was empty. With them pressed up against a wall, it would be bad if a fight broke out, but these thoughts got shoved aside as Push realized he'd somehow gotten stuffed between Scratch and Wrath.

Scratch's body was warm, yet somehow felt cooler compared to the heat coming off Wrath. Push could smell Scratch's aftershave. It was musky, yet subtle, not overpowering. Wrath wore nothing of the sort. The smell wafting off his skin, though, was spicy and darker, like some sort of potent herb. Being caught in the middle drove Push mad.

When the elevator doors opened at their floor, Push was the first one out. He was on the move before the doors had time to close. Right now, he didn't feel too terribly concerned about Wrath's health. The raging hard-on straining against his pants, as well as the tight control he'd once mastered slipping out of his grasp, were making him reckless. It was a relief when he spotted Margaret at her desk.

"We're here to see the Cape Cabinet," he said, pressing himself against it to conceal his protruding erection.

"They're waiting," she said absentmindedly. "Just go right in."

Push started to leave, but Wrath unexpectedly came up behind him. "Ma'am," he said softly, as though afraid she might scream. "I'm sorry to bother you, but if a package were mailed to this address, where might it have ended up at?"

Margaret looked up at his question and flinched. "Um," she said, sounding like Scratch for a moment. "In the mail room, I suppose."

"Thank you," he said, backing away.

"Not a problem." Her words were polite, but if the look on Margaret's face were any indication, she was the mouse who'd just been spared being eaten by the lion. "Would you like for me to check and see if there are any packages down there for you?"

Wrath lowered his head slightly in gratitude. "If you would, please."

Push turned to go and heard Wrath's footsteps following behind him. "Why would you be getting mail here?" he asked as they stood outside the Cape Cabinet room.

"No reason," Wrath replied evasively.

"It's not a bomb, is it?" Scratch asked, making Push stop short of opening the door. "Please tell me you didn't mail a bomb to this building, because they check for those things."

In answer, Wrath summoned a flume of fire into the palm of his hand. "Why would I waste time using a bomb?"

Push opened the door without another word.

The Cape Cabinet was filing in as they entered. Push made sure Wrath went first, then held the door out so Scratch could follow. The eyes of each member of the Cape Cabinet were fixated on the three of them as they lined up in a row. Push had expected Wrath to try and move off to the side, or at least put up a little resistance. However, the ex-con stood front and center between Scratch and himself without any sort of prompting.

"Welcome back, gentlemen," Shadow Devil said in a grave voice. "We need to have a little talk."

Mr. Answer glanced from where Scratch stood, over to Push, before finally settling on Wrath. "We'd like to applaud your responsible behavior, Mr. Wrath. Are you certain you're feeling up to speed?"

"I'm fine," Wrath answered in a polite tone.

"We're glad to hear it," Star Lantern said, folding both hands in front of her on top of the counter. "If the reports were any indication, the scene you escaped from was ugly. It's good to see you in such good spirits."

"There is still the matter of your real name," Rocket Grasshopper added abruptly. "Our records didn't yield any results as far as searching for your birth certificate."

"It's just Wrath," he replied. "I've gone by that for years. It might as well be my real name."

Rocket Grasshopper's eyes narrowed. "I see. Still—"

"It will have to wait," Patriot Arrow interrupted.

"Right," Booster Hawk jumped in. "The fact is, we called the three of you here because there is a situation. The villain you apprehended, the one calling himself the... Pranksta Gayngsta"—Booster Hawk's mouth twisted as the words came out, like they tasted sour to him—"escaped roughly two hours after he was arrested."

Push's eyes widened. "What?"

Scratch scowled. "How did they lose him in less than two hours?"

"We're not sure," said Star Lantern, twiddling her thumbs. "The police are still looking into it, but our preliminary report suggests he may have had help. Either way, it seems the man has fled the state and is headed south. We'd like for you to retrieve him."

"Why?" Scratch asked automatically. "Isn't that the sort of thing the police are for?"

"You turned him over to the police," Star Lantern replied pointedly. "And then he got away. How much luck do you think they'll have chasing down a man they couldn't hold onto for a whole night?"

"Besides," Mr. Answer brought up, coughing, "as we stated, it looks as though the Pranksta might have had help. If he is headed south, there's probably a reason."

None of them said a word at first. Wrath had nothing to add, standing there as though waiting in line at a truck stop. He was being utterly cool about all of this.

"If that's what you want," Push said, conceding. "When do we leave?"

"Right away," Patriot Arrow replied. "We sent word for Iron Mechanic to prep the Pussy Wagon for you. It's being upgraded right now with new features. The three of you will depart the moment it's done."

Push blanched at the thought of being back in that eyesore on wheels, but then froze as something struck him.

"We will?"

Scratch's mouth turned into a half frown, yet Push thought he heard his friend snicker for a second.

"Wrath was instrumental in the capture of your target," Mr. Answer stated, giving Push a hard look from underneath his fedora. "You'll find the Pranksta must faster this way."

"Agreed," said Rocket Grasshopper. "Mr. Wrath, we were going to give you time to get settled in and come up with your own costume, but it will have to wait. Once you return, we'll send you to a respected tailor in the industry to design something. In the meantime, I hope this won't be too great an inconvenience?"

"It's fine," said Wrath, folding his arms behind his back. "A nice view of the countryside would make for a good change of pace after being in a prison cell for so long."

"Well, try not to do anything that'll get you sent back." Rocket Grasshopper laughed, as though this statement should have been funny.

No one else on the Cape Cabinet so much as chuckled. Push was relieved. "Good luck, gentlemen," Patriot Arrow said, saluting them. "Keep us posted."

Push wanted to give them the middle finger salute, but resisted. His tongue stayed locked between his wisdom teeth for good measure until all of them were out of the room. The air in the hallway felt significantly less stale. Taking a good, deep breath, he followed behind Scratch as they walked with Wrath toward the elevator.

Margaret wasn't sitting behind the desk.

"Which floor is the mail room on?" Wrath asked, hitting the button.

"It's in the basement," Scratch told him while the doors rumbled open. "What did you have sent here?"

"You'll see."

WHATEVER modifications the Pussy Wagon was undergoing, it took half the afternoon to finish. Push and Scratch wound up going to lunch and leaving Wrath behind to pick up whatever package was waiting for him. First, of course, Push had confirmed that there had been no bomb threats. He wasn't thrilled with leaving Wrath alone, but neither he nor Scratch was in a mood to babysit after hearing what their latest assignment was.

The Burger Joint was located down the street from the RLSA building. He and Scratch would go there from time to time between missions, or when their beat was done. The place was crowded right now, but the owners were good about getting their food out to them in a hurry. Push had once helped their younger daughter when she'd been in an accident, and the father hadn't forgotten.

He and Scratch took their usual booth in the back near an old pinball machine. No one was playing on it, so the two of them took a moment to take out their frustration with a quick game. When their food arrived, Scratch was ahead by a hundred thousand points and had won two free games. Push sat down without a word and let the man finish while he ate.

"How can they lose the guy overnight?" Push grumbled as Scratch sat down opposite him.

"How are we supposed to find him when we don't even know where he's going?" Scratch wondered, munching on a fry as his eyes swept the room.

"We know where he's going," Push pointed out sarcastically. "South, remember? We just have to look all over one quarter of the country and hope our mark doesn't skip across the Rio Grande."

"Or jump on a boat headed for Cuba," Scratch added, picking his hamburger up. "Or sail across the Gulf to South America."

Push started to add something, but got cut off as he spotted Wrath coming through the front doors. The ex-con stood there sweeping the room before spotting them in the back. He had shucked the suit from earlier in favor of a long coat that came down past the knees. The sleeves of the coat had been rolled up to expose his taut forearms, and a thin shirt detailing a twisted skull was painted over the front of the T-shirt clinging to his chest. Leather pants with some sort of belts crisscrossing the lower legs clung to his body like he'd been poured into them. The boots looked heavy and surprisingly expensive. Everything he wore was solid black.

The man—and dressed as he was, there was no doubt in Push's mind that Wrath was all man—looked like he was ready for a death metal concert.

Scratch looked up from his burger as Wrath approached. "What are you wearing?" he asked around the bite in his mouth before swallowing. "Actually, screw that. Where did you get it?"

"It's my costume," Wrath replied in his calm tone, though Push thought it carried an edge to it now, like the answer should have been clear. "It's what I wore when I worked in New Orleans. I had a friend ship it to me."

Push put two and two together. "This is what was waiting for you in the mail room?"

"I couldn't send it to the hotel," he pointed out as Scratch moved over to let him sit down. "We weren't going to be there long, and I didn't know your address. The RLSA headquarters was the only thing that came to mind."

Scratch was giving Wrath's costume an appreciative look now, which made bile rise up Push's throat. "I like it," Scratch admitted. "But the Cape Cabinet will probably make you wear something else."

"I'd rather wear this," Wrath replied. "It feels comfortable, and was tailored to fit me. Plus, the fabrics are flame retardant."

"They'll still raise hell about it," Push insisted, looking away from both of them. "The members of the Cape Cabinet have this idea that all of RLSA members should dress like they're from the Silver Age. The debate was still going on when I joined about the necessity of capes versus their impracticality in a fight."

"I'll never forget when that Las Vegas trick gunslinger tried to join, and they raised hell about the fact that guns were a bad influence for children," Scratch added.

Wrath said nothing in response to this, but watched Push closely as he went back to eating his hamburger.

"Did you want something?" Scratch asked after a minute. "We weren't sure if you were hungry or not."

"I haven't got any money," Wrath reminded him, though not unkindly.

In answer, Scratch hailed a waitress and asked her to bring another burger and fries. The girl noticed Wrath and promptly blushed before walking off quickly with a nod.

"She's cute," Wrath noted.

"I like coming here," Scratch said, grinning. "Most of the servers are really hot. The food is awesome too."

"It's a burger," Wrath pointed out dryly. "It could taste like cardboard and would still be a welcome change compared to what I've been chewing down for the last ten years."

Scratch laughed at this. Together, he and Wrath began counting down the number of attractive waitresses who passed near their booth. Push listened, feeling sorry for himself and wishing they'd shut up and eat. Even after Wrath's food arrived, they kept at it.

Push had thought after the incident in the go-go bar in Grand Rapids that Wrath might pitch for his team. He hadn't considered the possibility of Wrath being a potential fuck friend. Being his parole officer tasked his patience enough as it was, but the thought of there being another superhero in the RLSA who was gay did have its appeal. Push would have picked just about anyone besides Wrath to fill that role, but it was a testament to how sad his life had gotten that he'd looked forward to Wrath being gay.

Now he was watching his best friend bond with the guy over which pair of tits bounced the best and learning just how far off base he'd been. Feeling more than slightly dejected, Push finished his meal and waited on the other two to polish theirs off. He was getting angry now, and that was never a good sign.

It was a relief when his phone went off. Margaret was on the other end, sounding bereaved and highly agitated about something. The new and improved Pussy Wagon had just left the garage and was being delivered as they spoke. Push gave their location quickly so she could update the onboard computer, and she hung up without another word. It sounded to Push as though the Cape Cabinet had her doing twelve different things at the same time. Pocketing his phone, Push informed Wrath and Scratch that it was time to go, then slapped a fifty down onto the table as payment. The two continued their conversation as they followed Push to the door. They had since moved on to some of their favorite actresses. Scratch had the leg up in this, being that Wrath had been out of circulation, and was filling the ex-con in on the many virtues of Milla Jovovich.

It was going to be a very long drive.

CHAPTER
FIVE

THE amazing part was that the Cape Cabinet had some idea of where to send them.

Of course, none of them found this out until they were inside the remodeled Pussy Wagon and on their way out of Chicago. The truck had indeed been upgraded. All three men had stopped dead in their tracks when they saw it. A pair of cat ears had been mounted on the roof above the windshield. Iron Mechanic's crew had, he later learned after calling the man to find out what the hell he'd been thinking, added some colorful purple stripes to simulate a cat's patterned fur. The paint was a new fast-drying variety that was donated to the Association for testing purposes, so the company could gauge its endurance during stressful driving situations.

The changes were, the mechanic swore, not his idea. The orders had come from the Cape Cabinet, but because of last minute repair problems with several other cars, his crew hadn't gotten to the truck before Scratch and Push took it out on the road. Upon hearing this, Push swore loudly and hung up on the man. It had been bad enough when they were riding around in an STD incubator. Now they looked like an advertisement for cat chow.

Scratch, naturally, found the whole thing funny. Only Wrath seemed to take it in stride, and he settled down in the back without a word. Once they were all inside, the GPS screen brought up the coordinates for where the Pranksta Gayngsta had been spotted last. It seemed a number of reports had already come through about possible sightings. Some, Push knew, were either common mistakes, or deliberate attempts to throw them off. From the looks of the line of dots, however, it was his theory that the Gayngsta had already left Illinois.

"We've got a long drive ahead of us," Push muttered as Scratch pulled out into the street.

The drive started off quiet, though not of the uncomfortable variety. Push hit the radio without being asked and pulled up a station both he and Scratch enjoyed. It occurred to him that he knew nothing at all about Wrath's musical tastes, much less if the man had any. He considered dismissing this, but it kept nagging at him. After a moment, he looked over to where Wrath was sprawled out in back.

"Is this okay with you?"

Wrath opened his eyes at the question. His face looked surprised for a second, but quickly shifted to a more neutral expression, and he cocked an eyebrow, curious as to what Push meant. Push pointed toward the radio in answer.

"Do you like this sort of music?"

"I'm more of a classics guy myself," Wrath said, shutting his eyes halfway.

Push thought for a moment, and started to reach for the knob.

"That doesn't mean you have to change it," he added, opening his eyes again. "You're the one riding shotgun."

"Um, we can listen to something else if you want later," Scratch said, turning the wheel gently. He was far more of a defensive driver than Push. "Once we get far enough out of the city, we won't be able to pick up the signal."

Wrath said nothing, so Push settled back into his seat. Once again, the man's politeness was getting under his skin, and he couldn't put his finger on why.

They didn't make it out of Illinois before dark. Reports kept coming in regularly over the computer, and each one showed the Gayngsta's location further south than before. In the beginning, the sightings were somewhat scattered, and the Pussy Wagon doubled back a couple of times before they got word that it was a false alarm. Pretty soon, though, the dots were coming in on a straight line. Every so often one would jump off to the side, but Push could see how they were forming a path southwest from Chicago.

"We're about to hit Missouri," Push said, glancing at the screen while Scratch went over the data. They had stopped at a gas station at one point to take a piss break and switch drivers. "Maybe he's headed for Texas?"

"If he wanted to jump the border, he wouldn't have come this far south," replied Scratch, hitting a couple of keystrokes. "It would have been easier to just swim to Canada."

Wrath rose up from the backseat. "Something is coming through," he noticed. "There's been another sighting."

"This one says he's in Arkansas," Push read. "How in the world did he get that far south so fast?"

"Furthermore," Scratch added, "what would he want in Arkansas? Um, something about this doesn't sound right."

Wrath looked over Scratch's shoulder at the computer screen. "That's Shove Point," he said, sounding upset.

Scratch frowned, and looked Wrath square in the face. "That's where you were captured after the Deadly Seven broke up, wasn't it?"

Wrath sat back in response. "This is all wrong."

Scratch glanced at Push. "Is there something in Shove Point the Pranksta Gayngsta might want, or somebody he could ask for help?"

"No," Wrath answered stiffly.

"Level with us, man," Push said, watching Wrath closely via the rearview mirror. "If you know something about the place, fill us in. Why would a crackpot like the Pranksta Gayngsta break out of prison to go there?"

"Yeah," Scratch agreed, giving Wrath a look of his own now. "You gotta admit, this sounds really odd."

"I never said it wasn't odd," Wrath replied, looking out the window at the darkness. "Shove Point is just a Podunk town surrounded by trees. I think there may be a sawmill there, but overall, it's a two-story town with maybe a couple thousand people to its name. There's very little anyone could call remarkable about it."

The air inside the truck was thick. "Still," Wrath added, shifting in the backseat. "Your mark drove about ten hours to get there, so perhaps he knows someone."

Push said nothing in reply. As fishy as it all sounded, there was little in Wrath's voice that suggested he was lying to them. That wasn't to say Push trusted the man. Wrath did not lie back down on the seat, opting instead to sit up and watch the road. The man was visibly uncomfortable, and though Push told himself it was likely because the town of Shove Point held unpleasant memories for him, he didn't believe it. At one point, he chanced a glance back at Wrath in the mirror. Something about the look in his eyes and the way the man held himself so stiffly made Push think they were headed for trouble.

Unfortunately, there was no way of getting around it. Push hoped the Pranksta would keep going and another sighting would come up on the screen. Nothing happened, however, and before long, they were coming into the city limits of Shove Point, Arkansas. Wrath flexed his fingers into a grip as they passed the city line, and a small plume of fire erupted out of his palm as he opened it back up.

"Sorry," he apologized. "My fault."

They had been on the road for hours, and it was well into the dark hours of the morning. "Any idea where we can find a motel?" Push asked.

"Turn left up here," Wrath said. "Then hit a right and go for about ten miles. There was an old motel near the interstate at one point."

Push reacted without thinking and spun the wheel as Wrath directed. Scratch, however exhausted, was much faster on the uptake. "I thought you were here for a couple of hours before that cop caught you," he wondered. "How is it you remember something like that?"

"Who knows?" Wrath replied evasively.

Push was far too tired to care at this point. He kept his mind focused on not running off the road and turned whenever Wrath directed him to. The town was indeed small. None of the buildings were higher than two stories and most of them looked old. It was the sort of place you might see on an old television program. Something about it gave Push the creeps.

Thankfully, Wrath turned out to be right. On the far end of the northwestern side of town, the interstate cut through. Push noticed that this appeared to be the most industrial part of Shove Point. A Wal-Mart was centered practically a few steps further uphill and surrounding it were all sorts of stores and eateries. The motel was located on the left just before the turnoff exit. Push was able to pull in without any interference. Being so late, there was no traffic on the roads.

The lit sign in the window said they were open. All three men climbed out without a word and marched through the door up to the front desk. A pot-bellied man in a dark T-shirt was staring at a TV. He looked up as the bell jingled above the door and froze.

"Can we get a room for the night?" Push asked sleepily, pulling his wallet out to retrieve the Association card. "With two beds and a shower?"

The man didn't move. His eyes kept darting from Push to Wrath and Scratch standing behind him. Push held the card out farther, but the man didn't take it. Finally, after letting out a deep sigh, he reached behind him for a key card off the wall and tossed it onto the counter. The card skidded over the side and landed near Push's feet. Push waited until the man jerked the credit card out of his hands before bending down to retrieve it.

The machine was printing out the receipt when Push rose back up. Push signed, mindful all the while of the man staring daggers at him, then pushed the paper back to him with a nod. The man accepted it, then presented all three of them with his back. It was clear they were supposed to leave.

"Great service," Scratch commented once they were back outside.

"Who cares?" Push replied. "I just want to crash for about eight hours or so, then find this lunatic so we can get the fuck out of here."

"Sounds good," his friend said.

Their room was on the very end of the farthest row, well out of the way of any ice machine. Push opened the door, needing to use the key card three times before the lock would accept it. The interior was nothing to talk about, but he could not have cared less at that point. All three began stripping out of their clothes. One of the problems with spandex was that it clung to the body. When a person sweats, the fabric is even more averse to letting go. Wrath freed himself first and, to Push's surprise, was not wearing underwear underneath.

Scratch shucked down to his boxers and climbed under the covers of the opposite bed without saying goodnight. Push stood for a moment, still in his spandex pants, suddenly facing a conundrum. He and Scratch didn't share a bed with one another. Push had always been too terrified of the prospect. There was always the fear in his mind that he would do something unforeseen to his friend while half-asleep, assuming he was able to sleep at all. Now, as he struggled with his pants, he felt himself torn in two. He could either bunk down with the convicted killer who had the ability to incinerate him, and had demonstrated poor self-control just recently inside the truck, or he could risk humiliating himself with his long-time friend and partner.

The fact that he chose to climb in next to the naked supervillain spoke volumes. Push was not oblivious to this as he lay back against the pillow. His mind must have been shot to hell from the stress of the day, because the first image to hit him as he shut his eyes was of Wrath snoring in the raw just inches away.

That was what Push told himself for the next half hour, until sleep finally claimed him.

THE pounding on the door only woke Push up part of the way. Rolling over and feeling the heavy erection pressing into his ass sent him flying out of bed. Push whirled around, unsure at first of where he was, and accidentally sent out a telekinetic burst that made the waste basket and coat rack flip through the air. This was enough to bring him out of his stupor, and the last twelve hours came rushing back almost all at once. Wrath rose up out of bed, watching Push through a curtain of tousled hair. The bed sheet had spilled off his lower half thanks to Push cartwheeling to the floor in a panic, displaying Wrath's manhood for the whole room to see.

Push felt his throat dry up as Scratch looked around through half-closed eyes. "What?" he mumbled. "Did somebody knock?"

The pounding on the door came again, nearly shaking it off its hinges. "I'll get it," Push said, grateful for anything that would keep him from staring at Wrath's thick shaft, not to mention the heavy-looking pair of low hangers spilling out onto the fitted sheet. The image burned into his brain as Push reached around clumsily for his pants.

Scratch stood in the meantime and staggered past Push toward the bathroom in only his boxers. Push was fighting with his left pants leg as his roommate trudged past, still not quite awake, and in Scratch's stupor, he accidentally brushed his crotch across Push's toes.

"Hm, sorry," Scratch mumbled, continuing on in his quest to relieve himself.

Push forced himself to remain in control. His frustration and anger were enough to help him push his leg all the way in, and he stood with his pants on a few seconds later. The pounding was echoing through the room now. Behind him, Wrath was zipping up his leather pants and coming around to join him. Push considered ordering him back, but thought better of it immediately. They were in a strange town and weren't expecting visitors. Best to have the guy who could set the building ablaze with a snap of his fingers close by, even if Push was still leery of him.

Push was undoing the chain and bolted locks when someone shouted on the other side. "Open up!" a man's voice yelled gruffly. "Police!"

Push paused. "The hell?" he wondered, looking back at Wrath.

"Sorry," he mumbled around a very big yawn. "I haven't done anything yet."

"Right," said Push before opening the door.

Two men stood side by side in the morning sun, dressed for bear in their uniforms and wearing dark shades. Push squinted and saw their badges marked them both as deputies.

"Can we help you?" Push asked.

"Sure," the taller of the two replied in a thick Southern drawl. "You boys mind telling us what you're doing down here?"

Push felt Wrath come up behind him. "Morning," he said, sounding very cheerful all of a sudden. "It's been a long time, hasn't it, Officer Fortenberry?"

Push saw Wrath was speaking to the shorter and rounder of the two men. "Forgive me," Wrath amended quickly. "It's Deputy Fortenberry now, isn't it?"

The deputy frowned as he reached up with one hand to lower his shades. "I know you, son?"

"Briefly," Wrath replied, smiling now. "About ten years ago, to my recollection."

Push moved back slightly as Wrath extended an arm out toward the two cops. Fire crackled to life in his palm as he held it up level with their eyes.

"We didn't get much of a chance to talk, though."

Deputy Fortenberry went pale. His skin faded from a healthy pink color to the sick shade that only corpses were supposed to have. The now paste-colored skin shone in the sunlight as Wrath closed his fist, extinguishing the fire. Fortenberry stepped back, clipping the other deputy on the shoulder as Scratch finally came to the door.

"Problems?" he asked, glancing from Wrath to Push.

"I'm not sure yet," Push admitted, looking from Wrath to Fortenberry, who was already headed back to the squad car parked illegally some twenty feet away.

His partner kept turning from them to the squad car, looking confused. When his eyes turned back to Wrath again for the last time, though, something seemed to click in his head, and the man was gone in a flash. Push saw Fortenberry speaking to someone over the radio very quickly.

"Yeah, I'd say we're going to have problems," said Push, letting out a very long sigh. "Care to explain what that was all about?"

"Fortenberry was the one who arrested me," Wrath answered simply.

Everything fell into place. "Great," Push groaned.

"The cops would show up on our doorstep the morning after we arrived," Scratch grumbled, watching both men now with interest.

"And while traveling with what they believe to be a known fugitive," Push reminded. "I doubt word of Wrath's release made it all the way down here."

Scratch just rolled his eyes and shut the hotel room door. "Um, this is going to be one of those days, isn't it?"

The three of them opted to finish getting dressed while they waited for the shit to hit the fan. The squad car was still parked in the same spot as earlier when Push walked out into the parking lot in his Association uniform. The moment they spotted him, the squad car roared to life and peeled out of there like a bat out of hell. Push watched it leave, shaking his head.

"That could have gone better," Wrath mused, coming up alongside him.

"If you hadn't rattled the guy, we wouldn't be in this mess," Push reminded him.

"It would have happened anyway." Wrath shuffled his feet in the gravel as he spoke. "Better to go ahead and get it over with now. Besides, aren't you under the Association's protection?"

"The Association walks a thin line when it comes to the cops," Push replied. "And I'm pretty certain the locals here will like us stomping all over their territory even less than the average cops do. The last thing we need is for them to go *Deliverance* on our asses and force us to defend ourselves."

"I wouldn't mind. The thought of putting my hands around Fortenberry's fat neck kept me warm on a lot of cold prison nights."

"No," Push said flatly, turning to face him. "Let's get something straight. You are with the Association now, and we have enough problems as it is getting the authorities to accept us without you going off on some personal vendetta. The Association managed to get you out on parole. Like it or not for either of us, you're a part of the team, and that means acting like it."

"Fine," Wrath said at once. "I never actually said I would actively try to kill him, if you will recall. However, Association or no, if the man tries to pull something, I won't hesitate to burn the fat off his thick bones."

Push glowered, but did not protest. "If you have to defend yourself, that's fine. I don't think it'll come to that, but so we're clear, you are within your rights to protect yourself from an attack."

"I would have done it anyway," Wrath replied. "But thank you for filling me in."

"What's going on?" Scratch called out, coming out of their hotel room to meet them. "I thought I heard a car peel out of here."

"You missed it," Wrath told him. "The police just left."

"We're going to have problems with them here, I think," Push explained, glaring back at Wrath again. "Of course, it would have helped if somebody hadn't scared the shit out of that one deputy."

"He asked for it," Wrath said flatly.

"The fat one?" Scratch asked, and there was no mistaking the impish smile on his face now. "What was the deal with him?"

"Fortenberry was the one who arrested me." Wrath quickly filled him in. "It would seem this helped him become a deputy in the local police department."

Scratch's mouth twisted into a half frown. "You got arrested by that guy?"

"Good point," Push mused, giving Wrath a look. "How did that happen, exactly?"

It was Wrath's turn to sigh heavily now. "I had just fled New Orleans after the Deadly Seven's big fight with the Association."

"Why come here?" Push interrupted.

"I was just passing through," Wrath replied quickly. "Anyway, Fortenberry was on patrol and flashed his blue lights at me for trespassing. I had just ditched the car I'd ridden in at a parking lot and was on foot. Apparently, he thought I looked like a shady character and decided to toss me in the cooler."

The same squad car was coming down the main road toward the hotel parking entrance now, its lights flashing. A second one was right behind it, its own strobes on. Wrath saw this, but kept talking.

"I was going to walk off," he explained. "Even back then, the man weighed three hundred pounds easily. I didn't think he would shoot."

"He shot you?" Scratch asked, stunned.

"No," Wrath replied. "He hit me on the side of the head with the butt of his gun."

Push cocked an eyebrow skeptically. "He pistol-whipped you?"

"Um," Scratch stammered. "I'm pretty sure that's illegal. Unless you were trying to set him on fire or something?"

"No."

The squad cars came to a stop near the front of the hotel, far away from the three of them.

"I was keeping a low profile," Wrath continued. "If I'd started throwing fireballs, it would have clued people in to who I was. I just told him to get lost. The next thing I knew, the lights were going out and I had a migraine. I woke up in a jail cell the next morning. Apparently, while I was out, a news report had come on TV with my face all over it. The sheriff had phoned it in, and the FBI was at their doorstep a few minutes after my head had cleared, armed with these weird foam guns that they hosed me down with."

Scratch laughed, but Wrath didn't appear upset. "To hear Fortenberry talk, he had wrestled me singlehandedly into his car while I was setting the whole town ablaze."

Push waved for the two of them to quiet down as the sheriff approached. The man looked to be in his fifties, with a weather-beaten face that seemed perpetually run down.

"Can I help you gentlemen with something?"

"It's good that you're here, Sheriff," Push told him, using his best approachable voice. "We were just on our way to pay you a visit at your office."

Push's tone seemed to catch the man off guard a bit, which was exactly what he'd hoped it would do. Most cops expected Association members to brush them off as nonexistent or get in their faces.

"The Association put us on assignment chasing after a dangerous escaped criminal," Push went on. "We were the ones who helped the authorities in Grand Rapids bring him in, and after word came through that he'd busted out, they asked us to go after him. We've been following him half the night and think he might have stopped here."

"Is that right?"

The sheriff was a tall, thin man, not as tall as the unnamed deputy standing far back behind him, but imposing. He seemed unnerved by the sight of all three of them, but hadn't threatened to run them out of town or make them disappear yet, which Push took as a positive sign.

"Um, has there been anyone strange lurking around since last night?" Scratch chimed in.

"You mean aside from you three?" the sheriff countered.

"Aside from us, yes," Push clarified.

"No," the sheriff answered. "Any chance this runner you three are chasing after could have kept on going?"

"It's possible," Push acknowledged, knowing what the sheriff was really asking. "His trail stopped cold here, though. There weren't any other sightings after the one here."

"Here?" The sheriff frowned hard at this. "Ain't nobody I know reported anything about seeing an escaped felon here in Shove Point."

"We thought it was strange," Scratch readily admitted. "At first, we suspected he might know someone here in town."

The sheriff thought this over for a moment, then looked past Push at Wrath. "Don't I know you from somewhere, son?"

"I just have that sort of face, sir," Wrath replied.

It was clear the sheriff didn't buy it for a second. "Well," the sheriff went on, looking back and forth at them. "You three have sure as sin managed to cause quite a stir. My two deputies came running into the station saying we were being invaded by a horde of superpowered freaks like on the news."

"As far as we know, our mark doesn't have any powers," Scratch assured the man. "He just looks really weird. If you've seen the guy, you would remember him."

The sheriff nodded. "You got a picture of the guy?"

"We can have someone fax it to you," Push said.

"You do that," said the sheriff. "Then I think you boys better come down to the station so we can sort this whole mess out. This is supposed to be a quiet little strip, gentlemen, and I don't like surprises in my town."

Scratch locked their room up and checked them out of the hotel. It was more for show than anything, to help give the impression they would be on their way as soon as possible. The sheriff stayed by his squad car the whole time, then followed them with his gaze as they marched over to the Pussy Wagon. The two deputies started laughing as soon as they spotted it.

"How in the world did they miss this thing?" Scratch wondered, starting the truck up.

"You've just witnessed the competence of the Shove Point police department," Wrath noted in a heated tone. "Expect more of the same standard."

"Wonderful," Push said wearily, sending the information for the fax over his phone.

The squad cars went first and managed to ditch the Pussy Wagon at a stop light. Scratch started to run it, but got cut off by a beat-up old Chevy with mud-colored doors.

"Terrific," Scratch grumbled. "Wrath, I don't suppose you remember which way the police department was?"

"Turn left at the next light, then keep going straight," Wrath answered. "Though they could have moved it since I was last there."

"We'll risk it," said Push as the light turned green.

Wrath was right on target. The sheriff and his men hadn't bothered waiting on them, so Scratch pulled up and parked the Pussy Wagon in the parallel space directly in front of the building. Push had a gut feeling his partner had done this to tweak them off, since the words "Pussy Wagon" were emblazoned on the side for all to see. One woman with a four-year-old girl froze up as they climbed out. Her daughter stood beside her, staring for a moment, then found herself being jerked along down the sidewalk.

"Cute kid," Wrath noted. "She'll be the envy of her preschool class tomorrow morning when she tells them what she saw."

The sheriff was in his office, apparently. The trio found themselves greeted by a receptionist upon entering, who took up several minutes of their time openly staring before finally getting on the phone.

"Who… should I say is calling?" she asked, looking back and forth between them, clearly unsure which of them she should ask.

"We're with the Real-Life Superhero Association," Push said. "It's Push, by the way."

"Scratch," said Scratch, introducing himself with his best smile, which succeeded in making the red-haired woman blush.

"Wrath," Wrath said simply.

The woman started to speak into the phone again, then looked back up sharply to stare at Wrath again. Her eyes widened, but after darting a glance toward Push and Scratch, she went back to the phone.

"He'll see you in just a moment," she told them, keeping her eyes fixed on Wrath the whole time. "Please, have a seat… somewhere."

There was nowhere to sit, but it was clear they were making her uncomfortable, so Push motioned for them to stand against a wall farther down so they wouldn't be in the nervous receptionist's direct line of sight. This proved utterly useless, though, since she would periodically tilt her head to the side and sneak a peek at them.

Scratch thought it was hilarious. "What did you do while you were here?"

"Not much, really," Wrath said earnestly. "I wasn't in town long enough to cause any major trouble."

Push noticed Wrath was watching a door leading into the back closely. "Everyone here seems to know who you are," he said, seeing Wrath's expression deepen.

"A place like Shove Point doesn't get much excitement," Wrath replied halfheartedly, his eyes still focused on whatever was holding his interest beyond that one door. "The capture of a notorious criminal is the sort of thing that would stay in everyone's minds for years."

Wrath looked toward the receptionist, who had been watching him the whole time and quickly jerked her head back yet again. "Right now, she's trying to figure out if I'm the same guy or just someone who looks like me."

"What?" Scratch wondered curiously. "Are you a mind reader on top of being a pyrokinetic? Isn't that cheating?"

"I'm not a mind reader," Wrath insisted quietly, watching the receptionist closely now. "I'm just good at reading folks. Humans have such simple ways of giving away what they're really feeling."

A side door, different from the one Wrath had been watching so closely, opened, and out came the sheriff. Push realized he hadn't gotten the man's name, and he scanned the plaque adorning what was, it turned out, the sheriff's office door.

"Sheriff Black," Push greeted him, hoping a nod would pass for a handshake.

Black looked at all three of them and made a face, as though he were still having trouble accepting they were really there.

"I didn't catch you gentlemen's names," he stated, as if fighting off swallowing something sour.

"Push."

"Wrath."

"Scratch."

Sheriff Black looked from one to the other. His head jerked from Scratch back to Wrath again as realization dawned on him.

"It's been a while, Sheriff Black," Wrath said, as though greeting an old friend. "Does your prison cell still have the little memento I left in there?"

Scratch gave Wrath a hard look, while Black's eyes doubled in size. "He's with us," Push explained, hoping to defuse the situation before the man opened fire. "Wrath volunteered to join the Association in exchange for being let out early on parole. My partner and I are showing him the ropes."

Black didn't hide his disgust now. "You're letting some freak run around on the streets with you? What in the Sam Hill is going on up there in Chicago?"

Push wasn't sure how to respond, but Wrath saved him the trouble. "Don't feel too bad, sir," he said. "They've been wondering that for the past two days."

Scratch and Push glanced at one another.

"You look different," Black commented on Wrath, giving him a once-over now. "Even done up like you are, I didn't recognize you."

"No, you don't recognize me."

Push frowned at that statement.

"I was a lot skinner back then," Wrath went on. "I could barely fit into my clothes, and my hair wasn't quite as long as it is now."

"Huh, don't look too much longer," Black mused, turning his head from side to side. "But then, I really didn't pay that much attention to you. Those feds said you were dangerous, and I took them at their word. We were told to keep away from that cell you were in."

"I know."

Black looked nervous all of a sudden. Wrath had gotten under the man's skin somehow, and the sheriff was doing a poor job of hiding it.

"I learned something before you boys arrived," Black went on, avoiding Wrath completely now. "Early this morning, they caught some poor drunk bastard staggering along down main street. He kept saying something was after him, so my boys threw him in the cooler to sober up. Word is, he's still passed out in there."

Scratch looked at Push and shrugged. "It's worth a look."

"Let's see," Push agreed. "If you wouldn't mind, sheriff?"

"This way," the sheriff said, motioning for all three to follow. "The sooner we find this guy, the sooner you gentlemen can be on your way."

"Gladly," Push heard Wrath mutter.

The sheriff overhead it as well and gave him a hard stare before unlocking the door to the back where the cells were. "Try not to burn the place down," he shot at Wrath. "We've remodeled since you were last here."

"I'll keep it in mind," Wrath replied.

The walls in the cell area were concrete brick and had been coated in a fresh layer of paint. The bars looked brand new, and the floors looked as though they'd been swept recently. The air still stank of piss, however, and the overhead lights flickered as they walked under them. There were only a handful of cells, and out of those, two were occupied. The first held a woman with a birthmark on her exposed shoulder. Judging by her attire, Push figured she was the local prostitute.

"Howdy, sheriff," she said as Black walked past without acknowledging her presence. "Nice bunch of new deputies you've got there."

"Thank you, ma'am," Scratch obliged humorously.

"I'd appreciate it if you wouldn't speak with my prisoners, son," Black grunted. "Here we go, then. He's still out like a light, so it's you boys' call whether you want to go in there and see if he's yours. He puked all over Deputy McGee's shoes before, though, so be careful."

The sheriff had stopped in front of the next to last cell in the row. Inside, a figure was wrapped up in a blanket. Push was reminded of a small dog cowering in fear from thunder. The blanket rose and fell with each breath the man took, but it covered too much of the bed for Push to tell if it was the Pranksta or not. The prisoner had pulled the blanket up over his head.

"It's him," said Wrath without a trace of doubt in his voice.

Scratch rolled his eyes. "Sure," he said sardonically. "Why don't you go in there and prove it, then?"

Without a word of protest, Wrath stepped forward and turned toward the sheriff expectantly. The sheriff watched him for a moment before moving to unlock the door.

"Isn't this the same cell you were put in?" he asked as the heavy bars clanged open.

"It was," Wrath replied, stepping inside. "Try not to lock me in."

"Watch your feet," Scratch warned.

Wrath marched up to the cot hinged to the wall without hesitating, and yanked up the bundle, blanket and all. The figure underneath fought back, suddenly very much awake and sober enough to stand. Wrath resolved this with a chop to the back of his neck before wrestling him forward.

"Here," he told Push and Scratch, pulling the blanket away so they could see his face. "See for yourselves."

A good day's worth of stubble covered the man's face. His eyes were bloodshot, like he'd partied way too hard, and blood leaked from where his lower lip had been split open. Despite all this, Push recognized him as the Pranksta Gayngsta. It was surreal seeing him this way without the makeup, get-up, and attitude.

"It's him," Push confirmed. "A little worse for wear. What happened to his lip?"

Black looked at Push like this was the stupidest question he'd ever heard. "Take him outta here, boys, and best you don't come back for a while."

"Let me go, bitch!" the Pranksta shouted as Wrath began manhandling him down the hall toward the door.

"Nice meeting you, boys," the woman in the first cell called out coyly as they passed.

"Delilah," Wrath responded, giving her a nod.

"Delilah?"

Wrath looked at Push as they entered the main area. "In a town like this," Wrath explained, accepting the cuffs Push offered him to restrain the Pranksta, "there's always a Delilah. People here have this thing for Biblical sin. It's sort of like truth in advertising."

Push didn't believe it for a second. The Pranksta continued giving Wrath a hard time as they dragged him over to the sheriff's office so they could fill out the release papers. After a moment more of this, Wrath got him to sit still by flashing flames in his face. Push started to protest but ultimately looked away.

"Officially, what'd this joker do that they'd send you three after him?" the sheriff asked.

Push looked up from the forms while Scratch went over to give Wrath a hand. "He orchestrated several bank robberies and almost drove the guy who owns them into bankruptcy."

"That fucker had it coming," the Pranksta growled in the same nasally voice he'd used in the warehouse after they'd caught him. "First he said I wasn't good enough for his daughter, then he tried to run me into the ground."

Everyone ignored him.

"Not like I could've pulled that shit off without help, anyway!"

Wrath let go of the Pranksta and held both of his hands up on either side of his face. Flames burned out from his fingertips, licking their way through the air toward the Pranksta's eyes.

"Be quiet," he growled.

The Pranksta went deathly silent, save for a squeaking noise that escaped out through his tightly pressed lips.

Sheriff Black's eyes never left Wrath as the flames eased back away from the Pranksta's face. Push saw the sheriff's hand grip the gun hanging from his belt and quickly scribbled down the rest of the information as fast as he could.

"Done," he said, sliding the papers over the crowded desk. "We'll get out of your way now, Sheriff Black."

"See that you do," Black said, watching as they left.

"This was almost too easy," Wrath commented as they exited the building. "Is it always like that?"

Scratch gave the receptionist a wave before turning around. "Sometimes," he said, smiling to himself. "But not always. If something bad were going to happen, it would have by now."

The rear window to the Pussy Wagon shattered as a gunshot rang out through the air. Everybody froze except for the Pranksta Gayngsta, who slipped out of Wrath's fingers and bolted like a jackrabbit, zig-zagging through the parking lot.

"Shit!" Scratch cursed. "Um, I should not have said that."

"Dammit," Wrath growled. "He's getting away."

Shots rained down on them, spraying the concrete in front of them with bullets. Push and Scratch both ducked down, but Wrath started to move in the direction of the Pranksta, who was out of the lot and already moving down the street with both hands still cuffed behind his back. Another shot stopped Wrath cold, and without thinking, Push jumped up to yank him down to the ground.

"Stay down!" he shouted in Wrath's ear. "We'll get him later."

"Over here!" Scratch, who had already rolled back behind the truck, was motioning to Push and Wrath.

Wrath, however, looked around as more gunfire rained down on them. "There!" he said, pointing up to the roof of the sheriff's department. "He's on the roof!"

The shooter was already moving. Push thrust out with his palm, letting loose with a telekinetic shock wave that could have brought down a horse. Time and distance still mattered with his powers, and with his target so far away, Push had no option but to risk injuring the guy. The blast shattered the edge of the building as the figure started running, knocking him forward off his feet. Sheriff Black came charging out the front doors as Wrath broke into a run.

"The fuck is going on out here?" Black shouted, his gun aimed upward.

"Sheriff!" Push called out.

Debris was on its way down over the exact spot where Sheriff Black had planted his feet. Wrath saw this and made a beeline for the armed man. Black saw Wrath coming and pointed his gun, but then froze as the first piece of stone, about the size of a man's fist, shattered against the concrete. Sheriff Black looked up as Wrath reached him. Their bodies connected, sending each one rolling over on top of the other back toward the door as brick and mortar rained down, missing them by but a few feet.

"Um, nice hit," Scratch said, getting out from behind the Pussy Wagon. "Getting a little carried away, aren't we?"

"We need to get to the roof," Push barked, ignoring his comment for now. "Please tell me you have your grappling hook on you!"

Scratch smirked and charged forward with Push at his side, whipping the two pieces of the specially made cue stick out as he went. Scratch fired the tip into the air as they slid to a stop near Wrath and the sheriff, who were getting to their feet.

"Go around the back," Push ordered Wrath, grabbing hold of Scratch. "If he tries to get away, do whatever it takes to stop him, but try not to burn the man to death."

"No burning," Wrath repeated, nodding. "Got it."

Sheriff Black stood for a second as Push ascended into the air with his arms wrapped around Scratch's waist. "Where the hell do they get that stuff from?" he muttered.

"eBay," Wrath quipped, already on the move. "You coming or not?"

Push and Scratch reached the roof's edge as Wrath and Sheriff Black rounded the corner of the building. Seizing the edge, Push launched himself off Scratch's shoulders in a flip. The instant his feet touched the tar, he reached around to help his partner up the rest of the way.

"Forget me," Scratch protested, even as he was being dragged up. "He's getting away."

Push didn't let go of Scratch. "No, he's not," he insisted.

Once Scratch was settled, Push rounded on their escaping sniper. The creep had made it to the other side of the roof and was securing a rappel line to his belt. He was dressed all in black, wearing a ski mask of some sort to conceal his face. Push didn't hesitate and thrust his palm out. The telekinetic blast slammed into the man, making him stagger. Push had held back deliberately to avoid sending him over the side, but this turned out to be a mistake. The perp shrugged the force blast off like it was nothing and kept going. Push tried again, this time putting much more "oomph" behind his attack, but the man only flinched like he'd been slapped.

"What is this guy made of?" Push wondered as Scratch moved in to give it a try. "That one should've blown him off the building."

"He must get a lot of iron in his diet," quipped Scratch, tossing a green billiard ball into the air. "Let's get sticky."

The more weighted cue stick was in his hands and assembled in a flicker of movement. As the ball came back down, Scratch took aim and sent it flying with one jab. The green ball flew toward the surface of the roof in a diagonal line, ricocheting off to strike the sniper in the gut. Upon impact, it shattered into bits, releasing a sticky, off-white cream that folded around its target. The sniper found himself encased in a coat of glue.

Push smiled as he watched the perp fight to free his arms, which were glued solid to his sides. "Nice shot," he commented. "As always."

"It's a gift," Scratch said. "Um, wanna give it one more go?"

"Nah," Push replied, looking back toward the trapped sniper. "He's not going anywhere now."

In answer, the sniper let out a roar. A wet tearing sound rang in Push's ears, and he watched in utter disbelief as the sniper tore his arms loose.

Scratch was dumbfounded. "That stuff was made to stop a charging elephant," he gasped. "Who the hell is this guy?"

The sniper didn't waste his time with them, surprisingly. Grabbing the rappel rope, he vaulted over the side, bouncing off the building on his way to the ground.

"Getting away," Push answered. "Let's hope the sheriff and Wrath haven't killed each other yet."

"Freeze!" they heard Sheriff Black's voice shouting from down below.

"Great," Scratch muttered as he and Push ran to the edge. "Now let's just hope that guy doesn't get his hands on them first."

"If he gets his hands on them, he won't be letting go," Push reminded. "He's still covered in all that glue, remember?"

A gunshot shut Push up. Down below, Sheriff Black was returning fire. The sniper had pulled out a .357 Magnum. The recoil didn't so much as shake his arm as he fired straight for the sheriff's head. Wrath sent out a fireball that sailed over the row of cars he and Black had taken cover behind in an arch. The sniper leaped back as the fireball landed where his feet had been, engulfing the area in a rush of flames. The sniper took aim again, but Wrath was already sending out more.

The fireballs exploded all around the sniper, disorienting him. The heat from the blasts caused the air to waver. Push watched as Black took advantage of the distraction to get in a shot to the sniper's shoulder. The bullet caused him to stagger, but the man just reached into the wound and yanked the bullet back out. It didn't look like the shot had gone any deeper than the surface of his flesh.

Push brought his hands together and concentrated. Scratch recognized the pose and backed away, keeping his face hidden. The air around his partner rippled as power built up. When Push felt it peak, he raised both arms over his head and took aim. The sniper was still down there. Praying that Wrath and the sheriff could take cover in time, he hesitated a moment more before letting go.

There was no scream to accompany the release of his full power. Push watched the blast go down, traveling at maybe a mile per second. The blast was on the sniper before he could blink, and flattened him into the concrete like a pancake. Rocks, dirt, and pieces of sidewalk flew high into the air. Wrath and Sheriff Black were thrown back, but rolled with the momentum, coming to a stop safely outside the range of the miniature explosion. As they stood up, the cloud of dust began dropping back down like bits of dirty rain in slow motion.

As the smoke cleared, the sniper stood up.

"I'll be goddamned," Wrath whispered. "It is him, isn't it?"

Sheriff Black looked at him. "Who?"

The sniper was watching Wrath closely now, as if trying to come to a decision. His eyes drifted toward the sheriff for a moment before turning back to the man whose dark hair whipped back and forth angrily in the wind.

"Sloth," Wrath said, his eyes narrowing as he spoke.

Hearing this, the sniper broke into a run. Wrath started to give chase, but the sniper fired several shots back at him that took out car windows. Wrath ducked out of the way of the flying glass, keeping his head down as he continued his pursuit.

Scratch, meanwhile, was lowering himself and Push to the ground with his grappling hook. Push watched Wrath take off and called out to him, but his words fell on deaf ears.

"The hell did you just do?" Sheriff Black demanded, stomping up to them like an ornery bull. "Was that supposed to be some sort of bomb?"

"It was a telekinetic blast," Push explained, still looking at where Wrath had gone. "I rarely use my powers at that level. It's not exactly safe."

Black cocked an eyebrow and took a step back. "You mean to tell me all you boys in spandex have honestly got superpowers?"

"Nah," said Scratch dismissively, pointing at Push. "Just him. And Wrath, really. Nobody else in the Real-Life Superhero Association is what you would call 'superpowered'. We just try to stay in shape."

Scratch's eyes drifted to the slight gut sticking out from the sheriff's uniform. The glance was not lost on Black, and he stared back at Scratch, furious.

"The Pranksta Gayngsta got away," Push interjected, hoping to stop a fight before it broke out. "Whoever that sniper was, I don't think he wanted him dead. He could have shot the Pranksta before he ran off, but didn't."

"He seemed more interested in keeping us away from him," Scratch added.

Black sighed and holstered his gun. "Look at this mess," he grumbled, glaring around in a circle at the damage. "You boys bring nothing but trouble, you know that?"

"We've heard that before," Scratch admitted. "Honestly, though, I'm more worried now that we know Push's powers don't affect that guy. That telekinetic bomb he used once took out a truck, and the guy ran off like he wasn't even hurting."

Push frowned. "It could have killed him," he said, thinking hard. "The sheriff shot him, and that didn't bring him down."

"Must've been wearing a bulletproof vest," the sheriff suggested, though he continued looking around at the destroyed section of parking lot every few seconds.

"I hit him twice while he was up on the roof," Push insisted, shaking his head. "He barely flinched both times."

"You're thinking this guy has some kind of superpower?" Scratch asked, seeing where this was going.

"I hope not," Push said earnestly. "Not if it makes him that tough."

Black pursed his lips. "Why would some freak be hanging around in my town? Isn't the one you boys chased here enough?"

Push didn't have an answer that he felt would placate the irate sheriff.

"It doesn't look like Shove Point is going to be a quiet town for much longer," Scratch said.

CHAPTER
SIX

WRATH came back shortly after, looking pissed. Push, Scratch, and the sheriff were waiting for him outside the department building.

"He got away," Wrath stated sourly after coming to a stop in front of them.

"Who was he?" Push asked, arms folded. "The sheriff said he thought he heard you say the guy's name."

Wrath met Push's eyes before answering. "It was Sloth," he said. "From the Deadly Seven. Sloth was the sniper. That's why nothing we tried worked on him."

"Fuck," Scratch said flatly.

"We may very well be that," Wrath agreed, giving him a slight nod.

"Wait," Sheriff Black interrupted, holding his hands up. "What's this all about here? You're telling me the guy that was on my department's roof shooting the place up was the same guy you used to take your marching orders from?"

"Yes," Wrath answered gravely. "Sloth was the leader of the Deadly Seven."

"And he's in my town?" the sheriff pressed.

"Yes." Wrath gave another nod, then added, "Still."

"How'd he get away?" Scratch asked.

Wrath let out a sigh. "He's much faster than people give him credit for. I think whatever it was Push did caused more damage than we thought. He was moving like he was injured but kept going. I kept up at first, but he gave me the slip near the old tire warehouse past that patch of forest in back. Sloth loved staying one step ahead of everybody else, so it shouldn't surprise me that he'd have an escape route planned."

Push mulled all of this over. "I've got to report it in," he said at last, reaching for his phone. "The Association will want to know. Plus, they'll also need to hear that the Pranksta got away."

Wrath waited until Push wandered off before speaking again. "Better you than me."

In a little bit, Push returned, looking the worse for wear. "How did it go?" Scratch asked, preparing for a bomb.

"We've been reassigned," Push told him, ignoring Wrath completely for the moment. "The Association is making arrangements as we speak for the three of us to remain in Shove Point."

Wrath's eyes nearly popped out of their sockets. "What?" he shouted.

Scratch and Push gave him a look. "We're going to be stationed here until the Pranksta Gayngsta and Sloth are captured."

"The hell you are!" Black barked. "I've had me one hell of a migraine from the minute you three set foot here. I'll be damned if I'm gonna endure this sort of thing on a daily basis."

"For what it's worth, Sheriff," Push told him sadly, "I'm not happy, either."

"None of us are, apparently," Scratch noted, still looking squarely at Wrath.

"The Association already cleared our transfer with the Arkansas governor," Push continued, though noting the quiet fury in Wrath's face. "They are searching for a place we can stay in while we're here and having our things shipped down. We are to make finding Sloth our top priority, but locating the Pranksta Gayngsta is still on the list."

"I guess that sort of makes sense," Scratch mused. "Between the two, the Pranksta wasn't wanted by the feds."

"And hasn't eluded capture for a decade," Push added. "Yeah, they pointed that out to me. And it seems the Association thinks having Wrath on hand will help, since he and Sloth were once part of the same outfit. I couldn't think of a good argument against that, since it's pretty solid reasoning."

"So, the three of us are going to be roommates?" Scratch asked.

Push nodded. "Speaking of which," he said, turning to Wrath now, "they told me you will be shipped an account card. Apparently, someone in the Association set you up with a bank account and transferred an advance and utilities bonus to buy clothes and stuff with. You're also being given an Association BlackBerry communicator."

"Wonderful," Wrath grumbled. "Would it be too much to ask for me to be shipped back to prison instead?"

Scratch's shoulders shook a little as he laughed. "Come on," he tried. "It won't be that bad here."

Wrath said nothing in reply.

"I've got to put up with you boys blowing my town up and burning things to the ground?" Sheriff Black wondered. "My God, and to think I turned down retirement this year."

"We were told to try to cooperate with you," Push added.

"Thanks," the sheriff moaned, rolling his eyes heavenward. "That makes me feel so much better."

THE Association worked fast. Within two hours, Push's phone rang with the news that a place had been secured for them. It was Margaret, and she sounded as harassed as ever.

"I've got the address right here," she insisted as a separate phone rang impatiently in the background. "Hold on. Just give me a second."

Push waited while she gathered herself. "Okay," Margaret breathed into the receiver. "I found it. The information is logged into your GPS system in the truck. Just follow the directions and it will take you right to it. The place is furnished, but your things won't arrive until tomorrow."

Margaret got cut off as the phone in the background rang loudly again. "Please inform Wrath that his bank card should arrive within two days. I think I've got that sorted out. If there are any problems, have him get in touch with me. I've got to go now."

Margaret hung up without saying good-bye. Push closed his phone, chuckling at how busy she seemed these days, and made a mental note to find the woman some of those chocolates from Canada she liked so much.

The three of them loaded back up in the Pussy Wagon, with Wrath once again taking the backseat. Push noticed now tired the man looked, a stark contrast to the calm facade he'd maintained up until now. Wrath would periodically press a hand to his temple, looking frustrated, as they rolled leisurely through town. The people they passed by on the street took one look at the truck and averted their gaze.

"Kind of, uh, a different reaction from before, isn't it?" Scratch said, as one woman shielded her daughter's eyes.

"And that was before the cat ears," Push pointed out.

Wrath ignored both of them and focused his attention on his booted feet. Push kept his eyes on the road, following the GPS computer's directions whenever it signaled for him to turn. Soon, they were off the main road and headed down a quaint, narrow street with potholes every few feet or so. The houses here varied greatly. Some looked like they belonged in a neighborhood with better street surfaces, while others were dilapidated. One or two fared somewhere in-between. The Pussy Wagon passed several of these in a row before arriving at the spot on the digital readout map.

Wrath froze as he was climbing out of the truck after them. His eyes grew to the size of dinner plates as they swept the road from one end to the other. Push started for the door, but went rigid as the look of horror registered with him. Wrath jerked sharply toward the house in front of them.

"You have got to be fucking kidding me," he said in barely a whisper.

Scratch obliged by moving out of the way as Wrath stomped past. "What's with him?" he wondered, looking toward Push as though he had the answer.

"No idea."

The inside of the house felt nice after the slight chill in the air. It was much less cold this far south, but the air was much damper. Push felt his nose itch and hoped he wasn't catching a cold. That was the last thing he needed right now.

The front door opened up into a foyer with the floor slightly lower. A coatrack and shelf had been set up against the wall. Push and Scratch deposited their coats first, followed by Wrath. Push decided to leave his boots on the shelf as well. Apparently, this was what it was intended for. Scratch kept his on, as did Wrath, but both followed him when he went farther in. The living room was expansive, divided unequally by a gorgeous rug with a white tiger emblem emblazoned on its surface. Resting on top of the rug was a poker table surrounded by standing lamps. A great big china cabinet had been propped up against the wall beyond that, and someone had left it open to show several decks of playing cards as well as a number of board games.

The actual living area had a wide-screen television set on top of a bookcase, where an Xbox and several games were laid out. A three-corner couch, with each section separated to let people walk through, faced the entertainment area. A pair of French doors and a window on the far end kept the place well lit with sunlight during the day.

The kitchen was on the other side of the wall beyond the living area. It was narrow, but well stocked. The refrigerator was one of the biggest Push had ever laid eyes on. The kitchen even had a breakfast area set up beside a large bay window facing the backyard. To the right was a short hallway leading to the back door, where a screened-in porch was set up. In the opposite direction, Push found the laundry room complete with washer, dryer, and a spare sink before coming to the master bedroom at the end.

The others hadn't gone with him. Wandering back the way he'd come, Push found them down the main hallway, looking into a second master bedroom.

"Dibs," Wrath called out.

"Fucker," Scratch replied, though he didn't protest.

Wrath was watching the room, looking very worried now. Push noticed how his eyes would drift toward the walk-in closet, as if expecting someone there. After a moment more, he pushed away and kept going. Push and Scratch followed, finding another bathroom—the only one not stationed in a bedroom—followed by two rooms shoved together beyond a sharp right turn.

"I guess I'll take this one," Scratch said, speaking of the larger of the two. "That leaves you with the smallest one, Push."

Push shook his head. "I've already found mine."

Scratch frowned. "It's not bigger than this, is it?" he asked, pointing to the room he'd just claimed.

"A lot bigger," Push said, smiling now. "It's got a bathroom and a walk-in closet too."

"I hate you both," Scratch declared, looking over his prize with disdain now.

The three of them spent a good hour or more looking the place over thoroughly. Since their stuff wasn't going to arrive until tomorrow, there was nothing for them to unpack. Wrath had nothing besides the clothes on his back. Whatever became of his suit from before, Push had no idea and didn't bother asking. He would have some clothes soon, and that was one less thing for Push to deal with.

In the meanwhile, though, there was a far larger problem on their plate, or lack thereof. Push wasn't surprised, but there was no food whatsoever in the whole house. Scratch drew the short straw and, after a bit of grumbling, consented to go shopping.

"Just get the basics," Push told him. "We can make a real grocery list tomorrow."

"Why don't I just get some chips and stuff?" Scratch suggested. "We can break the place in tonight with some booze."

"Shove Point is a dry city," Wrath countered, looking up from the couch he'd sprawled out on. "You can't buy anything stronger than beer here."

"We passed a liquor store on the way here," Scratch informed him. "It was open for business."

That got Wrath's attention. "What?"

Push nodded. "It was right across the street from that Subway."

Wrath was floored. "There's a Subway in Shove Point?"

Both ignored him after that, and Scratch made a list of what chips and snacks to buy, what sort of alcohol they needed, and what Push wanted on his sub. Wrath called out his order just as Scratch reached the door, which delayed the man a good five minutes, because Scratch misplaced his pen somehow.

Push bumped knuckles with his partner, then went back to the living room. Wrath was resting on the far corner couch, staring at the TV screen. It was turned off.

The awkwardness was breathable. Push struggled to think of something to say, but after several minutes of fruitless searching, during which Wrath didn't so much as look at him, he gave up. Luckily, Scratch was not out for very long. Shove Point was a much smaller town than Chicago. He was back in a little over a half hour with a sack full of unhealthy junk food, several smaller bags of whiskey, rum, and cocktail mixes, and two sandwiches each.

"I thought we might want one for later," Scratch explained as they put the booze in the refrigerator to chill. "Saves me the trouble of making a second run."

"Wrath could do it," Push pointed out, storing his second sub in the back.

"Do you really want him driving the Pussy Wagon?"

Push let the subject drop. He had just taken a bite into his sandwich when the doorbell rang. "Here," he said, tossing Wrath's lunch to him as he passed through the living room. "Enjoy."

When Push opened the door, the first thought that entered his mind was that a very excited-looking, overweight clown was standing on the front porch. After he blinked, and took a second assessment, he realized it was just a woman in her forties with far too much makeup who'd taken someone's bad fashion advice.

Most likely on a dare.

"Good afternoon, sir!" she said in a shrill voice that might have sounded more professional without the exaggerated redneck twang.

"Good afternoon, ma'am," Push answered automatically. Inside, he was desperately praying to whatever god didn't hate him that she wouldn't want to come in.

"My name is Laura Thompson," the woman introduced very quickly. "My husband owns this house. He's the one that the Association called to rent the place out to you fellas."

"Nice to meet you," Push said, offering his hand.

Her fingers were large and coated in some kind of lotion that felt slimy to the touch. It made Push set his sandwich down, even though most of it was still wrapped up. With what clung to his hand, he wasn't going to take any chances.

Mrs. Thompson, meanwhile, was staring at Push as though waiting for him to do a trick. The Association, of course, had to give the name of their organization, and the names of who would be staying in the house. Given Sheriff Black's reaction, Push had assumed no one here would know who they were. Apparently, Mrs. Thompson was much more informed than the local law. She was staring quite openly at him, to the point where it would have been considered rude in any circle. Each time Push shifted his weight even the slightest, her eyes followed like a hawk.

He noticed how she paid especially close attention to his crotch. Luckily, he hadn't taken the cup he wore to conceal that very problem off yet.

"I just wanted to come by and say hi, see how you boys liked the place, and to ask if you needed anything," Mrs. Thompson went on, still talking a mile a minute. "I bet you haven't had time to get settled in yet."

"No ma'am," Push told her. "We just made a run to Subway for lunch."

"Oh, well ain't that wonderful!"

Push had no idea what she meant, so he didn't reply.

"My great-aunt's cousin's daughter works there. I bet she was the one who made it for you. The next time you stop by, be sure and ask for her. I bet she'd just love to speak with you."

"I will," said Push, crossing his fingers behind his back.

Mrs. Thompson continued to rattle on as Push's sandwich grew colder by the minute. "...So I told her not to bother with it," she finished, before taking another deep breath. "Anyway, if you fellas find the time, come on over to church with us on Sunday. I'm sure the kids would think it was fun to spend some time with you."

Push was saved by the sound of footsteps. Wrath had wandered over to the china cabinet and retrieved a deck of cards from inside. His fingers flew through them, shuffling the deck with a professional's ease.

"Oh, don't mind any of that stuff," Mrs. Thompson said, still speaking to Push. "My husband set that up years ago, but I finally wore him into giving it up. I told him it just wasn't in the good Lord's plan for our family to gamble."

Wrath looked up from the cards and stared right at her. Laura Thompson's face went rigid, as if she'd been stung in the back. A lump formed in her throat. For a moment, Push thought she looked afraid. Wrath was doing nothing, however. He wasn't even looking at her as his fingers worked through the deck again and again. When he did finally meet her eyes, however, Mrs. Thompson jumped slightly.

"I'll be seeing you boys around," she said nervously, backing up. Push watched as she staggered from stepping in a hole. This wasn't enough to slow her down, and she limped down the street as fast as her injured foot would carry her.

"That's what happens when you put five-inch heels on a size twelve foot," Wrath sneered.

"Thanks," said Push as he collected his sandwich with one hand.

"Don't mention it," Wrath replied as Push made a beeline for the kitchen to wash his soiled hand off. "Ever. The woman is a complete idiot."

The hand soap, it turned out, was in the cabinet under the sink. Push used a liberal amount before scrubbing himself off.

"We just met her," he pointed out, turning the hot water on all the way. "Anyway, what happened to Scratch?"

"He went to take a dump. What's with all the booze in the refrigerator?"

"It's sort of a tradition with him and me," Push explained, drying his hands on a towel hanging nearby. "This isn't the first time the Association has placed us in an area for an extended period of time. Sometimes a case we're helping the police with runs longer than expected, or we're helping to clean up a bad neighborhood. Whenever we're put somewhere and know we'll be there for a little while, he and I throw a party for ourselves so that it feels a little bit more like home."

"Ah," was all Wrath said.

"That," Push went on, avoiding looking at Wrath now, "and we do this sort of thing whenever a new Association member is assigned to us."

"You get him drunk and embarrass him?"

Push laughed. "No! Well, there was that one time, but the Demolition Tank was an exception. Nobody knew he couldn't hold his liquor."

Push was still chuckling when it hit him that he'd just laughed at something Wrath said. Wrath either didn't notice when he stopped suddenly, or didn't care.

"Shouldn't we do something more constructive? Like finding the two guys we were put here to hunt down so we can leave?"

"It won't take long," Push assured him. "This isn't our first manhunt. Scratch and I have been doing this sort of thing for a while."

"Except nobody knows how the Pranksta Gayngsta got away," Wrath pointed out. "And Sloth has evaded capture for years."

"The Pranksta got lucky," Push insisted dismissively. "And we've got you on our side now. You know how Sloth thinks better than anyone, I'd wager."

It felt weird talking so casually with the man who, only a few days ago, had been released from prison after serving time for more crimes than most people could list. Push kept waiting for Scratch to come back. It was getting awkward talking to Wrath like they were friends now.

Wrath, meanwhile, had gone back to eating his own sandwich. This made Push remember his, and he picked it up off the counter. Even cold, it tasted good.

"Pride knew him better," Wrath said after swallowing, almost as an afterthought.

"Who?" Push looked up from his own bite. "What did you say?"

"Nothing," Wrath replied, looking away. "Just that Pride was the one who always figured out Sloth's plans. She was great at reading people, and it got to where we all depended on her to think several steps ahead in case one of Sloth's crazy schemes went bad. That happened a lot after we started getting big."

Wrath was staring out the window behind Push, wearing a forlorn expression. Push opened his mouth to ask him to continue, but Scratch picked that moment to return.

"Sorry about that," he said, shambling past the two of them, snatching his sub from the breakfast table where he'd left it. "I used your bathroom, Push, since it was closer. You might not want to go back there for a little while."

"Thanks a lot," Push grumbled.

The three of them stood around eating together in silence. Once that was done, Wrath hunted down some trash bags in the laundry room so they could bag everything up.

"It just seemed like the place for them to be," he insisted quietly, even though neither of them had asked.

"I'm stuffed," Scratch lamented. "I think I saw some DVDs on that shelf in the living room. Who's up for some cheap whiskey and bad action flicks?"

"If they've got the Green Lantern movie, let's watch it," Push suggested. "We can make fun of all the things they got wrong."

Scratch laughed. "It's been a while since we did that."

The *Green Lantern* DVD was sandwiched between *Iron Man* and *X-Men Origins: Wolverine*. Push fished it out and got the DVD player ready while the other two took a seat on the couch. Wrath sat in silence, watching them point out the film's various flaws and bad acting.

"Please tell me you both are aware of the irony in this?" he asked at one point, when they were a little over halfway through.

"What?" Push wondered, laughing at Ryan Reynolds.

"Dude, we're comic book geeks," Scratch explained, looking away from the screen for a moment. "Why do you think we wanted to be in the Association in the first place?"

"Yeah," Push said, getting a hold on his emotions before stuff started getting blown across the room. He wasn't sure if the Association had put down a damage deposit on the place. "Most of the members of the Association were comic book fans at some point. We always have to take care of business real quick at meetings, because someone will eventually start bitching about DC Comic's *The New 52*, the *Identity Crisis* storyline, or Spider-Man forgetting he was ever married to MJ."

"Dear God!" Scratch yelled, throwing his head back while an explosion rocked the screen. "Don't ever bring that up again! I thought Scarlet Queen and the Wiccan Witch were going to need sedation."

"Both of them were huge Spider-Man fans," Push explained, filling in a confused-looking Wrath. "Up until 'One More Day', anyway. Scarlet Queen and the Wiccan Witch are good friends of ours."

"You guys trade comics with each other?" Wrath asked jokingly.

"I'm more into figurines," Scratch corrected, before frowning sharply. "Um, speaking of which, I left a bunch of unfinished figures I was customizing out to dry in my room. I'd better call and make sure whoever packs that shit up is extra-careful with it."

Scratch ran out of the room to use his phone. By the time he got back, the movie was almost over.

"It could have been worse," Wrath was saying to a now-tipsy Push. "But then again, I never read much of the *Green Lantern* series, so I can't compare it to the comics."

"Did you read comics growing up?" Scratch inquired, sitting back down in his spot near Push.

"Some," Wrath replied evasively. "My parents would sometimes buy me reprints of the old Carl Barks and Don Rosa stories."

"So you used to read Disney comics?" Push pressed.

"A little." Wrath kept his eyes glued to the TV as the credits began to role. "I guess this means Sinestro will be the villain in the sequel."

"I doubt there's going to be one," Scratch told him. "Nobody likes this movie. It tanked at the box office. People are still making jokes about how bad it was."

"Too bad," Wrath said, getting up to stretch. "I liked Sinestro's character."

"He's better in the comics," Scratch insisted, following Wrath's lead. "So, we've made fun of the Green Lantern movie. Let's put this shit up, polish off the whiskey, and play a few rounds of poker. How does that sound?"

Wrath nodded. "I deal," he said. "After I take a piss."

"Use your own bathroom," Push said, pointing down the hall.

Push decided to relieve himself also. The damage from Scratch's little visit to his bathroom was still lingering in the air, so Push fumbled around for the switch to activate the air vent. When he returned, Wrath and Scratch were already situated at the poker table on opposite sides, waiting for him. Wrath kept busy shuffling the deck of cards as Push eased by Scratch to sit in the chair next to the wall. Once he had parked himself, Scratch poured him a shot of Bacardi while Wrath began dealing. They were starting off with a basic game of five-card stud.

The first round went to Scratch.

An hour later, they had moved on to Texas Hold 'Em. Wrath had won twice, Scratch two more times, and Push three.

"Flush," Wrath declared, laying his cards out for them to see. "That comes to a three-way tie. How are we going to settle this?"

Scratch looked over to Push. "Want to play something else?"

Push shrugged, tossing his cards into the center. "I'm still game, unless somebody had a better plan. How much rum is left?"

Scratch held the bottle up for him to see. They'd worked their way through one bottle already, and the second was over halfway down.

"Shit," Push grunted. "How the hell did we drink so much?"

"We've got an extra glass, remember?" Scratch pointed out, lifting his glass toward Wrath before pouring himself a refill.

"I've been drinking rum since I was twelve," Wrath informed them. "Care to pour me another round, bartender?"

Scratch obliged. "I think I was around fourteen or so when I had my first beer," he said, passing the glass back to Wrath. "It was at a party. At the time, I never thought I would be able to keep it down. It was really cheap stuff."

"I don't like beer much," Wrath replied, saluting both of them. "The aftertaste is too strong for me. I can drink rum or whiskey until the room sinks, though."

"I drank Jack Daniel's whiskey when I was in high school," Push told them, passing his glass to Scratch for another round. "Not very often, but a friend of mine worked part-time at a gas station, and the owner would sometimes look the other way when he wanted some."

"Lucky bastard," Scratch grumbled, tossing his own round back.

Push chuckled softly to himself. "The night before graduation, he came over to my place with a bottle of Jack and a six-pack of beer as chasers. We were going to celebrate getting through high school together. At one point...."

Push went rigid as he realized what he'd been about to say out loud.

"Go on," Wrath insisted.

Push hesitated again for a moment more. "It's nothing, really," he said evasively. "My friend got so drunk that he actually asked if I would kiss him, just to see what it felt like. I turned him down flat. The next morning, he claimed not to remember it."

"You should have kissed him," Wrath said simply.

Push gave him a look. "What for?"

"Why not?" the ex-con asked, finishing his drink off. "It's pretty clear you wanted to, and the guy was drunk enough to not care."

"I didn't want to make things weird for us," Push said, staring down at the cards on the table. "He was my best friend, really."

"You weren't the one making things weird, though," Wrath went on, not letting the subject go. "He brought it up and was the one wanting to know. Plus, he was willing to play the 'too drunk' card, so if he was like that without you kissing him, I doubt it would have been all that much worse. Weren't the two of you going off to college?"

Push didn't like where this was going, mainly because Wrath was making too much sense. "We didn't go to the same college," he admitted, nevertheless. "I haven't heard from him in years."

"Too bad," Wrath said, leaning back in his chair a little. "I bet he would have been a great kisser."

"He was straight," Push informed him in a flat voice. By accident, he found himself glancing over at Scratch and averted his eyes back to Wrath.

"Not too straight, apparently," Wrath challenged.

"Let's talk about something else," Push declared, setting his glass down too hard. "What can you tell us about Sloth?

"Well," Push pressed, perhaps a bit too harshly, when Wrath didn't respond. "Let's have it. You were all fired up to go out and beat the bushes earlier. What can you tell us?"

"He's an asshole," Wrath blurted out.

Scratch snickered. "Yeah, um, we're gonna need a little more to go on than that."

"Seriously," Wrath said, and he shot Scratch a piercing look. "Sloth is a complete bastard. He likes to imagine himself superior to everyone around him. If the man is in a crowded room, you'll find him in the center, waiting for everyone's attention to focus on him. It's about pleasing him and nothing else."

"He's an egotist," Push summed up.

"Megalomaniac would be a more accurate term," Wrath corrected. "But he hides it fairly well. For the most part, Sloth comes across like that dumb jock everybody supposedly knew from high school. He's big, strong, fast, and loves picking on anyone smaller or weaker than him. In his case, that means everyone."

"And?" Scratch asked, sensing there was more.

"He's brilliant," Wrath continued, moving his glass aside for now. "Very shrewd and clever. Sloth was a genius at planning on long and short terms. He's obsessed with preparing for every eventuality."

"A perfectionist," Push assumed.

"Very much so. The thing is, Sloth is also lazy. He never liked getting his hands dirty if he could help it. His method was to get other people to take the fall for him. As far as he was concerned, everyone else was expendable."

"What happened today, then?" Scratch wondered, putting the now-empty bottle down out of his reach. "If he doesn't like taking big risks, what was he doing up on the sheriff's department roof taking shots at us?"

"Good point," Push said. "He already had an escape route planned out, but that sounds like the type of job he'd give to a grunt, from what you've told us."

"Assuming he has them," Wrath pointed out. "He may have been working alone because nobody else would go near him. Or, maybe he thought the risk was minimal. Shove Point isn't exactly a metropolis. Sloth probably figured he would be dealing with a couple of hick cops and nothing more. That was his weak point. He had a tendency to underestimate people."

Wrath was eying the bottle as he filled them in. "There's one other thing, though I hate bringing this up."

Push and Scratch waited. "What?" Scratch asked, looking mildly irritated now at being dragged along verbally.

Wrath let out a long sigh. "It didn't get around New Orleans," he explained. "This wasn't the type of thing the locals would talk about openly. Some of the Deadly Seven suspected this too after a while, though. Pride especially."

"Spit it out," Push insisted.

"There was a theory going around among the other members of the Deadly Seven that Sloth got his marching orders from somewhere else."

Push and Scratch each blanched. "Say that again?" Push asked, certain he had heard wrong. "You're telling us Sloth was taking orders from someone?"

"Pride thought so," Wrath admitted, looking down into his empty glass. "So did I, after a while. We thought it would be better to keep a low profile, but Sloth overruled us. Granted, as our reputation got bigger, we got more powerful. Some of the missions he sent us on were just plain stupid, though. It was almost as if he wanted us all to be caught."

"That's information the Association will want to know," Scratch stated, glancing over at the clock. "Probably better to report that in tomorrow."

"Agreed," said Push. "But thinking about the Deadly Seven being ordered around by somebody else… that's a whole hell of a lot to take in."

"We couldn't prove anything," Wrath told them. "Sloth didn't want to get caught, remember, so he was very careful about not leaving anything just lying around for someone to stumble across."

"I wonder why, though?" Scratch mused, pulling out the last bottle of rum from the brown paper bag on the floor next to his chair. "If the Deadly Seven had just been a group of enforcers working for the mob, that would be one thing, but you guys took over the New Orleans criminal syndicate. Why stay in the shadows for so long after the fact?"

"No idea," Wrath confessed. "It's something we all asked at one point or another."

Wrath passed his glass down the table for Scratch to fill, helped along by Push, who also handed his over for another round.

"If there was someone pulling the Deadly Seven's strings," Push asked thoughtfully out loud to himself, "what did they gain? If they didn't want to take over the New Orleans underworld, what was the point?"

"I have asked myself that very same question a number of times while sitting in that jail cell," Wrath told him, reaching across the table to take his drink from Scratch. "There's something about the set-up that I've missed, I think. I don't know what it is, but odds are Sloth will have the answer."

The three men toasted each other before throwing their glasses back. "If possible," Wrath said, setting his down, "I'd like to find out once we locate him."

"I'd say that's something we'd all love to know," Scratch told him, looking across the table. "Don't worry about it. Just as soon as we track him down, Sloth's going to have a lot of questions to answer."

"Like why he helped the Pranksta Gayngsta get away," Push said while fiddling with his glass.

"Maybe they're working together?" Scratch offered. "Or Sloth works for him now?"

Wrath laughed. "Not a chance," he said. "Sloth was a raging homophobe. He'd consider taking orders from a guy like the Pranksta beneath him. Odds are it was the other way around."

Scratch frowned. "The Pranksta was working for Sloth?"

"More than likely," Wrath said seriously. "I told you back at the warehouse that the Pranksta was wired with this Bluetooth, and it sounded like he was getting orders fed to him through it. Sloth was probably the guy lurking up in the rafters of the building, watching the whole scene go down."

"Then why didn't he come out and help?" Push wondered.

"He's wanted for federal crimes," Wrath reminded him. "And he never liked directly confronting anyone unless he had the upper hand."

"Weird," Scratch admitted. "But it makes a fucked-up kind of sense. If Sloth was the one who broke the Pranksta out of jail, though, how come they didn't just stay together?"

"I don't know," Wrath said, thinking it over. "Something about that doesn't make sense. If they're in this together, Sloth would have kept an eye on the Pranksta so he didn't do something stupid, so why did he let the Pranksta get locked up in the local tank?"

No one could come up with a satisfying answer. Scratch kept the rum flowing, and soon, the conversation started to drift away from more serious business.

"I still say you should have kissed the guy," Wrath muttered, circling the top of his glass with a finger, then licking the droplet collected there off.

"Who?" Push mumbled. The whiskey and rum was really socking it to him now. That, and being on the road for two days had him almost completely wiped out.

"The guy from high school," Wrath clarified. "The one who asked you to make out with him before you both graduated. At least you would have known, and not spent all this time wondering."

"I don't wonder about it," Push insisted, and even to his ears, it sounded like a bald-faced lie. "He and I haven't spoken to one another in a long time."

"He'd probably do it now," Wrath continued, not letting the subject drop. "You're a famous celebrity crime-fighter. Get a straight guy drunk enough and there's little he wouldn't do."

Push rolled his eyes. Scratch, on the other hand, was laughing his ass off. "Would you make out with somebody famous if they offered?"

"Depends," Wrath told him, smirking. "I wouldn't say no to Hugh Jackman if he promised to take his shirt off first. They showed that X-Men movie about him while I was locked up once. The other cons thought they were being punished for something, but I actually enjoyed it. Of course, I spent the rest of that night beating off to the image of him and that dark-haired chick making out with each other."

Scratch smiled and didn't look particularly put off by this bit of news. Push cocked an eyebrow at his best friend, then turned to face Wrath.

"I thought you were..." he began, before his tongue slipped. "I thought you liked girls. What was all that before with you two going on with how hot the waitresses were?"

"I'm bi," Wrath answered at once.

It took a second for that statement to work its way through the cloud of alcohol fogging Push's brain. "What?"

"I'm bisexual," Wrath said again, tilting his head sideways now. "Wasn't that in the file the Association had on me?"

Push shook his head. "No, it wasn't. I didn't know."

Scratch smiled as he looked toward Push. "So, we've got one gay superhero, and one bisexual one. The Cape Cabinet will be thrilled. I guess this means you won't be doing all those stupid fundraisers and junk alone now."

"Oh, joy," Push grumbled.

"I don't do fundraisers," Wrath replied flatly.

"I wish I didn't most of the time," Push said, the alcohol really loosening his tongue now. "It's a pain in my ass."

"Have you been with many guys before?" Scratch inquired, speaking to Wrath again.

"No," said Wrath, looking down into his glass. "Very few. The New Orleans underground is not very forgiving of people who prefer any sort of alternative lifestyle, even though a lot of them pitch for more than one team every now and then. None of that changed when Sloth finally reached the top of the ladder. I was always being watched."

"That sucks," Scratch said sympathetically.

"Sloth had a gay prostitute on the side," Wrath told him, leaning forward as he spoke. "Actually, he had something like four mistresses, two girlfriends, and that one gay prostitute. I don't know what it was, but he would sometimes go to the guy and force him to give free head. Sloth wasn't the sort who took no for an answer, so the guy didn't dare object. I tried to look after him, but it wasn't easy."

"Funny how that works," said Scratch, frowning hard.

Push was feeling left out and more than a little uncomfortable now. For some reason, it felt like Scratch and Wrath were getting cozy with one another and leaving him out of the loop.

"Yeah," Wrath was saying now. "Power does weird things to some people, makes them push their boundaries or feel like normal rules don't apply to them. Plus, I guess everybody has some kind of exception to the rule floating around in their head. I've never heard of a straight guy who'd turn down free head once enough beer was in him."

At this, Push stood up and made tracks for the kitchen. After dropping his glass in the sink, he stumbled awkwardly down the shorter hallway to his room. Wherever the conversation was going, he wanted no part of it. After spending two minutes or so trying to find the light switch, he gave up and tripped his way through the darkened room to the bathroom, hitting his knee twice in the process.

After taking a much-needed piss, Push flushed and staggered back to his bed. Scratch and Wrath were still talking in the living room. Push tuned them out, stripped all the way out of his spandex, and promptly passed out cold on top of the covers.

His feverish dreams consisted of him lost in a crowd of screaming women who cheered wildly as Scratch stripped out of his clothes on stage. Each time his partner got down to his boxers, he would call out for Push to join him. And each time, Push would get close enough to the stage where Scratch could hear him and demand to know what was going on. The dream would end, everything faded to black, and then started back all over again.

Push cycled through the same dream four times before waking up. His body felt sticky with sweat, and he'd cum on himself at some point. He had to piss again, and his mouth tasted like rubber.

"That's it," Push grunted as he raised up amid protests from his aching muscles. "No more rum and whiskey nights for a long while."

Wrath was standing in the doorway wrapped in a towel. Apparently, Push hadn't shut the door before losing consciousness. Through his haze, Push noticed that Wrath was still dripping wet.

"I don't have any other clothes," he answered, though Push didn't remember asking. "We got a call."

"What?" Push grunted, rubbing the sleep from his eyes.

"Sheriff Black wants to have a word with us," Wrath explained. "They may have found the Pranksta Gayngsta."

CHAPTER
SEVEN

THE body had been charred black by flames. The mouth lay wide open, exposing nothing but raw gums. Somebody had gone to a great deal of trouble yanking all the teeth out.

"Is this him?" Sheriff Black asked, keeping both eyes on Wrath as he spoke. "Is this who you came all the way down here for?"

The body in question had been left in the mouth of an alley in plain view. Clearly, it was meant to be found. The smell was horrible, but Push held his stomach in and silently thanked himself for having the foresight to not eat breakfast.

Wrath and Scratch were by his side, looking down at the charred corpse, each silently taking in the sight. Sheriff Black had brought along his two favorite deputies, Fortenberry and McGee. Each one was watching the spandex-clad trio instead of the body. Push had a sneaky suspicion they did so on Black's orders.

"No clue," Push told him dryly. "Whoever it was, they must have gotten into a fight with an angry dentist wielding a flame-thrower."

"Sloth must have found him first," Wrath said, studying the scene.

"Did he have a thing about removing his victim's teeth?" Scratch asked, frowning down at the burned corpse.

"He preferred doing damage to people while they were still alive to feel pain," Wrath informed. "Then again, at this point, all we've got is a dead body with no positive identification. It could be anybody."

Black was sizing Wrath up like a horse for sale. "Care to tell us where you were last night, son?"

Not one of them moved. "He was with us," Scratch said, as the deputies snickered.

"Doing what?" McGee asked leeringly. "Trying on each other's spandex?"

"Scratch is a medium, just in case you were wondering," Wrath quipped.

"You just don't know when to shut your mouth, do you?" Black demanded fiercely.

"Enough, Sheriff Black," Push said, feeling more tired now than when Wrath woke him up earlier. "Wrath was with us all day yesterday and throughout the night. The only time we can't vouch for his whereabouts is when we all fell asleep, so why don't you tell us the victim's time of death so we can get that settled."

Wrath was watching Push, wearing a small frown. "It was about one or two," he said. "When I fell asleep. Scratch and I played a few more rounds of poker before calling it a night."

"That don't matter now anyway," Black replied dismissively. "The coroner hasn't had a look at the body yet, so we won't know anything until then."

"Don't you think it's a little early to be suspecting people, then?" Scratch pointed out.

Black narrowed his eyes at that. "I don't like queer little pricks coming down to my town from some big city and telling me how to do my job. I've got me a burned corpse and a firebug who wandered in the other night. It don't take no bat-computer, or whatever the hell you bastards call it, to add that much up."

"Fine." Push hated to admit it, but hearing the "queer" remark from the lanky redneck got him riled. "If Wrath is going to be formally charged with a crime, I will personally contact the Association."

"What for?" Deputy Fortenberry wondered, running a hand along his swollen belly.

"Wrath is a member of the Real-Life Superhero Association now," Push reminded the man. "The Association keeps an entire law firm on retainer. If a member is formally charged, they are automatically given legal representation. The Association can also fly down a professional forensics team within a few hours to examine the body."

Black looked like he wanted to sucker punch Push in the face. Both deputies behind him were holding their hands uncomfortably close to their guns now.

"Well?" Push asked.

A moment later, they were headed back to the Pussy Wagon together. "That could have gone better," Scratch grumbled, climbing into the backseat without hesitating. "Definitely worth getting out of bed for."

Wrath paused outside the truck for a moment before getting into the front seat next to Push.

"Um, any idea where we can get some breakfast?" Scratch continued. "We still haven't gone grocery shopping yet."

"There used to be a diner at the four-way stop leading into town," Wrath told them. "If it's still there, they ought to be open by now."

"Sounds good," Push said, peeling out into the street.

The diner, it turned out, had been converted into a truck stop at some point. The building looked fairly new, with parking spaces for eighteen-wheelers and more compact cars. An eatery of some kind was built on to it, so Push pulled into the nearest space before a Kia rolling out from one of the gas pumps could take it.

"You don't exactly drive defensively, do you?" Wrath noted as they all climbed out.

Inside, the three stood around in front of the entrance. All of them stood out like sore thumbs, yet the inhabitants sitting around at their tables acted as though there was nothing unusual going on. The eatery was, in fact, two separate areas: one for ice cream, and a buffet-style setup with a variety of scrambled eggs, sausage patties, bacon, tater wedges, and the like. Push and company made tracks for the food. As they walked, he noticed several people watching him out the corner of their eyes. One elderly man stared openly for a moment before turning back to his Styrofoam cup of coffee.

They had lucked out. There was no line at the counter. The woman standing behind it, however, spent several seconds staring at them while smacking on a large piece of gum. When she finally asked them what they would like, it was in a stern tone that reminded Push of a grumpy librarian.

Once they had paid for their orders, Push and Wrath took an empty booth near the back while Scratch ran to the bathroom.

"Thank you for what you said earlier," Wrath said, choosing to focus his energies on opening his dinner box instead of meeting Push's eyes.

Push sighed. "I'm going to ask you this once, and I hope it won't be a problem for you."

Wrath immediately folded his hands in response and waited.

"Did you do it?" Push asked him, the words sounding weighted as they left his mouth.

"No," Wrath answered. "For one thing, we don't know that it was the Pranksta Gayngsta's body. This could be one of Sloth's little games, and even if it wasn't, I was under the impression we were supposed to bring the man back alive. If I did have to kill him, it would have been because my life was threatened, and had that been the case, I would have known better than to burn the corpse so badly that it wouldn't be recognizable."

"Thank you," Push said. "I had to ask."

"No, you didn't," Wrath contradicted him. "But I don't mind either way."

Scratch emerged from the bathroom a moment later. Push kept his eyes on the table as he tugged open his dinner box. Scratch often had a problem with morning wood, and today, Push didn't trust himself not to sneak a peek. The last thing he wanted was for Wrath to notice, though their new "teammate" seemed too preoccupied with gorging himself on tater wedges to notice.

"Hey, guys," Scratch said, his eyes stuck on the window as he walked up to their booth. "Um, is that plane crashing?"

Push frowned, and looked out the window. Wrath did the same just in time to spot what looked like a short-haul commercial jet heading down fast toward the middle of town. The back part of the jet was in flames, leaving a trail of dark smoke through the air as it descended in a shaky line.

Others in the dining area were getting to their feet now and moving toward the window to watch.

"It's going to hit the town," Scratch shouted, running for the door.

Push was already getting out of his seat, with Wrath surprisingly close behind. Wrath gave one last glance over his shoulder toward his missed meal before continuing. Scratch was already unlocking the truck doors for them and climbed in to rev the engine. Push and Wrath joined him a second later, and they were off.

"It looked like it was coming down near Main Street," Wrath said, directing Scratch down a side street. "This way will be faster."

The sound of metal tearing through brick, mortar, and wood filled the air amid the roar of the jet's engines and the spreading flames. Debris was flying through the air as Scratch slammed down on the gas, urging the truck faster toward the demolition.

They reached the point where the jet first touched ground a moment later. It looked like a war zone, and the carnage hadn't stopped there. The momentum and still-firing engines were carrying the jet farther into town, carving a path straight through buildings and city streets. Cars had been smashed, torn in half, or blown completely apart.

Push felt as though something in his stomach had been torn out. He clammed up for a second as his eyes took in the full scope of the damage.

"These people need our help," he said after clearing his throat. "Pull over. We'll be better off from this point on foot. There's no way the Pussy Wagon can handle that kind of track right now."

Scratch came to a stop, pulling the truck up along the side of the road before killing the engine. All three of them got out without a word between them. The situation spoke for itself.

"What do we do first?" Wrath asked.

Push had to clear his throat again. "Check the area for survivors," he instructed. "The rescue teams and ambulances will be on their way soon. Wrath, can you put out fires as well as start them?"

Wrath nodded. "Yes."

"Then see if you can't get some of those fires under control before they spread and burn the whole town to the ground," Push ordered. "A lot of these buildings are old. It won't be long before they go up like kindling."

Wrath took off for the nearest one without another word. "And be careful!" Push shouted after him quickly. "Scratch, we need to see what we can do for the people who were out in the streets when that jet hit."

The two of them made tracks for the nearest street, taking a detour around the path that the jet had carved to avoid some of the rubble. From the sound of things, people were already starting to panic. If things went wrong, they could have a full-blown riot on their hands.

Push and Scratch came to a car first. It had been flipped over, it looked like, by the jet stream. A woman was trapped inside, screaming her head off, begging for God to help her. Push whipped out his telescopic bo staff and jammed the tip into the space between the door nearest to her. Professor Trixter had designed the thing to withstand almost a ton of pressure. Push was less worried about breaking his favorite weapon, though, than he was at the thought that the metal might have fused together. Scratch joined him with one of his cue sticks, and a few seconds later, the door popped open.

"Ma'am," Push shouted, calling out to her. "Are you all right?"

"Please, help me!" she screamed.

Despite being upside-down and majorly freaked out, the lady didn't appear seriously injured. There were visible scrapes and cuts on her body, so Push took great care when he reached down and undid the seat belt holding her in place. Both he and Scratch managed to catch her and helped her out as the stink of gasoline filled the air.

"There's nobody else," Push assured them, checking the inside of the car one last time. "Let's get clear in case this explodes."

"My car," the woman screamed as they helped her along. "My husband is going to kill me!"

Once they were far enough away, Push let go of her to see if she could walk. Her ankle appeared to be giving her problems, but it didn't look broken.

"Find a safe place," Push instructed, keeping their eyes locked so she would have something to focus on. "Do you have any family in town with you?"

"I…." The lady stammered for a moment. "No, I don't think so."

"Good, then find someplace safe," Push said, giving her a pat. "When an ambulance arrives, make sure they look you over. You may have injuries that you're not aware of yet."

Scratch had already moved on, having spotted several older men digging through a broken pile that had been a building at some point. Apparently, somebody was trapped inside, and the part of the roof that was still holding up had caught fire. Scratch yanked out his cue stick, along with several of his trick balls, and sent them flying through the air in a complicated pattern. The balls exploded on impact, blanketing the smoking areas with asphyxiating foam. Push decided to leave him there to help and continued on.

Push began working his way down the path the jet had taken, helping where he could, directing folks to where they would be safe. An air raid siren was blaring now, drowned out at some points by the sound of approaching fire trucks. It looked as though things were coming together slowly. With that in mind, Push decided to move a little farther down.

Everything was in shambles. Whole buildings had been torn in half or ripped to pieces entirely. Cars were strewn everywhere, lying on their sides or upside down. Some were even stacked haphazardly on top of one another. Broken glass, pieces of brick, and busted water pipes lay scattered over what remained of the city street. There were more bodies here, some that might have still been alive, but Push couldn't distinguish them. Moving anyone so critically injured was a bad idea anyway, though he hated leaving anyone behind. The heat vision on his goggles was shot thanks to the flames and exhaust from the jet. Push tried a different setting but only got static. He was left on his own with his protected eyes, at least for the time being.

The jet had left the more urban area and come to a stop in a rundown derelict sprawl of houses. The remains of one were spilled over the undersides of the jet. Push winced but kept moving. He couldn't hear anyone screaming. For the moment, all the noise was echoing back behind him from the region he'd just left. This part of town was eerily silent, like it had taken a deep breath when the jet crashed and was waiting to exhale.

Strangely enough, one small miracle was that the tail end of the jet wasn't on fire anymore. Scraping along the ground for so long had apparently snuffed the flames out. The tail had been badly damaged, the metal blackened and warped. Push wasn't sure, but it looked like something had hit it before it crashed.

Shaking the thought off for now, he edged toward the front of the plane, keeping an eye out for survivors, as well as any signs that the jet might ignite again. Nothing happened, so Push decided to risk it and see if anyone on the inside was still alive.

As he approached the bay door, it shifted and swung open. A woman appeared on the other side, bleeding from the forehead, dressed in a pilot's uniform. She looked around in a daze for a moment before zeroing in on Push.

"Ma'am," Push called out, getting as close to her as he could from the ground.

"Please," she called out. "There are people inside who are still alive!"

"The fire is out," Push assured her. "I don't know for how long, though. Can you find the emergency ramp?"

The pilot nodded. "I know where it is," she said, turning around.

"Get someone to help you," Push told her.

A moment later, the inflatable ramp was hanging down from the door's edge. Push seized the opposite end as it filled with air, making sure it was secure. Several other men were watching the door, helping the elderly and young out first. Push caught each one in his arms as they flew down the ramp, moving them out of the way before another came along.

"Once everyone is out, I'll find an ambulance," Push told them. His cell phone was still working, but the emergency lines would be too tied up at the moment to get through. He had a much better chance of going back into the main part of Shove Point than trying to call anyone.

"There are still people inside," the pilot told him once the last mobile passenger was off the jet. "We're afraid to move them, though. I think a few are dead."

"Come on down," Push yelled, moving up to the ramp to catch her. "We'll get a medic team here so they can examine them."

"I can't," she insisted. "They're my passengers. These people were my responsibility."

Push nodded in the end. "One of you is in charge until I get back," Push said to the group who'd helped the others out. "Make sure you keep everyone together. I'm going to find an ambulance."

"Who are you?" a nearby woman asked, clutching her arm in pain.

"They call me Push," he said, before taking off. "I'm with the Real-Life Superhero Association."

It took Push less than a minute to follow the path back. Several ambulances had already arrived on the scene and were checking the strewn bodies.

"I'm with the Association," Push told one of them, flashing his ID badge. "The Real-Life Superhero Association."

"Push," the man said, nodding. "I remember you."

For once, it was good to be recognized. Push wasn't sure anyone this far south would know him by his face. "The jet crashed just beyond here," he explained. "I've gotten a lot of the survivors out, but there are still people trapped inside. The pilot says they're too injured to be moved down the ramp. The rest are waiting outside beside it."

The technician looked back toward where Push had come from. "We've got our hands full here," he said gravely. "I'm going to get on the horn and send word out. They said more help is already on the way. It should be here within a few minutes. I'm going to let them know where to go. Did you get the name of the street?"

Push swore loudly. "I didn't think to look."

"Doesn't matter," the guy said, turning around. "In all this craziness, the name of a street won't mean much. Besides, a jet is going to be hard to overlook."

It was still chaos. Firefighters were helping to clear the area of as much rubble as they could. Citizens were volunteering their services to help. People moved back and forth, passing out drinks and blankets to those with only minor injuries. Others stood in circles praying together. Some simply stood off to the side, looking lost.

Push took a deep breath, steadied himself, and went back to work. There would be time for him to break down later. Right now, these people needed his help.

PUSH worked well into the day. Exhaustion did nothing to slow him down. Once a medic team arrived at the crash site to take care of the passengers, he moved on to help wherever he could.

Push was always near a medic team. His powers came in handy moving toppled cars and helping to clear away rubble. Overexerting them left him with a screeching headache, but he kept going. When he had a spare moment, Push touched base with Scratch over their phones. Wrath didn't have his, and Scratch hadn't seen him in a while, so Push was left with no choice but to believe the man was doing his job and hadn't skipped town.

Little by little, like chipping away at a stubborn old rock, the battle was being won. The aftermath would linger for a long time, but as the sun sank down into the west, Push looked around and felt a sense of relief beginning to creep over. Thanks to him, and everyone else's help, the town was going to make it.

The basement of the hospital had been reorganized into a shelter for the mild-to-moderately wounded. Those who were alive and well, but without homes, were packed into buses with whatever they could carry with them to be taken to the local convention center. Blankets, food, and water were being set up there so people could eat and get a good night's rest. Some were opening their homes up to their neighbors and relatives while arrangements were made. Insurance adjustors would be arriving soon, most likely within a couple of days, to survey everything.

For him and Scratch, though, the day was over with.

Sheriff Black found him as the last of the survivors were being loaded up. Push was signing autographs for a couple of younger kids whose parents had asked, knowing their children needed something to take their minds off things. When Push felt a pair of eyes watching him, he looked up and saw Black standing beside his patrol car, waiting patiently. Telling the kids good-bye, he made sure they got on the bus before walking over to where the sheriff stood.

"Need a lift?" he asked, pointing to his car. "I'd like for you to come by the station for a minute, if you've got time."

Push climbed in without a word, not in the mood to argue. The sheriff was blissfully silent as he drove them the short distance to the station. It had survived the crashing jet's destructive rampage, being northwest of the damage area. The courthouse hadn't been so lucky, however. Part of it had been taken out by one of the jet's wings. A fire had done the rest.

"That was one of the last places your boy got to," Black explained softly, noticing where Push was looking. "You'd have been proud of him today. He just marched right up to the places that were burning like it was nobody's business. The flames jumped into the air toward him, spun in a circle, and then snuffed out up. That sight would've made a believer out of anyone."

"I'm sorry he didn't make it to the courthouse," Push said absentmindedly, even though he wasn't sure why he was apologizing to the man.

Sheriff Black just shrugged. "It's only a building. He saved a lot of lives today; some of them were kin of mine, and others I've known since I was knee-high to my own pop. They won't forget it, neither."

"Good," Push said, giving the sheriff a look now. "I don't think he killed whoever it was in that alley."

Black smiled a little. It looked strange on his face.

"You actually believe in the man, don't you?"

Push had to think that over for a moment. "It looks like I do."

CHAPTER
EIGHT

WRATH was waiting in the building's entrance area. The black coat flowed around him like a cape as he knelt down in front of a harried-looking elderly man. Someone had brought out a chair for the old guy to sit in. Wrath was speaking to him in a hushed voice as Push paused just inside the door.

"I'll go out and look again in a little while," Wrath was saying in a reassuring tone. "I have to touch base with my… superior first, but once that's taken care of, I'll keep searching."

"You be careful out there, son," the old man said, giving Wrath's shoulder a squeeze.

Push kept watching, expecting Wrath to pull away. Wrath remained where he was, though, and gave the old man an amazingly reassuring smile.

"I don't know what I'd have done if you hadn't pulled me outta that burning building," he said. "I just wish I knew where she was right now. Even if she was dead, that would be better than not knowing."

"I'll take a look at the deceased," Wrath offered tentatively. "If you want, that is, just to scratch that off the list."

"I don't have a picture of her with me for you to take with you," the old man said miserably.

"It's okay," Wrath insisted, giving the old man's hand a gentle squeeze. "It's a small town. Somebody here will know what she looks like."

Wrath started to get up, but the old man stopped him. "Thank you for doing all of this, son," he said, the tears in his voice audible from where Push stood watching the scene unfold.

"It's no trouble at all, sir," Wrath said, getting up slowly. "I'm merely returning the favor."

Wrath spotted Push in the doorway as he stood. He moved a bit more stiffly than usual while approaching Push, but Push attributed that to his being exhausted. They were all tired, and it was a good enough reason for now. Later, maybe not, but Push wasn't curious enough to press for details.

"Who was that?" he did ask, however.

Wrath looked behind him. "I think they said his name was E. J. Glennwood. I found him inside one of the burning buildings earlier. His wife is missing, and they haven't located her yet. I promised him I would find her once I reported to you." Wrath hesitated. "Is that all right?"

Push couldn't resist smiling. "Permission granted," he replied in a very stiff, authoritative tone. "I'm shocked you're taking such an interest in these people. Yesterday, it seemed like you didn't want to be here."

Wrath glanced toward the man named E. J. Glennwood again. "Some of them aren't all bad," he mused. "Before I leave, though, is there anything I should know?"

"If you know where Scratch is, get the keys to the Pussy Wagon and take it," Push instructed. "Better for you to drive than go out there on foot. I'll see if I can't get the sheriff to drop him and me off once we're done here with whatever he wants."

"Good luck with that," Wrath muttered, reaching into his pocket. "Better you than me. Oh, and I already have the keys. A little while ago, Scratch sent me out to bring it around and pick up anybody that needed a lift."

"That'll save you some time, then," said Push. "Stop by the house while you're out and see if your BlackBerry came in. If there's any other mail for us, just leave it on the kitchen counter. I'll give you my number so you can call me once you get it set up. Right now, more than ever, the three of us need to stay in touch with one another."

Wrath obliged, borrowing a pen from the secretary so he could jot Push's number down on a slip of paper, then headed out the door.

"That's a good man you've got there," Mr. Glennwood said after Wrath was gone.

"Yeah," Push replied thoughtfully. "Maybe."

"Oh, that one's been through the wringer," Glennwood insisted firmly, nodding his head. "Ain't no disputing that fact. The ones who've been dealt a rough hand always have a tough time of it at first, but you can usually sort out the good ones from the bad in the end. He's got a mighty fine spirit to him. He just hasn't had someone believe in that for a long-ass time. It'll be good for him to have somebody who'll treat him right."

Sheriff Black had gone straight to his office. Push gave Glennwood a nod and headed for the cracked-open door, knocking first before nudging it open.

"Come on in," Black said. "I wanted to talk with you about something first before giving you and your other boy a lift. I saw the one in black leave already."

"He's got the truck," Push explained. "We could use a ride later, if you can spare one."

"I'll drop you two off on my way home," Black said, gesturing to the chair in front of his desk. "But first, I wanted to ask you something."

Push sat down. "Okay."

Black motioned for the door, which Push had left open a crack. With a flick of his hand, Push closed it using a very mild telekinetic burst.

"You boys are full of surprises," Black muttered, before folding his hands on his desk. "Word has it you were the first one to reach that jet. Is that true?"

"As far as I could tell," Push replied.

"I see." Black rolled his tongue on the inside of his cheek thoughtfully. "Any idea what brought that jet down into my town?"

Push thought hard for a moment. "I can't say," he began hesitantly. "But…."

"But?"

Push held his breath for a moment. "It looked like something had hit the tail."

Black narrowed his eyes. "Like, another plane?"

"I don't think so," said Push, thinking back to the crash site. "A jet like that should have spotted another plane coming toward it, and vice-versa, although I guess it is possible. If another plane had hit it, though, it should have done more damage. Whatever hit that jet was too small to be a plane."

"What could it have been, then?" Black wondered. "Some sort of radioactive space rock? That's the sort of stuff you boys deal with, right?"

"Not every day," said Push, smiling slightly. "Most meteorites burn up as they pass through the atmosphere. The ones that do make it are usually small. The odds of one bringing down a whole plane are pretty wide, but again, anything is possible."

"So, not another plane," Black listed off. "And not a space rock. What else could have done it, then?"

"It could have just been some sort of accident," Push offered. "This isn't my area of expertise. Maybe I got it wrong. At the time, I was more focused on the people trapped inside the plane."

Black gave Push a droll look. "Are you honestly going to sit there and tell me all of this was just an accident?"

Push thought hard for a long time, not wanting to give his opinions voice. In the end, though, he couldn't hold back.

"No," he admitted. "I don't think it was an accident, not a normal one in any case. Whether on purpose or not, something else brought that plane down."

"Onto my town," Black finished, looking grim. "Onto people I have known for years, so what the hell am I supposed to do about it? I'm not as thick as I seem, you know. I'm just a simple local sheriff. Somebody's fucked me over royally, so what am I supposed to do?"

Push met the sheriff's eyes. "We find them," he answered simply. "And put a stop to it, whatever 'it' is."

"SO HE thinks it wasn't an accident?"

Push regarded Scratch for a moment. "This is his town," he explained. "He won't accept that something fell out of the sky and played havoc with everything he knows by pure coincidence. I can relate to that much, at least."

"Yeah," replied Scratch, looking away. "I remember."

They were at the poker table, drinking what remained of the beer from the previous night and eating chips. Push wasn't sure if there was a grocery left standing in Shove Point, much less if it was open for business, so they'd gone with leftover snack food. He forced himself to not think about all the ab crunches he'd have to do to make up for it later on, since this was the first meal he'd had all day. He'd barely taken two bites out of breakfast before that jet had belly-flopped across Main Street.

"How much longer do you think he'll be gone?" Scratch wondered, looking past Push to the front door.

"I can call," Push offered, stirring the salsa with his chip. "He remembered to send me his phone number at least, so we know he got the BlackBerry."

The daunting task of having to unpack had been rendered unnecessary. The grunts sent by the Association had arrived with their stuff already and set it up in each room. Somehow, and in a way that made Push highly suspicious, they'd known which room each one had picked out for himself. Everything was laid out for them; all of their clothes were unpacked and stored in the closets and dresser drawers. It had saved them a lot of time and energy after such a grueling day, and while a small portion of Push wanted to debate the ethics of Association members ignoring a crisis to help them get unpacked, in the end Push was far too exhausted to care much.

"We could call," Scratch was saying, not aware that Push had drifted off. "But I don't feel like breathing down the guy's neck. So far, he hasn't done anything that I'd call suspicious."

"No," Push acknowledged. "He hasn't. In fact, the sheriff of all people said what a good job Wrath had done keeping the fires out. Apparently, the fire department was able to go right to getting the trapped locals out."

"Amazing," his friend replied dryly. "Considering his department was in such a hurry to toss him into the slammer this morning."

"I know. That's been bothering you too, huh?"

Push watched as Scratch took a long drink from his beer bottle. "So, what did you two do last night after I went to bed?"

Scratch snorted. "More like passed out cold. I went in to check on you about an hour after you left, and you were dead to the world. Apocalypse could have come knocking and you wouldn't have noticed.

"It was… interesting," Scratch continued after a moment's silence. "He's not a complete dickhead like I was expecting. For the most part, he struck me as somebody who'd been run over one too many times and fought back because he had to."

"Did he say anything about his past?" Push pressed, now very interested. "Like, before he joined the Deadly Seven?"

"Um, we didn't talk about it," Scratch admitted. "He was very reserved about anything concerning himself. I tried a couple of times, but he just shrugged it off."

"Oh," Push replied, feeling a little let down.

"Except, there was something really weird," Scratch told him suddenly, leaning forward in his chair a little as he spoke. "At one point, I was telling him about the comic book shop you and I sometimes visit whenever we get a chance back home. He mentioned there used to be one in the next town, about thirty minutes away."

Push frowned. "Okay?"

"So," Scratch insisted, "how would he know that?"

A light went on in Push's head. "That is strange," he said, thinking hard. "Wrath got arrested here after the Deadly Seven broke up, but how would he know that much about the area?"

"And have you noticed how familiar he is with this town?" Scratch added, getting excited. This was obviously something he'd wanted to discuss for a while. "It seems like he knows this place pretty well. If he'd only been here for one night, and was locked up for most of it, how does he know where so many things are?"

"Let's see if we can't find out when he gets back," Push suggested. "Maybe with a little bit of coercion, we can get something out of him."

"And I thought you were against roughing people up to get information," Scratch joked, finishing off his beer.

"We don't have to play rough," Push replied. "There's no reason why we can't do this in a civilized way."

"What were you thinking?"

Push smirked slightly. "Would you be up for another round of poker later?"

Scratch's eyes grew serious. "That's one thing about him," his friend warned, pointing a finger at the table. "After you left, Wrath suddenly got damn good at poker. I lost big time to him."

Something on Scratch's face caught Push's attention. "What'd you lose to him?"

"Later," Scratch said nervously. "I wouldn't mind having the chance to win it back, though, and if you're up for it, putting the squeeze on that cardsharp should be a hell of a lot of fun."

Push smiled conspiratorially. Both men paused at the sound of the Pussy Wagon rolling into the garage. A minute later, Wrath came stumbling in with both hands loaded with plastic bags.

"Young man," Scratch said in a mock-stern voice, "what sort of hour do you call this?"

"Sorry, Dad," Wrath jeered back, kicking the door closed. "I had to run out to the grocery store in the next town to pick up some stuff, since the one here is closed. It took me a while to find the place."

Push stood up without a word and headed out to help unload their bounty. With Scratch's help, it only took a couple of trips.

"Did you buy out half their stock?" he wondered, once everything was laid out on the kitchen counter. Some of the bags had to be set on the floor.

"Be glad I got anything at all," Wrath replied as he began placing things neatly on the cabinet shelves. "The people here in Shove Point who didn't lose their homes all drove out there to pick the shelves clean. I had to fight one woman off for that bag of marshmallows."

"I hope you let her live," Scratch said, stacking several pizzas into the refrigerator freezer. "I'd hate to think a woman died just so we could have marshmallows."

"If you killed her for steak, he'd be more forgiving," Push explained, placing the canned soups next to one another in rows.

"The steaks are in that bag next to the sink," Wrath said, pointing. "I thought we'd grill some up tonight, assuming no one here is a vegetarian."

"Not me," Push said. "Where'd you get the money for all this, though?"

"My bank card," Wrath told him, like it was obvious. "It came through the mail, just like you said.

"Don't worry," he added when Push looked apologetic. "I wouldn't rob a bank just to buy food. It's much easier and simpler to steal the food directly. Eliminating the middle man is something we're taught at the Supervillain Academy."

"I knew I was right about that," Scratch muttered, stuffing a gallon of milk into the back of the fridge.

Moments later, everything but the ingredients Wrath had set aside to cook the steaks with had been put away.

"Since you bought the food," Push told Wrath, "one of us will cook tonight."

"I don't mind cooking," Wrath said as he reached for a skillet. "I enjoy it."

"Have you ever cooked steak before?" Scratch wondered.

"Rare, medium, or well-done?" he asked in answer, giving the skillet an expert spin.

Scratch put a DVD in while Wrath got to work. "We were thinking about playing poker later," Push said, leaning against the counter casually. "Care to join us?"

"Sure," Wrath said absentmindedly as he poured a liberal amount of vodka over one of the simmering steaks.

"Great."

It turned out that Wrath was not merely adept at cooking breakfast. The steaks were seasoned just right, juicy but not tough. Their knives sliced through the meat with a single, clean cut. They took their seats in the living room as the movie played. Scratch had found a copy of *Daredevil*, and the film was a little over halfway done already.

"Say." Push spoke up suddenly while Ben Affleck dodged a sai-wielding Jennifer Garner. "Did you ever find anything on that guy's wife from the sheriff's station?"

Wrath froze midbite. "Yeah," he said slowly, setting his plate back down. "She's dead."

Scratch looked over toward Wrath as he ate quietly. "What happened?"

"They found her body in some rubble," Wrath explained curtly, swallowing his food. "Or, I should say, they found most of her. Apparently she got cut in half by the plane. The Glennwood man has already been told. They're going to have a memorial for all the people who died in a few days."

"Poor guy," Push said, remembering how it felt to lose a loved one.

"I think I'm done," Wrath announced, getting to his feet. "I don't know if you saw, but there's more booze in the refrigerator. We're going to need it if we're playing poker when this goes off."

Wrath stayed in the kitchen, moving around and making a lot of noise all the way through to the end credits. Curious, Push got up to see what he was doing, and found him cleaning the dishes in the sink.

"I forgot to buy dishwashing detergent," he mumbled, low enough for Push to wonder if he wasn't talking to himself.

"What's eating at you?" he asked, hoping Wrath might be in a forthcoming mood without the need for a binge drinking session.

"Nothing," Wrath replied, now clearly aware of Push's presence. "Nothing at all."

Scratch got the cards out, lined up the bottles of liquor in the middle of the table, and poured a glass for each of them. Once Wrath was finished and had dried himself off, he joined them at the poker table. Scratch dealt first, seven-card stud, and won the first hand.

Wrath didn't look put out by it at all.

Push gathered up his next hand and resisted frowning. Ever so carefully, he reached out with his right foot and applied just enough pressure to Scratch's so he could feel it. It was a signal they'd used once years ago during a rigged card game. Scratch coughed once to signify that he remembered and laid down two cards. Push called for three and was rewarded with two pairs, albeit low ones. Scratch did much better and won the next round.

Wrath beat them in the next hand, though that might have been Scratch's intention. Push won two rounds, before and after Wrath's next win, followed by Scratch getting a third. Scratch was keeping the hands more or less even so that no one at the table got too far ahead of the rest. If Wrath picked up on this, he gave no indication of it. It was more or less how things had gone last night, only this time, Push knew it was on purpose.

After a few more rounds, Push stood up. "I need something to chase this stuff down with," he said, heading for the kitchen. "Anybody else want something to drink?"

They'd all been drinking pretty heavily. Push grabbed a handful of sodas from the refrigerator per request, and tossed one each to Scratch and Wrath on his way back in. The others he sat down on the table next to him.

"How about we make this interesting?" he said, getting comfortable in his chair again.

"Like how?" Scratch asked. "You want to bet money?"

Push turned toward Wrath. "Nah," he said. "Let the new guy keep his earnings. He more than deserves them for today."

"There are worse ways to earn a paycheck," Wrath stated, picking up each card as it landed in front of him.

"I guess you'd know," Scratch ribbed, placing the final card in front of him.

"Maybe," Wrath replied. "What did you two have in mind?"

"Well," Push began, choosing his words with great care. No matter how heroic Wrath had been today, Push wasn't foolish enough to trust him completely.

"You're the odd man out here. Scratch and I have known each other for years."

"You have my file," Wrath reminded them.

"A file isn't the same thing," Scratch insisted. "I've seen the Association's file on me, and they haven't got a clue as to some of the stuff I've done."

"Same here," Push added.

"I see," Wrath said quietly, looking at them over his cards. "So, the two of you think there aren't any secrets between you?"

Scratch looked at Push, who tried to conceal the lump in his throat with little success. That, he hadn't been expecting.

"We know one another pretty well," Scratch admitted, giving Push a nod. "But who knows? There are probably still some surprises here and there."

"Are you brave enough to find out?"

Push stared hard at Wrath. "What did you have in mind?"

"Nothing much," replied Wrath, moving his cards around. "Keep things real simple. Whoever wins this next hand can ask anyone at the table one question. It can be about anything and directed at anyone. The winner picks the question and who to ask it to. Whoever gets asked a question has to answer with the complete truth. No exaggerating or lies."

"So, you're suggesting we play Truth or Dare," Scratch concluded. "Without the 'dare' part and with playing cards."

"Essentially." Wrath looked from one to the other. "Either of you game?"

Push won the first round. "Wrath," he stated, taking a drink from his soda can. "What is your real name?"

"Wrath is my real name," he answered at once, placing his cards back in the pile. "I was tried and convicted under 'John Doe as Wrath'. If you check my legal records, I have a Social Security number."

"How did that happen?"

"That's two questions," Wrath reminded him. "Deal."

Push accepted the cards from Scratch and dealt. Wrath won the next round and stared down the table at Scratch.

"Have you ever had sexual feelings for another man?" he asked bluntly. "And I'll accept a simple yes or no."

Scratch went tense for a second before reaching over to bring the bottle of Black Label over for a long, healthy swig.

"Once," he answered, sighing as he set the bottle back down next to him. "Back when I was about thirteen or so. A buddy of mine and I were watching porn at his house while his parents were out. His dad kept a stash of tapes in the back of the hall closet, and he'd come across them by accident a couple of weeks before. We both decided to jack off together, and during the…."

Scratch paused, searching for the right words. "During the 'moment', I guess, I looked over at him and wondered what his dick would feel like in my hand."

Push felt his eyes go wide. "Wait, when you were thirteen?"

"Sorry," Wrath informed him. "You'll have to win your own hand to ask."

Push glowered at him before turning once more to Scratch. "Your best friend when you were thirteen was Jimmy Hartgrove," he continued, mindful not to phase it as a question. "I remember you mentioning him before."

"That was him," Scratch admitted, keeping his eyes glued firmly to the liquor bottle as he ran his fingers along the neck. "He went around telling everyone at school that I was queer the next year because I stole his girlfriend and she gave me a blowjob. He'd been begging her to give him head the whole time they were together. I think she did it out of spite, honestly, but at the time, I wasn't about to complain."

Wrath's mouth turned sideways in a kind of half smile. Clearly, he had not been expecting Scratch to be so forthcoming. "New deal," he said.

It was close, but Push won the next hand. Wrath didn't look the least bit surprised when Push turned to stare him down.

"What was your name before you were tried as 'Wrath'?" he demanded.

"I went by Wrath for years," he said, smiling as he ran a finger around the rim of his glass. "People in New Orleans didn't know me by anything other than Wrath, and I had several aliases set up."

Push started to get pissed, but Wrath spoke up quickly. "But," he added. "I guess it wouldn't hurt. It was John."

Push waited. "And?"

"And what?" Wrath was obviously enjoying himself. "You didn't ask for my full name."

Scratch chuckled, then gave Push an apologetic smile as Push dealt the next hand. It might have been funny were Push not so annoyed.

"I win again," Wrath declared, showing a straight flush. "Push, the first time you ever laid eyes on Scratch, did you think he was cute?"

Push shrugged as casually as he could and made sure not to look directly at Scratch's face when he turned toward him. "He's not really my type," he insisted, somewhat feebly. "I don't waste my time chasing straight guys."

Wrath smiled. "You knew he was straight just by looking at him?"

"No more than one question," Push reminded, feeling a bit of satisfaction at turning that back on him.

"Very true," Wrath acknowledged, holding his hand out. "My turn to deal."

Wrath won again, this time with four kings. "What is your full real name?" he asked Push while motioning for another soda.

"Garfield Barnes," Push told him, passing the can along. "You could have looked that up in the Association records. Full-time members get access to the RLSA's database."

"I'll keep that in mind," Wrath said. "Next deal."

Scratch dealt again. Both he and Push came out ahead, surprisingly, with a Full House each, trumping Wrath's straight. Scratch had the higher cards of the two, though, making him the winner. Push expected him to press for Wrath's last name, but Scratch caught him by surprise.

"What made you join the Deadly Seven?" he asked, after chasing a mouthful of liquor with the rest of his soda.

Wrath shrugged in that nonchalant way of his. "That's easy," he said. "Power. Money. Respect. It wasn't a hard decision for me."

Wrath won yet again. "Let's see," he mused, looking back and forth between them. "Who should be next?"

Push watched as Wrath pointed his finger from one to the other, feeling apprehensive. When Wrath's finger landed on him and stayed there, he felt his hands clench involuntarily.

"Hmm," Wrath hummed, thinking carefully. "No, that's too easy, and not something I really find interesting. What else?"

"Is that your question?" Push asked boldly.

Wrath shook his head. "No, I think I've got it. Push, how is it you've known Scratch for as long as you have and yet have never made a pass at him?"

Push raised an eyebrow at this. "You're serious?"

"Utterly," Wrath said. "Answer the question."

"Because he's my friend," Push stated, as if that should have been obvious. "And he doesn't like guys. I know he's not interested in guys. Scratch is one of the biggest horndogs I've ever known. Hell, I'm usually the one setting him up with women. If he ever turned gay, I think some of the Association's female members would probably kill me!"

Push didn't realize how loud he'd been talking until his words echoed back to him from across the room. Even then, they sounded forced and unconvincing. Wrath had folded his hands in front of him during Push's brief rant. Scratch was looking down at the table when Push finally worked up the nerve to face him.

"My deal," Scratch said, reaching his hand out for the cards. "I think we've learned more than enough about one another for one night. This'll be the last hand."

Scratch won. "Wrath," Scratch said, getting his full attention. "What was your connection to that old man at the station, the Glennwood guy?"

Silence fell over the room like a dark cloud. Push watched as Wrath stared at Scratch across the table for a moment, before raising his still-folded hands up so he could rest his chin on them.

"Very good," he praised softly. "You're getting the hang of this."

"Answer the question," Push said, leaning on the edge of his seat now.

Wrath sighed. "Right, I was the one who made the rules after all, wasn't I? There's no point in turning back now."

Both waited as Wrath adjusted himself in his seat. "E. J. Glennwood was my babysitter," Wrath told them. "He and his wife used to watch me when I was a little kid."

Push waited a moment, sure he hadn't heard right. "Wait," he began, wrestling with the bomb Wrath had just dropped on them. "He knew you when you were little?"

Wrath nodded. "Exactly."

"But that means…."

Scratch was the one who finished the sentence. "…this used to be your hometown?"

"I was born in the hospital at the next town," Wrath began, hunching up slightly as his gaze drifted out toward the living room.

"Back then, Shove Point didn't have one of its own. I was raised here until I was eleven, I think. It's hard to remember exactly when now, but I wasn't any older than that when Sloth's men found me."

"You were eleven when you first met Sloth?"

Push expected Wrath to bring up the one-question rule, but all Wrath did was nod. "I had been walking down the road when a van pulled up and someone grabbed me. Looking back on it, I think Sloth must have been watching me for a while. He knew a lot about me, knew how to approach me. The man really can be brilliant when he wants to."

Wrath took a drink before continuing. "Anyway," he said, setting the can back down hard. "The men took me to him, and he asked if I wanted to join his gang. At first, I thought it was some kind of practical joke. I was only eleven, after all, but then he told me that he knew about my powers, how nobody believed me when I said that things setting on fire weren't my fault. People thought I was some kind of pyromaniac."

"Even your parents?"

Wrath scowled at Push's question. "Especially my parents," he said through gritted teeth, and it was such a contrast to how calm the man usually looked that Push found himself memorizing the rage set in Wrath's face.

"They hated each other," he went on. "Always had. I never knew why they married, or decided to have a kid, but here I am. They weren't prone to fighting, or having loud arguments. Both of them were paranoid about what other people thought, so they kept it all inside. I didn't know it at the time, but I was...."

Wrath clammed up suddenly. "Go on," Scratch encouraged in a careful voice. "We're still listening."

Wrath swallowed. "I am not just a pyrokinetic," he said slowly, keeping both eyes fixed on the table's surface now. "My powers are fueled by my empathic abilities."

"You're an empath?" Push quickly recalled what the word meant. "So, you can control other people's emotions?"

"Not to that degree," Wrath replied. "Although some people find it difficult to control their impulses when I'm around, especially if they've been suppressing them for a long time."

Wrath glanced up at Push as he said this. "My pyrokinesis is fueled by the rage and hatred of people around me. I draw it into me by instinct, then convert it into flames."

"And with your parents always quietly seething at one another," Scratch said, putting it all together. "That must have made things rough."

"My father would force us all to sit at the table together," Wrath told them. "It was like their feelings boiled over out of their bodies and into me. That was when I had the most trouble controlling myself. Other kids at school thought I was disturbed, or had some kind of mental problem. A lot of the adults avoided me and wouldn't let their kids come over. When Sloth found me, he made going away sound exciting. I'd never seen New Orleans, and he promised to take me to somebody who could show me how to control my abilities. It seemed like a good offer, even though I knew he was hiding things from me at the time."

Wrath let out a deep breath. "Sloth brought me to New Orleans and introduced me to some people who had limited knowledge of psychic abilities. They were able to help some, but overall, I was basically learning how to teach myself. Sloth was still gathering some of the other members of the Deadly Seven during my training period. By the time we were all together, I'd figured out just what I'd gotten myself into. By that point, though, I'd started getting the hang of controlling and mastering my powers. Being a crook seemed nowhere near as bad as Sloth sending me back to Shove Point, which he threatened to do several times."

"That was the big threat Sloth used to control you?" Scratch wondered, and even Push had to agree a little. "He was going to ship you back home to your folks if you didn't do what he said?"

"At the time," Wrath said emphatically, looking mad, "it seemed much worse. I was still a minor and had no real legal recourse. I couldn't prove I hadn't been starting fires on purpose without exposing myself, and there was no telling what would have happened if my powers had become public knowledge. And assuming my parents were still around, they'd have most likely taken turns beating the shit out of me."

"Where did you live?" Push asked.

The question had come out unbidden, but Wrath didn't appear to mind now. "You're both sitting in it," he told them, gesturing around the room.

"Shit," Scratch said flatly.

"This is your place?"

Wrath gave Push a small nod. "It was my parents' house," he said stiffly. "I grew up here. Back then, the room you're sleeping in hadn't been built. Jimbo Thompson must've added on to it after they seized the property. They went to the same church that my parents always dragged me to."

"You knew the Thompsons?"

Push wasn't sure why he was asking all of this.

"I knew Jimbo Thompson," Wrath clarified, no longer minding the topic of conversation, it seemed. "Back then, he wasn't married to that Laura woman. She used to be what my mother called a 'bad woman', meaning she'd been married more than once. The Thompson guy must have lowered his standards for her to get that close to his wallet."

"So how come nobody here recognizes you?" Scratch asked suddenly.

"Good question," Push said. "I was thinking about that, too."

"No idea," Wrath replied earnestly. "I was a lot skinnier back then, and my hair was short. It may be that people just forgot about me after a while and found something new to talk about. Or maybe they don't associate the kid I was with who I am now. When people look at me, they tend to think 'dangerous supercriminal'. A painfully shy eleven-year-old boy who panics at the sound of thunder doesn't exactly strike fear into the hearts of others."

Something occurred to Push upon hearing this. "Does that mean you were lying to us?" he asked. "No offense, but you were a member of the most notorious gang of criminals this country has ever known. How do we know any of this is the truth?"

"If you have to ask me that," Wrath said, getting up, "then I guess there's no point in me being honest with you at all."

Wrath headed for his room without another word. Push watched him go and heard the door slam shut while Scratch frowned at him.

"You didn't have to go that far," he said once Wrath's door closed.

"I know," Push agreed, feeling lousy all of a sudden. "I guess I just can't get used to the fact that our new roommate used to be a famous contract killer and criminal muscle. He keeps throwing me curve balls, and I don't like it."

"He's waiting to see how you react," Scratch told him in a firm way, like Push was suddenly a teenager again. "I think he wants to know where he stands with us and whether it's going to last. If I were in his shoes, I'd probably be real suspicious right now, especially with how things have turned out."

"Yeah," said Push, thinking back over that. "Do you think the Association knows?"

Scratch had to think that one over. "Probably not," he said at last, running his fingers through his hair, a gesture Push often found irresistibly cute. "The Cape Cabinet are dicks, but I don't see why they would want to put all three of us here so Wrath could confront his childhood trauma. You know as well as I do that the Cape Cabinet doesn't go for that bullshit. They don't even like having therapists on the roster. The member vote was what got us that. More than likely, this was just a coincidence."

"You know I refuse to believe in those," Push said, standing along with him.

"I don't know what to say," Scratch confessed, heading toward his room now. "But it's late, and I am exhausted. We can worry about this later. Right now, I just want some sleep."

Push watched his friend head down the hall. "Night," he said, not moving until Scratch was out of sight. "Sweet dreams."

CHAPTER
NINE

SOMETHING was wrong.

When Push woke up, this was the first thing to run through his mind. He'd been dreaming, about what he couldn't be sure now that he was awake, but the house felt wrong. The air in it was still, as if waiting for something. With his eyes now open, Push felt wide awake. He also realized as he glanced toward the digital clock next to his bed that his throat was bone dry.

He'd gone to bed under the covers, and wearing his boxer shorts this time. The urgent need to piss overtook him as he threw his legs over the side of the bed, so Push took care of that first and foremost. He would probably have to do it again once he drank something, but nature wasn't giving him much of a say in the order of things.

Upon leaving his room, Push fumbled around blindly for a light switch. It took him a while, but he finally came across one near the refrigerator that lit up the florescent bulb hanging over the kitchen sink. Spots swam in front of his face for a moment before his eyes cleared up. Able to see, he pulled a glass out of the cabinet in front of him, then filled it up using the filtered-water dispenser on the refrigerator door. It felt amazing going down his throat. All of the alcohol he'd drunk in the last two days, as well as the frantic pace he'd run on after the crash, had apparently dried him out. Push drank two more glasses before he felt somewhat satisfied.

The lights were off in the rest of the house. Push had paced back and forth as he had downed his third glass, and while pacing, he had noticed something odd about the hallway. Wrath's bedroom light was off, yet his door was wide open. Push remembered it being closed when he went to bed. Something that sounded like a painful moan drifted faintly into the kitchen from that direction. Suspicious now, Push set his glass down and moved as quietly as he could across the tile floor.

Wrath's bedroom was empty. The sheets on his bed were rumpled, signifying that the man had at least gone to bed at some point. The sound came again, and this time, Push realized it was originating from further back.

It was coming from Scratch's bedroom.

Push's mind raced as his feet dragged him unwittingly down the carpeted hall. It was none of his business. Scratch must have brought a girl home after he left. It was far too late for Scratch to be on a booty call. Wrath could be anywhere right now. It didn't mean anything had happened. It was none of his business, after all.

He shouldn't have looked.

Scratch was naked, sprawled out across his bed on his back with his head raised up, watching as Wrath's mouth sank down on his dick. Push's throat went dry all over again as the thick head of what had to be at least eight inches slid down Wrath's throat.

Scratch had a death grip on the back of Wrath's head, shoving him down hard on his slicked cock. Push felt the head of his dick pop out of the fly in his boxers as he watched. Despite his erection, another feeling like writhing, angry snakes churned in his stomach. For a moment, the scene shifted in his head. He was the one buried between Scratch's legs, sucking the length of him down like there was no tomorrow. It was Push who was making Scratch writhe on top of the bed, naked, who made his best friend scream now.

"Yes! Fuck, keep going!" It almost sounded like Scratch was begging him. "Dude, I'm gonna cum soon if you keep that up."

Wrath released Scratch's dick from his mouth briefly. "Go ahead," he encouraged. "I want you to."

Even in the darkness, Push could see Scratch's eyes widen. "You don't mind?"

Wrath ran his tongue up the underside of the shaft playfully. "I really want you to," he said softly, gripping the base with his thumb and forefinger. The two couldn't connect with one another. Scratch's girth was too much for it to happen.

"I like the taste of it," Wrath was saying now. "And I want to see how you taste."

The look on Scratch's face was a mix of confusion, adulation, and smoky desire. Beads of sweat glistened in the dim light peeking through the window as Wrath picked up speed. It didn't take Scratch much longer.

It felt like Push was about to go off in his pants. His hands remained by his sides, unwilling to move. He hadn't lost that much of his dignity yet.

Scratch was cumming now. His best friend's eyes widened to the size of saucers as his load exploded down Wrath's throat. Push watched and waited as Wrath's tongue licked around the sides of Scratch's cock, writhing like the nest of snakes still coursing in Push's belly, waiting to be let out.

"That was fucking amazing," Scratch gasped.

"You want to do it again?" Wrath asked, applying pressure slightly to the thick vein on the underside of Scratch's dick, moving it up and down a little to coax out more jizz.

"Uh, I don't know," Scratch said hesitantly, between breaths. "Maybe."

Push heard himself speak. "You could have always asked me, you know."

Scratch jerked his head in shock, but Wrath turned slowly, as though expecting to find Push there. The rage boiling inside of Push flared at this, and he lashed out without thinking. Wrath was still crouched down on the bed half-dressed, looking utterly calm as the telekinetic blast flung him through the air. Push moved his hand to throw another one as Wrath crashed against the wall, but something made him look to where Scratch was.

Scratch had risen up off the bed, still nude, and was looking at Push like he didn't recognize him. "Jesus, Push!" he screamed. "What the hell?"

Their eyes met, and Push felt his begin to fog over. "Motherfucker," he swore at Scratch, hating himself. "It just had to be him, didn't it?"

Scratch looked confused for a second. "It wasn't anything serious," he insisted, covering himself up now. "I just… I lost a bet with him the other night."

"And what?" Push demanded. "This was how you were paying him off. What the hell did you gamble with, and what made you want to with a convicted murderer, for God's sake?"

Push saw Scratch was still hard and having trouble hiding his shame. "Oh, don't bother covering up now," he jeered. "Why the hell bother? Let's see the whole show once and for all!"

A hurt look flickered on Scratch's face. "What the hell is wrong with you, buddy? I've never seen you like this before."

Wrath chose that moment to speak up. Push had nearly forgotten he was in the room, or that he'd blasted the man right off the bed in his anger. Wrath didn't look angry. If anything, the man almost looked like he felt sorry for both of them.

"He's in love with you. Push has loved you for a long time, I think."

This hit Push like a punch to the gut. It felt as though he were on the receiving end of one of his own telekinetic bubbles.

"What?" Scratch looked over at Wrath as he stood up. "Push isn't…."

Scratch jerked his head back at Push then, however, and saw the look on his face. "Oh my God," he said breathlessly. "Push, you didn't…."

Push turned to go. He wasn't thinking about where he was headed, or what he was planning to do. All that mattered then was getting out, as far from those two as he could. His hands dressed himself in record time, moving of their own will, while the remainder of him was on autopilot. Push grabbed his costume, foul-smelling though it was, wallet, bo staff, goggles, and house key before making tracks for the front door. He saw Scratch coming down the hall toward the kitchen as he left, but didn't stop, not even when his friend called out his name. The sound felt like a dagger in his heart.

He broke into a run the minute he felt his feet hit pavement. The rhythm carried him down the road at a breakneck pace. He didn't care which direction he went in. None of that mattered right now. The point was to run until he couldn't go any farther and couldn't see that house anymore.

The road was a blur. His footsteps hit the ground to the beat of his frantic heart. Everything went by him in a haze. There weren't many lights on at this time of night. The residents in the areas still intact after the crash were sleeping, dead to the world, letting their dreams take them away from the horror that had taken place today. Push closed his mind to them and their troubles, as well as his own, and moved on. He was coming up on the center of town now, near where the jet had cut through. Push had no idea how fast he'd been going, or how he made it this far in such a short period of time.

Push kept running until he came to an area where the damage had been especially bad. The buildings were in ruin, the streets torn apart under the stress of a puddle-jumper scraping along it, and the air still stank somewhat of smoke and jet fuel. It fit Push's mood perfectly.

Coming to a stop, he wandered over to where a car had been left turned on its side. If it hadn't fallen yet, Push didn't see it happening anytime soon. Mindful of the glass, he located a spot near the back and parked his ass on the ground. Now that he'd stopped running, his thoughts were beginning to clear.

The truth had come out. Scratch knew, and this could very well be the end of their friendship. It wasn't that Push hated the thought of losing Scratch as a partner in crime-fighting, though that played a significant part in it all. He and Scratch worked perfectly together. Push never felt more at ease than when he knew his best friend had his back. It had been that security that kept Push going during more than one bad period in his life.

Push was afraid of facing the future without Scratch at all. Scratch was straight and wouldn't want Push fawning all over him while he got on with his life. Hell, Push didn't want that for either of them. He'd spent years forcing himself not to care for Scratch as more than a friend. It had hurt more than he cared to admit. Now, all of that hard work had blown up in his face thanks to Wrath.

Then again, Wrath hadn't been solely responsible, though it felt good to blame the asshole for everything at the moment.

Footsteps came closer. Push didn't react to them, didn't consider the possibility that it could be someone looking for trouble. It didn't register with him that he knew the sound of those steps, yet it came as no shock at all to look up and see Scratch looking tentatively around the side of the car at him.

"Hey," Scratch said feebly.

Push stood up. "Yeah."

"Don't leave," Scratch said as Push started to walk off. "I was worried I'd have to spend the rest of the night driving around this burg looking for you."

"You took the Pussy Wagon?"

Scratch turned around and pointed a little ways down the road. "I drove past you just before you got this far. By the time I'd parked it, you were going behind the car. I came the rest of the way on foot because of all the glass."

"Oh."

Push kept his gaze turned away slightly.

"How long?" Scratch asked. "How long since…?"

"Years," Push said, the bitter words leaving an acid taste on the tip of his tongue. "Not since the very beginning, though. I didn't become your friend because I wanted to get inside your pants, if that's what you were worried so much about."

"That's good to hear," Scratch replied. "But I honestly wasn't worried about that."

"Yes, you were."

"No," Scratch insisted, moving toward Push just a little. "You always despised people who did that sort of thing, and you're not a hypocrite. I was just wondering… how long you had been keeping this from me, is all."

Push sighed. "I honestly don't know myself," he confessed. "I just know it's been a long time. I always thought you were good-looking, don't get me wrong. Remember, how we used to joke about it?"

"Yeah," Scratch said, and it sounded like he was laughing. "I used to joke all the time that I could get more gay guys than you."

"I know," Push said in an irritated tone. "Looking back on it, I think I stopped doing that because I realized I was beginning to have feelings for you. At that point, I could shove it aside and not worry, though. In some ways, it felt like you were made just for me. We both liked the same things, had a lot of the same opinions about stuff, and you were so accepting and easy to talk to. When we became roommates, I thought it might be a problem, but I was in a bind at that point. I couldn't let my feelings wreck our friendship and leave me homeless. After that, it seemed easy, until one day I looked up from something I was doing, and you were just suddenly *there*."

Push felt his throat tighten. "I couldn't explain it, but at some point, it got too big for me to ignore. You were right in front of me, and it took everything I had not to reach out and touch you. If I hadn't been so scared of freaking you out, I might have done it." Push scowled suddenly. "I'm going to choke that son of a bitch!"

"Don't," Scratch told him. "It was my own damn fault. After you went to bed the other night, we played several more rounds of poker. I was shit-faced at that point, and somehow, we got on the topic of what a straight guy would and wouldn't do. We played one last hand, and the winner was supposed to name his reward."

Push snorted.

"Wrath won, obviously," Scratch continued. "And told me he wanted to give me a blowjob at the time of his choosing."

"Ah."

"I had gotten up to piss, and he heard me coming out of the hall bathroom. I guess that seemed like as good a time as any, so I told him he could. It had been a little while since I got head, so…."

"Right."

Scratch was looking around at the damage. "Maybe if I hadn't made that stupid bet with him?" he offered.

"He knew already," Push reminded him. "He's an empath, remember? Chances are he would have blabbed it at some point."

"I forgot."

Scratch stared down at his feet, keeping his eyes away from Push. "This isn't how I imagined things going, but…"

A noise cut Scratch off, startling both of them. "Stray cat?" Scratch offered as the sound came again from one of the partially-crumbled buildings. "I hope so. There have been enough surprises for one night."

"Understatement," Push muttered. "We'd better make sure, though. A stiff breeze would bring some of these places down. It's no place for anyone to be screwing around."

"Then again," Scratch pointed out, as they both started toward the source of the noises, "neither one of us should be doing this, either."

Scratch's statement, however true, did nothing to deter either one of them. A moment later, Push was stepping over the threshold of the ruined structure, taking a quick look around before signaling Scratch that the coast was clear. A part of him felt uncomfortable doing this, what with everything that had just happened. Scratch had been in the middle of saying something, but Push was convinced he didn't need to know what it was. Investigating a derelict building on the verge of collapse sounded much more appealing.

The building creaked ominously then, changing Push's mind.

"It could have been rats," he said, sounding hopeful to himself. "Let's make this quick so we don't get buried under."

"No problem," Scratch replied, taking his place at Push's side.

The interior of the dilapidated building was dark. Push pressed a button on his goggles and switched them to night vision mode.

"I'm not getting anything," he said uneasily. "Hold on, let me switch to my motion sensor."

The light from his goggles flickered as he changed modes. "This is really strange," Push said, keeping his bo staff at the ready. "We both heard something, but I'm not picking anything up. Even rats or a stray cat would trigger the sensor a little."

"I hate it when that gizmo of yours messes up," Scratch grumbled, holding his cue stick up. "Because it always means something bad is about to happen."

"Either we were both hearing things," Push went on as he slowly raised his head up toward the ceiling. "Or whatever was in here climbed up to...."

Something that could have been a snarl echoed down at them. Push jumped back out of the way, but not fast enough to avoid getting hit. Whatever struck him felt like it was armed to the teeth. Scratch tackled Push hard as two more came down, each one crashing against the places where they'd been standing.

"Sorry," he apologized, helping Push back up.

"Forget about it!" Push shouted, readying both his staff and a telekinetic blast. "What the hell are those things?"

They were balls. At first glance, at least, that was what they looked like to Push. Each one came up to about Scratch's waist. They reminded Push of giant pill bugs, which would have been silly, except that one started rolling along the concrete toward them.

Push and Scratch scattered as the first one rolled between them, then stopped short of the wall and changed directions. The others were already rolling around as more dropped down to the ground. Push counted a total of eight.

"Here goes nothing," he said as one changed directions to run him down.

The telekinetic force bubble caused the roller to ricochet back in the direction it had come and crash against one of its own, both of them colliding with two more.

"That worked!" Scratch called out. "Kinda, anyway."

"I'll try again," Push offered, firing another bolt.

This one caused a chain reaction. The one he struck bounced back and forth off several of the other rollers in succession, causing a racket.

The last one it collided with caused the roller to bounce up into the air. When it landed, Push heard it make a loud cracking sound. A bunch of sinister clicks filled the room as the roller unfolded into....

Something.

It had two arms and legs, of that much Push was certain. Quickly, he switched back to his night vision to get a better look. Scratch apparently didn't need goggles to see it, because he gave a shout as the thing stood up.

"Fuck me running!" he cried out. "Is that...?"

Push had no idea. The creature's arms hung down past its waist, forming what looked like claws made for eviscerating someone. It stood duck-footed with its knees bent and the weight pressing down on its two-pronged toes. Mandibles surrounding the mouth made the clicking sound, sending chills up Push's spine. It reminded him of an insect monster from an old horror film.

Two more rolled up and unfolded out into the same shape. It was difficult to tell with his night vision on, but their flesh might have been dark-colored. All three of them were holding weapons of some kind. The first one pointed at Scratch, the closer of the two, and spoke in a kind of jibberish that made Push's eardrums throb.

The other two fired.

"Scratch!" Push shouted, as beams flew across the room and nailed Scratch in the chest. "You sons of bitches!"

Push let loose with a shock wave of telekinetic force that rippled the air. The three creatures, whatever they were, went flying as more unfolded out of their pill bug shape with weapons drawn and ready. Push dove behind a fallen bookshelf as they aimed their blasters and opened up on him. The lasers pelted the wall behind him with shots, throwing dust and debris up into the air. Push raised a hand up over the shelf and let loose another blast.

The firing ceased as one of the creatures cried out in pain. There was a weird noise for a moment, like thick rubber being stretched too thin, and then a loud pop rang in Push's ears. Unsure of what happened, but not willing to waste an opportunity, Push rose out from behind the shelf with both arms high over his head and unloaded on the remaining creatures with everything he had.

Two more went flying back through the air. One landed on a sharp piece of wood sticking up from the ground, impaling itself there. Half a second passed, then the body started to swell. Push stared in shock as the creature inflated to the shape of a balloon and exploded. Thick ooze that stank worse than Push's jock cup on a hot summer day flew across the room in all directions.

The other creatures didn't look bothered by this at all. Three opened fire on him, but were cut off by three bouncing billiard balls that rattled through the rafters before opening up. Bolas spun through the air out of each one of them, wrapping around a single target. Two had their arms pinned to their sides, while the last one's wrists were tied together.

Scratch was alive!

"I'm okay," Scratch called out, as if hearing Push's thoughts. "But damn, those things smart. Don't let them hit you if you can help it."

Push was too relieved to come up with a sarcastic comeback. Picking his targets off one at a time, he took aim for their chests and blasted each one. Two more of them exploded.

"Yuck!" Scratch groaned, sounding sick. "What was that all about?"

"Whatever these things are," Push said as the remaining four opened up on them, "I don't think they're very durable."

"No kidding." Scratch rolled forward and launched two more trick balls up at the ceiling, where they bounced back and forth off the rafters. "But what are they?"

"Not important just yet," Push replied. "We need to get out of here so we have more room to maneuver!"

The two balls hit the floor where the creatures were grouped together, releasing a thick cloud of green gas. The creatures kept right on firing, forcing Scratch to stay low to the ground as both he and Push made tracks for the gaping hole that had been their entrance.

The creatures took their time coming out of the building. Push and Scratch raced behind the overturned car, watching as their opponents looked back and forth, as though searching for something. After a moment, one of them pointed to the others and spoke in the same grating language again.

"Why aren't we being attacked?" Scratch asked.

"Don't sound so disappointed," Push chided. "We still don't know what they are."

"It helps me work out my aggression," Scratch insisted as the creatures began to separate. "It doesn't look like they're interested in us anymore. Should I be offended?"

"Not yet," Push muttered, keeping himself out of sight. "I want to know what they're doing."

"They're leaving."

The creatures were, in fact, splitting off into teams of two and leaving the area.

"I'm going to follow one of them," Push said, easing out from behind the car now. "Go home and pick Wrath up, then come and find me. I'll turn the GPS tracker in my phone on so you can follow me."

"This is messed up," Scratch muttered. "It's like we're trapped in a comic book or something."

"The irony wasn't lost on me," Push replied. "Go!"

CHAPTER
TEN

TRACKING the creatures turned out to be a lot easier than Push expected. Once the fighting stopped, it was like they lost all interest in him. He should have been spotted before now, but apparently, these guys had better things to do than tussle with him.

Not that Push felt offended, of course. He wasn't the stealthiest, so not having them turn those laser weapons onto him all over again made for a wonderful change of pace. Scratch had said they hurt, yet he hadn't looked injured once they left the building. Still, Push didn't want to risk those blasters having more than one setting. If those Clickers had been sending out friendly fire, he didn't want to see what happened when they got serious.

That was what he'd come to think of them after hearing that awful clicking sound they made over and over again. He was clenching his teeth now as they came upon the crashed jet at the end of its trail of destruction. Someone was coming to haul it off tomorrow, according to Sheriff Black. The thing looked like a sick monument to the town's tragedy.

The creatures were standing around it now at the tail end. None of them moved or made any kind of gestures, but it looked to him as though they were examining the damage.

"What in the world?" he wondered aloud softly.

In unison, the two made an about-face as though somebody had flipped a switch in their heads. Push hesitated for a moment in his hiding place behind some stacked rubble. He had hit the power for his GPS tracker almost immediately after he and Scratch separated. They were probably right behind him, so he took a chance and headed off down the crumbled road.

The streets here were even worse than the ones on his road. Push kept a safe distance from his targets as they strode calmly side by side. The houses here hadn't been damaged by the crash, though one look at them might make one think otherwise. It looked like a good stiff wind would topple any of them. How they managed to stay standing in spite of a jet crashing in their neighborhood was anybody's guess. Push had no doubt as to what section of the town he was in now.

Putting the thought out of his head, he kept on going. The street dead-ended up ahead. Beyond that was a field, and maybe a hundred yards further down on the other side of it was the edge of a forest.

The creatures kept going, as if the concept of leaving a road was foreign to them. For a little while now, in the back of his mind, Push had been debating a hypothesis on what he was currently tracking. Up until this point, it had remained dutifully back behind the solid wall of steel he'd trapped it in. Now, though, as the creatures got further away, it spoke volumes louder.

Feeling way out of his league now, Push nevertheless continued onward. Going through the field made keeping out of sight a lot harder. There was a significant lack of cover in this area, except for the tall brush and grass. Push had to keep low to the ground to avoid being seen, although he had lucked out thus far in that the creatures no longer seemed to regard him a priority.

Something stung him in the leg as he neared the end of the brush field. Looking down, he saw something stuck to his spandex pants. In the darkness, it was hard to see, and struck with a sudden fear of all manner of horrors lurking in nature, Push quickly switched on his night vision specs. Zooming in, he saw they were cockleburs.

He had cockleburs in his spandex.

Checking himself over, Push saw they were in his jacket, as well. The sleeves looked eaten up with them, as though the prickly seeds were trying to devour his clothes.

"Wonderful," Push grumbled to himself, forgetting that he was supposed to be stealthy at the moment. "My tailor is going to kill me."

A clicking noise sent chills up his spine. Push didn't waste time looking around, but dove forward into a roll. His body crashed right through a patch of brush full of burs, sticking to him on all sides. Rising up, his hair covered in the things, Push spotted several new Clickers standing together with weapons raised.

"Then again," he mused, raising his hands, "she may not get the chance!"

It was a choice between getting stabbed in the face with yet more burs or having his body riddled with laser fire. Taking into consideration the fact that his eyes were shielded and the burs were less likely to outright kill him, Push threw himself forward into the brush as the air overhead flashed with red beams. To his utter shock, he landed in a spot that was only dry brush.

The creatures—he refused to call them aliens just yet—began shouting at one another in their grating language and continued pouring on the fire. Push rolled out of the way, hoping to get clear so he could make a counterattack, but the beams followed him.

And yet, they weren't aiming at the brush directly.

"They must've gone to the Imperial Stormtrooper Marksmanship Academy," he told himself, still tumbling through the brush. "I guess I should be thankful they graduated."

A familiar sizzling sound burned through the air in the distance, and Push stopped short in his dizzying roll as he heard the rubbery sound of one of the creatures swelling. Two seconds later, a loud, moist bang filled the air, and goo went flying.

"Okay," came Wrath's voice. "I'm convinced now. Neither of you were having a go at punking the new guy. My mistake."

"Over here," Push called out, raising a hand.

One of the aliens, or creatures rather, opened fire on him again. The beams were cut off by the sound of fighting and more loud popping. Push raised up and saw Scratch taking on two of the things at once while Wrath shot flames in an upward angle through the chests of the remaining three. All three ducked down as the air was filled with a sticky, gooey mess.

Scratch stood up and looked around. "We're being invaded by alien zits," he commented. "Somehow, this isn't nearly as cool as I'd imagined it would be."

"Same here," Wrath mused as Push marched over to them.

"Cutting it kind of close, aren't you?" he asked critically. "You couldn't have just blown them up from way back?"

Wrath stamped the ground in reply. "Dry brush," he said pointedly. "A fire out here could spread and burn half the town to the ground. I think they've had enough problems for one day."

"You can put fires out," Push reminded him, getting angry again.

Wrath twisted his mouth into an uneven smirk. "I wanted a closer look, okay?"

Push looked away, unable to argue with that. However pissed he still was over what happened, the guy had just helped save his ass. Wanting a closer look at aliens—no, creatures—was hardly surprising.

"Thank you," Push said meaningfully. "I'm still pissed over the stunt you pulled, but you helped bail me out back there, and I appreciate it."

"Right" was all Wrath said as the awkward silence settled back down between them.

"So," he went on after a moment. "Do we stand around out here in the middle of the field and talk about our feelings, or go see what those walking pus balls were up to?"

"Monster hunting has my vote," Scratch said quickly.

"Same here," Push said. "It looked like they were headed for the woods."

"That was going to be my guess," Wrath said. "I wonder what's in there."

A wind rustled through the trees, followed by the sound of an owl hooting hungrily somewhere within the tangled mass of branches high overhead.

"They were looking at the crashed jet," Push told both of them. "I tracked them through the trail it left to where the jet is. It looked like they were studying its tail."

Scratch frowned at this, deep in thought. "You told Sheriff Black earlier that you thought something had brought down that jet. And you were the first one to see it after it crashed."

"It did look as though something could have hit the tail," Push said, nodding.

"And now aliens show up, searching for something to do with the jet," Wrath finished.

"We don't know they're aliens," Push insisted.

In response, Wrath picked one of the slime-covered weapons off the ground. Up close, it definitely resembled something from a horror film. The laser blaster fit like a gauntlet over the forearm. Wrath tried it out, aiming high in the air, and fired a single shot.

"Try not to bring down any more planes," Scratch advised as Wrath removed it from his arm.

"Right," he replied, passing the gauntlet to him. "You might want to take this. Nothing personal, but a little firepower couldn't hurt."

Scratch accepted it without looking hurt. "If nothing else, once the batteries die, I can keep it as a souvenir." He paused. "Assuming this thing even has batteries."

"Let's go," Push said. "Whatever they were here for, it must be in there. Wrath, you grew up in this town. Any chance you know your way around these woods?"

"Where do you think I spent most of my time?" Wrath replied, taking point. "There wasn't much else to do but go for walks in there. It shouldn't have changed too much, I hope."

This wasn't as reassuring as Push had hoped, but he was willing to take what he could get. Sparing one last look back at the remains of whatever had attacked him, Push swallowed his fear and kept his eyes sharp. He'd been caught off guard by these things twice already in the same night. They were obviously not very durable, yet the sight of them alone made him uneasy.

They seemed so… alien.

Just thinking of the word made his hands clench, so Push put it out of his mind for now. His goggles were still tuned in to night vision mode. Wrath led them down what might have been a hunting trail and through a thicket into a grove of trees. The air here was cold and crisp and tickled his nose. Even with that, though, Push felt himself quickly open up to the scope of nature they were surrounded by. Noises made by animals unseen echoed overhead and along the ground.

Wrath stopped a little further ahead. "Problems?" Push asked.

"I was just wondering which way to go next," he answered, looking around. "I don't see any tracks, at least none that look like they were made by aliens, or whatever those things were. You wouldn't happen to know which way those things were going, would you?"

Push shook his head, then remembered that the others couldn't see in the dark. "No," he said. "They just stood behind the jet, studied the busted tail, then headed toward the treeline."

Wrath ignited a flume of fire in the palm of his hand, which caused Push to stagger back. "Damn," Push cursed. "Warn me next time!"

Wrath looked back and saw the lights on Push's goggles. "Sorry," he said. "I was trying to get a better look at the area. It's been a while since I was out here, but there used to be a lake deep in the trees about a mile or two northwest of here."

"And?" Scratch asked.

It was the first time Scratch had uttered a word since they entered the forest.

"Animals tend to stick close to a water source," Wrath explained in a casual voice that irked Push. "When tracking something unfamiliar, you start with what you know and work your way on from there."

"Okay," said Scratch, keeping his eyes fixed on Wrath. "Who taught you that?"

"Glennwood," Wrath answered at once. "He was the only one willing to spend time around me for more than a couple of minutes and not flinch."

"Take us to the lake, then," Push interjected quickly. "It's better than getting lost in the woods, and nobody else seems to have any other ideas. Myself included."

Wrath turned away without another word and took them along a diagonal path down a steep slope. "Careful," he warned, getting farther and farther away from them. "If you aren't used to it, it's easy to lose your footing in places like this."

"Easy for you to…."

Push was cut off midsentence as the ground beneath his left foot suddenly gave way. For a split second, he felt his body fall slowly at a very dangerous angle toward a set of rocks several feet below him. Rocks that, of course, looked much more lethal now than they had at first glance a moment ago. Push started to flail, but felt a hand grab him by the bicep and hold him firmly in place.

"Stop struggling," Scratch commanded.

Push forced himself to go limp. Scratch gave his arm a hard jerk, drawing him back upright onto a much steadier piece of ground.

"Thanks," Push muttered, wanting to kick himself.

He could feel Scratch's eyes on him. "Did you think I was going to let you fall?"

It felt like he had been slapped. "No," he bit back, and even to Push, it sounded immature. "I just… I don't know anymore, okay?"

Push jumped down to the next ledge, leaving his concern for his own safety behind where Scratch stood, and made his way down to the bottom where Wrath was waiting. Somehow, Scratch was able to catch up to him very quickly.

"What did I do to make you angry with me?" he demanded.

"Nothing," Push said, realizing as he spoke that he was now parroting Wrath's very own words from before. "Nothing at all."

"Bullshit." Scratch seized Push by the shoulder and forced him to turn around. "You're pissed at me, and I think I at least deserve to know why!"

"Don't touch me!"

Push hadn't meant to shout so loudly. His words rebounded off the tree trunks surrounding them on all sides, making them bounce back into his ears.

It made his next breath feel like knives cutting through his chest. "Why did you have to pick him?" he asked, his voice barely a whisper now.

Scratch didn't answer.

"If you wanted to know what it felt like, if that was what it was all about, I would have volunteered. Hell, I'd have offered to pay for the chance at one point. You didn't have to go to someone we both hardly know."

"I didn't go to him," Scratch insisted, refusing to look away from Push. "It was a stupid bet I made while I was drunk. He came to me while I thought you were still in bed and told me he wanted to collect. I almost said no right then and there, but he said that a bet was a bet."

Push scowled, but couldn't bring himself to disagree.

"Besides," Scratch added, very reluctantly, "I wasn't sure I was going to enjoy it. Not from him, anyway."

"Then why didn't you just offer him something else?" Push demanded, tossing his arms up. "Why not pay him off with cash, or… wait, what?"

Scratch looked uncomfortable now, but didn't look away. "I said," he began, speaking each word distinctly. "I wasn't sure I would enjoy getting head from him."

Push felt he was missing something very big. "It sure sounded like he was doing okay," Push said, narrowing his eyes shrewdly. "You were less enthusiastic the night you finally got to bed Barbwire Beatrix."

Neither one seemed to notice that they were making their way down the slope again together. "I thought you had a date that night?" Scratch asked, helping Push down past a particularly rocky area.

"It ended early," Push told him, keeping a firm grip on the trunk of a narrow pecan tree. "I got back while you two were still going at it. I've never said anything, but the walls between our bedrooms aren't very thick."

Scratch went rigid. "Sorry," he muttered. "I never knew."

"I didn't say anything," Push pointed out, steadying Scratch with a hand to his shoulder. "It wasn't anything you could help, and who am I to say you can't enjoy yourself in your own home?"

They were getting close to the bottom now. "She wasn't as great as rumors said," Scratch explained. "I think we just didn't click together."

"Right." Push almost let the subject drop, but something compelled him to keep going. "You never did answer my question."

"No, I didn't," Scratch admitted, coming to a stop. "I wasn't worried about getting head from another dude," he explained. "That didn't bother me. You know I don't see people as gay or straight and nothing else. I'd never met another guy I felt attracted to, was all."

"So?"

"I always thought…." Scratch kept his eyes on the ground. "I always thought one day I'd get up the nerve… to ask you."

The last part came out in a rush.

"Scratch," Push began, feeling a little silly at the moment for stating something so obvious. "You're straight."

"Yeah," Scratch replied, and it sounded a little defensive. "So what?"

"You like girls," Push elaborated.

"So does Wrath," Scratch pointed out sardonically, waving down toward the bottom of the slope. "It didn't stop him from sucking on my knob."

"Wrath is bi," Push stated.

"So?" Scratch countered.

"What are you getting at?" Push felt himself get angry, and remembered to rein his powers back to avoid blasting the local flora. "You keep going around in circles."

"I'm not going in circles," Scratch yelled, glaring at Push now. "You're the one who keeps avoiding the issue."

"What issue?" Push demanded. "You're straight."

"But I think I might love you!"

Footsteps crunched up the slope toward them. Push had his bo staff out in under a second, but it was only Wrath.

"I was getting bored waiting," he said, looking back and forth between them. "Are you two done yet, or should I go back down and pretend I couldn't hear everything?"

Push scowled. "I know you used to be a crook," he spat. "But there was nothing in your file about you being an eavesdropper."

"I wasn't eavesdropping," Wrath replied, not offended. "You two were talking very loudly."

"We weren't being that loud," Scratch countered, though he didn't sound convinced.

"You were," Wrath stated flatly. "The denizens of Shove Point will be talking about your conversation at the four-way truck stop just as soon as the sun rises all the way. I might have been away for a long time, but I doubt this place has lost its love for juicy gossip. Plus, they'll want something to take their minds off everything else that's happened. A nice sordid scandal will be just what the doctor ordered."

"Why are you being such a dick?" Scratch demanded.

Wrath took a deep breath. "I didn't want to be," he confessed, surprising the both of them. "Nothing I say will ever make this believable to the two of you, but for an empath, emotions are like air. I breathe yours in as naturally as you take in oxygen. Plus, if you will recall, being around me tends to cause people to lose their inhibitions with emotions they're repressing. You two have done this awkward tango around one another for years now. I figured it would be better to force it out now instead of waiting for everything to blow up while we were surrounded and being shot at."

"You're full of shit," Push snarled.

"No," Wrath said. "But I don't expect either of you to believe me. It won't matter in the end if you hate me or not, because neither of you planned on trusting me with your lives. This way, you can hate me with something closer to a clear conscience and hopefully stop being such dumbasses in the process."

Wrath turned to leave, but Push moved quickly to catch up. "What's that supposed to mean?" he demanded, tripping over a tree root.

"Careful," Wrath warned.

"Answer my question," Push said, testing to make sure he hadn't injured himself.

"You both put too much emphasis on labels," Wrath told them, sounding strained now. "Each of you assumes everything in life only goes one way. People fall for others who are outside what they consider their scope of sexual attractiveness every day. A guy who loves big, beautiful women might fall for a woman built like a stick, or a woman who wants her boyfriends to be svelte and muscled might find herself happily married for life to a big, hairy bear of a man. People's ideas about attraction change over time. It's more common for people to develop a lifelong bond with someone who isn't their aesthetic ideal than it is for the opposite to occur."

Even in the dark, there was no way Wrath could have missed the look of skepticism on Push's face. "But Scratch and I are both guys," he pointed out.

Wrath rolled his eyes. "So?" he asked in a tired voice. "Why is that such a strange concept for you two? If everything else I've just said is true, why would gender be the great exception?"

Neither of them had an answer.

"Fine," Wrath said, turning around to leave again. "You know what? Make each other miserable for the rest of your lives. It's not my problem, and if you both die, maybe those geriatric pricks in Chicago will send me a chaperone with less emotional baggage."

Push said nothing as he and Scratch continued down the slope, helping each other when the trail got rough. Nothing seemed to deter Wrath from putting distance between them, though he never moved too far out of Push's sight. Scratch had nothing to say about Wrath's absurd theory. Push knew the man might have meant well in some perverse way, but there was no way he could buy into it. Scratch couldn't have feelings for him. They'd lived together for years and were best friends, but he had no hope of it ever moving beyond that.

Not without turning into a complete fiasco.

Besides, assuming he believed Wrath, it meant he would be asking Scratch to be something he wasn't. Push wasn't about to do that. Soon they would have to work things out. Much as he hated it, Wrath was right about that. This couldn't stay up in the air indefinitely.

Push had the sinking feeling, though, that it would come down in the end with the same force as that crashing jet on Shove Point.

When push came to shove, something always had to give.

CHAPTER
ELEVEN

IT FELT as though they had walked for hours. Push thought a sliver of morning sunlight was trying to creep through the trees now. He'd turned off his goggles a while ago, instead relying on the light from the fire clutched in Wrath's hand.

"How much further?" he gasped after a particularly rough uphill climb.

"We're almost there," Wrath told him, glancing back. "Can you smell the water now?"

Push sniffed, and to his surprise, the air did in fact smell moist in this part of the woods. As they reached the peak of the hill, he and Scratch looked down and saw the edge of the lake lapping up excitedly against the bottom of the incline.

"Something's wrong," Wrath said, looking very worried all of a sudden. "The water shouldn't be that choppy."

Wrath was sliding down the hill before Push had a chance to catch his breath. "How does he do it?" Push wondered.

"You got me," Scratch said.

The awkwardness from before returned in full force, but only for an instant. The two immediately switched over to hero mode, their mutually shared term for when things got serious, and took off after Wrath as fast as they dared. The slope down to the lake wasn't a clear path. There didn't appear to be any rocks here, thankfully, but trees made running down it at a breakneck pace implausible.

Well, for them, it was implausible. Wrath managed somehow while making it look cool at the same time. It made Push want to throttle him all the more.

Wrath was waiting for them at the water's edge when they arrived. "Look," was all he said, pointing at something along the shoreline not far away.

"What?" Push saw it before he had finished speaking. "…the hell?"

"Is that a…." Scratch began.

"Don't say it!" Push cut him off, sounding frantic. "Not yet. Let's not jump to conclusions."

"Because the upright-walking insects with laser blasters weren't proof positive enough for you?" Wrath asked derisively. "Well, I'd say this qualifies as concrete."

Scratch swallowed. "Um, I'm gonna have to take his side on this one."

One by one, each moved toward the craft that had parked itself on the embankment. Push started to protest, but then realized he was already moving, and getting ahead of Scratch in his eagerness.

The craft was roughly the size of a two-car garage. It was black in color, with ridges and sharp-looking prongs sticking out at weird symmetric angles. It was probably just because of the creatures they'd fought off earlier, but something about the craft reminded Push of a large, insectoid creature. Moss and algae clung to the sides and on the suspended pods in the rear, which Push assumed to be the propulsion system.

Going on looks alone, the craft appeared to have beached itself on the shoreline not so long ago.

"Forgive my lack of professional approach," Wrath said, his voice for once devoid of sarcasm, "but this is unbearably cool."

"Agreed," Scratch said.

"Won't get any arguments from me," Push rounded off. "I guess this must be what brought that jet down."

"Yeah," Wrath said, and there was an edge to his voice now. "Probably."

"Um, this is kind of overwhelming," Scratch whispered, taking a tentative step closer to the machine. "What are we supposed to do here?"

Nobody said a word. "We'll think about that later," Push replied, keeping his eyes fixed on the craft. "Right now, let's just enjoy the moment."

Together, the three stood at each other's side, mindful to maintain a safe distance from the craft, but unwilling to back any further away. None of them spoke. Light spilled over the lake through a clearing on the other side, illuminating the area. The region of the woods suddenly came alive with the sound of birds singing as the forest's denizens came out from their burrows to greet the day.

"This is so incredible," Scratch said softly.

"It's like," Push tried, grasping for words, "everything we ever wished for just dropped right here into our laps. I used to dream about this when I was a kid."

"So did I," Wrath croaked, bringing a hand up to shield part of his face from view. "I was going to be an astronaut and explore other planets."

"Now the planets came to us," said Scratch peacefully.

The snapping of a tree branch somewhere on the slope above them reverberated through the air, but Push gave no notice of it.

"What do you think is inside it?" Scratch wondered, sounding slightly panicked all of a sudden.

Push frowned hard. "More aliens?" he suggested nervously.

"This doesn't look big enough to carry that many," Wrath pointed out, taking a single step toward it now.

"It's as big as my bedroom back in town," Scratch pointed out, following his lead.

"But there were at least seven of those... whatever they were," Wrath said pointedly, giving Push a glance.

"Aliens," Push affirmed. "I've officially surrendered my stance as of this moment."

"Aliens," Wrath repeated. "And you two fought more of them in that wrecked building. Something like this shouldn't be able to fit that many."

"Unless they can somehow shrink down," Scratch interjected, utterly serious.

"Without taking that into account," Wrath amended.

"Or unless it's bigger on the inside somehow," Push added.

"That too," Wrath agreed, looking irked. "Getting back to my point, though, Push said that those aliens were looking for something. They were searching through the rubble, then checked over the crashed jet before heading toward the woods."

A light came on in Scratch's eyes. "So this is what they're looking for?"

"Probably."

A horrible feeling entered Push's stomach. "But they were headed this way when we fought them out in the field," he said, looking back toward the trees. "If there are more of them, and they already knew which direction this thing had crashed in, that means they'd be on their way here."

"Right now!" Scratch shouted.

Push twirled his bo staff out as he raised his palm up, ready to blast the first thing that moved. Scratch had several of his trick billiard balls in hand along with his cue stick, whereas Wrath summoned a great ball of flame over his head, held in place by both arms.

Nothing around them moved.

"Or not," Wrath suggested, as the ball of fire went out.

Scratch tentatively put his balls away. "False alarm?"

A laser beam cut through the air, missing his ear by a foot or so and striking the lake behind them with a noisy hiss.

"Nope!" Push said, ducking for cover. "False start!"

All three dove for cover beside the ship. It wasn't the best defensive position, but the area didn't offer a lot that would blanket all of them. Push also figured they each had banked on the theory that, assuming this was what the aliens were after, they would take greater care to avoid shooting it.

At least, that was the theory. In practice, it didn't look as though the aliens cared that much. The lasers they fired while descending downhill toward them came dangerously close to battering the ship. Scratch readied a brown-striped white ball in his hand. His eyes stayed sharp at a spot where there was lots of movement behind the trees. Once the aliens came into view, Scratch launched the ball through the air with a sharp jab from his cue stick. The ball broke apart into two halves as it reached the three creatures, releasing a net that snagged two, sending them down the slope at a breakneck speed.

"You have a blaster," Wrath reminded him as the aliens began to swell into balls.

"And you've got flame powers," Scratch shot back. "Feel free to jump in at any time."

"They're too close to the trees," Wrath countered. "I'd rather not waste time trying to put out a forest fire while these things shoot at us."

The two aliens exploded into pus as their bodies collided with the ground.

"It doesn't look like these things can survive much damage in this atmosphere," Push mused while more resumed their fire.

"It doesn't look like they can aim very well either," Wrath said as Scratch armed himself with the gauntlet laser.

"Be thankful for small favors," he said, returning fire.

A few reached the end of the incline. Wrath used his powers and sent out a few fireballs, guiding them with his thoughts to home in on the aliens. One or two aliens were set ablaze and exploded moments afterward. The rest, however, proved to be surprisingly more adept at dodging. Wrath raised his arms like a conductor before an orchestra and summoned the flames back into the air for a second attack. The aliens kept right on firing like the flames meant nothing to them.

"Are these guys kamikaze invaders?" Scratch wondered.

Push sent a telekinetic shock wave out that blew several of the aliens off their feet. "Must be," he replied. "They don't seem to care about what happens to their own."

It was not going well. The three of them were pinned down, and a few more of the alien shock troops had joined their brethren. Wrath spread a wall of fire out just past where the water reached the shore and strained to maintain it. The aliens stopped advancing, but continued to fire. Because their visibility had been reduced, this meant the shots came through the flames haphazardly, making them even more dangerous.

"Ideas?" Push asked.

"We don't know that this thing doesn't rightfully belong to them," Wrath pointed out. "Maybe if we leave, they'll take it and go."

"Except that they fired on us first," Scratch said.

"And haven't stopped shooting," Push added. "Still, it's worth a shot. I don't know that giving them this ship is the right thing to do, but at this point, it's worth a try. We don't have a protocol on what to do in case of alien contact."

"Bring it up at the next meeting," Scratch suggested.

"Sure," Push said sarcastically. "For right now, get ready to bolt on my signal."

"Make it fast," Wrath warned, sweating hard now. "The water makes it difficult to maintain the firewall. I can't keep it up much longer."

"Run!"

Wrath brought up the rear, keeping the firewall going as they tore across the lake shore. Falling behind slightly, he bent the firewall in a curve to keep the aliens from advancing on them too quickly.

"Hurry!" he shouted, catching up to the others. "That wall won't last much longer without me fueling it. Head for the path leading into the woods."

Push saw what Wrath was talking about immediately. On the far left, away from the lake, a natural ramp had formed from water run-off. He and Scratch turned on the steam and charged for it as laser fire flew around them. Push reached the upward incline first and kept going. Behind him, he could hear Wrath letting loose with more fireballs.

"So much for not wanting to burn the forest down," he muttered between gasps.

Looking back, he saw that Scratch had turned around and was spreading cover fire at the ground with the gauntlet, keeping the aliens back so that Wrath could catch up.

"Come on!" Scratch yelled to the firestarter. "They're gaining on you!"

At the top of the ramp, Push turned around and steadied himself. Breathing in, he drew as much power as he could from inside the space that gave him the strange, unique mutant ability. The telekinetic bomb formed in his hand as Scratch backed up alongside him.

"What are you..." his friend started to ask, but then saw the way Push's hands were cupped together and cut himself off.

"Shit."

Push opened his eyes as Wrath came up the ramp last. "Duck!" he barked, raising both arms up over his head.

Wrath saw what Push was doing and dropped to the ground. Bringing his arms down at the same time, Push unleashed the force down the ramp at the aliens, who were coming up it with lasers blazing. The ones nearest to the blast flew back. One or two expanded and popped as they hit the ground, but the rest kept coming.

Wrath cocked his head sideways and gave Push a look. "That was it?" he wondered. "What about before when you blew apart a parking lot?"

The others had already turned around and were running. "Give me a break," Push yelled back. "I can't do it that many times under the best of circumstances, and in case you forgot, we were walking through the woods half the night!"

Wrath caught up, breathing restlessly, as the aliens climbed the ramp. "This is stupid," he snarled. "We haven't done anything to these guys."

"Tell us something we don't know," Scratch bit back, ducking around some trees. "We can't keep this up forever, though."

"We still haven't tried communicating with them," Push said, taking cover behind a large oak as a laser blast singed the tip of its trunk. "If they would just stop shooting at us!"

"We could wave a white flag?" Wrath offered.

"They probably won't get the gesture," Scratch pointed out. "That's the problem with intergalactic relations."

"True," Push replied. "Plus, I don't have my white boxers on today."

The trio huddled behind a set of trees and watched as the aliens advanced closer and closer to their position.

"I say we take 'em out," Scratch whispered.

"We don't have much choice left," Push said, agreeing. "They're almost on us, and they seem more interested in taking us out now than getting that ship back. It looks like every last one of them followed us up here."

"Anyone got a plan?" Wrath asked.

"Sure," Push told him, rising. "Simple and straightforward. Attack!"

Scratch followed suit, sweeping the area with fire from his blaster to provide them with some cover. Wrath and Push charged out from behind him as the aliens were momentarily stunned.

"Take their weapons away," Push ordered, knocking the nearest one out of the alien's claws. "It's the only advantage they have on us."

Wrath swung up with a flash kick and his foot ignited in flames, blowing the arm clean off one alien. "Disarmed," he quipped, leaping back as the alien began to swell.

"Works for me!" Push yelled, firing a telekinetic blast into another's chest.

Scratch came forward and pressed his back against Push's, spreading more fire around to keep others from sneaking up on them. Push felt himself automatically relax as their bodies touched. His eyes narrowed as a sense of peace entered his mind. Strength returned to his body, the aches of walking on uneven terrain for so long vanishing in a heartbeat. Suddenly, the last six hours were gone. Nothing more needed to be said. He was together with his friend and comrade, fighting side by side with him.

The next alien that came for him was blown apart. The blast from Push's hand didn't even give it a chance to expand. Its chest burst open as it sprung backward through the air before splattering against a tree.

"Nice one," Scratch said as Push disarmed two more with his staff.

"Keep it up," Push told him. "Herd them toward me so I can knock their blasters away!"

Wrath, meanwhile, was unleashing a set of punches and kicks augmented with the power of his flame. Push spared a glance to see the former supervillain in action, moving like a break dancer to a rhythm only he could hear. Wrath swung both fists upward. The impact they made against the abdomen of two aliens created a small explosion that blew them wide open. Wrath back-flipped out of the way as they splattered.

"He's actually pretty good," Push mused.

"I was the enforcer for the Deadly Seven," Wrath called out, having heard Push's words over the battle. "Did you think I could have held that position not knowing how to fight?"

"Flash and substance," Scratch joked, firing into the chest of a disarmed alien that foolishly tried to rush him. "They go so well together."

The whole area of the forest was splattered in alien goo now. Only one remained, holding its weapon steadily as the three men advanced on it.

"We don't want to hurt you," Push tried, holding his hands up. "You were the ones who attacked us. If you can understand what I'm saying, give us some sort of sign."

The creature's eyes leveled with Push's face as he fired his weapon. The laser blast struck Push in the chest, sending him to the ground.

"Bastard!" Wrath snarled, unloading a wave of fire that cut the alien clean in half. "So much for fucking diplomacy!"

"Push," Scratch said, taking his friend in his arms. "Shit, don't let that thing have been set on high. Come on, say something to me, man."

Push's eyes came back into focus. "Ouch," he groaned, giving a small chuckle. "Those things really do hurt."

Wrath helped Push get up on his feet again, which the telekinetic accepted gratefully. "It doesn't look bad," he said, lifting up Push's shirt to see where the laser hit.

"They look worse than they hurt," Scratch informed him. "You'll just have trouble breathing for a few minutes. It passes pretty quickly, though."

"We can pick up a first aid kit on our way back through town," Wrath told them, letting go of Push's shirt. "There's a pharmacy in town that survived the crash."

"Assuming anyone bothers opening it," Push pointed out.

Scratch froze as something caught his attention. "Does anybody else hear that?" he asked, looking from one to the other. "That buzzing sound?"

Wrath darted his head to where the noise was coming from. "Shit," he swore, pointing at a nearby log covered in the alien goo. "Hornet's nest! All that fighting must have stirred them up. We'd better get out of here."

It was a quick dash back to the ramp. Before they reached it, the three had slowed their pace. None of the hornets had followed them, it seemed, and all were feeling a bit winded after such a big fight.

"I have to admit," Wrath told them, walking alongside Push casually, "when that lawyer came to East Arlenton asking if I'd sign up, I never expected Association work to be like this."

Scratch laughed, putting a hand gently on Push's shoulder to steady himself as they stepped lightly over an area of tangled tree roots. Push tensed for a moment, but then felt himself relax. It felt great having Scratch touch him, for once, instead of worrying how his friend would react.

"I can't wait to tell Wiccan Witch that we got to fight actual aliens," Scratch was saying, meanwhile. "She's wanted something like this to happen for years."

"I know," Push said, grinning. "Everyone in the Association is going to flip when this gets around. I wonder if the Cape Cabinet will believe any of it."

"There's the spaceship," Wrath reminded. "We still have it to back up our story."

The three froze as they came down the ramp leading back to the lake. Down on the waterline where the ship was still parked, a lone figure was crouched on top of it. Massive shoulders stretched against tight black fabric. He'd removed his mask, and as Push drew closer, he saw a pale albino head.

Cornrows hung down in back and on the sides, shielding his face from the sun. Each row was as pale as his skin. Sunlight, and the scope on his goggles, showed a pair of red eyes narrowing in frustration as the big man's enormous hands tinkered with a set of exposed wires on the ship's surface. Angrily, the man kicked against the ship in frustration.

Push readjusted his goggle's long-range vision and knew just by the look on Wrath's face that it was Sloth. Wrath was holding flames in his hands as they marched the rest of the way down to confront his former commander.

Sloth looked up as their footsteps approached. "I see you fellows took care of those ugly bugs for me," he said in a calm, gruff, yet oddly slick tone. "All that's left now is for me to get this fucking hatch open. Damn thing's sealed itself."

Sloth kicked at the surface of the ship again.

"Where is the Pranksta Gayngsta?" Wrath asked, keeping both eyes fixed on Sloth as he worked. "Did you kill him?"

"Not yet," Sloth said absentmindedly. "Haven't been able to get around to it just yet. Our bosses seemed to think this clunker was a much bigger priority."

The air around Wrath was heating up. Push could feel it just standing next to the man. It wavered now as Wrath's temper rapidly built.

The anger on his face was strangely quiet, like the stillness before a hurricane sweeps along the coast. Wrath raised both hands, the fire clutched in them building until they were twin columns of gold.

"I don't work for you," Wrath stated in an even voice that made Push think things were about to head south fast.

Sloth laughed casually in reply. "You still work for the same people as me," he said, not looking up. "Ten years hasn't changed that, kid."

Wrath moved before Push could stop him. Crisscrossing waves of flame arched out from the pyrokinetic's hands and slammed into Sloth, knocking him back.

"I want him," Wrath said softly, shrugging away Push's hand that gripped at his bicep. "I waited a long time for this."

Push turned to Scratch, hoping for a better solution.

"Let him have it," Scratch suggested. "I'd say our boy has some issues to work out."

"Okay." Push relented and turned back to Wrath. "Try not to kill him if you can."

Wrath cracked his knuckles in response as Sloth got to his feet.

"That's letting him have the easy way out," Push said, giving Wrath a pat on the back. "Let him live, and the Association will see to it he spends the rest of his life in jail."

Wrath frowned.

"He'll have to deal with worse than you ever did in there," Push added. "Plus, you'll be outside living it up while he rots away."

Sloth jumped down off the ship into the shallow edge of the lake. "Care to try that again?" he snarled as lake water splashed back down on him.

"Gladly." Wrath brought his hands up and blew Sloth backward again. "You win," he told Push, advancing forward. "He lives."

Push smiled. "You're learning."

Wrath stood on the shore's edge as Sloth got to his feet a second time. Water dripped from the albino's head as he glared furiously.

"You've picked up a few new moves," Sloth noted, shaking droplets out of his eyes as he sloshed through the shallow water toward Wrath.

"I spent ten years in prison," Wrath reminded him, crouching slightly in an offensive stance. "There wasn't much to do but read and practice."

"A shame, really." Sloth stood a few feet from Wrath now. "I was ordered to keep you alive, but if you're going to be difficult about this, Daddy will just have to give his boy a spanking."

"In your dreams."

Sloth laughed. "You've got some nice moves there, kid," he said, pulling a gun out from behind him. "But I'm the one with the gun."

A white billiard ball whipped through the air and knocked the gun out of Sloth's hand. "Play nicely, boys," Scratch scolded teasingly from farther back. "Don't make me come over there and separate you."

Wrath seized the opportunity while Sloth was distracted. A fiery strip formed in his right hand. Wrath brought it around in a spin, swiping Sloth across the face. A red scorch mark stretched across the albino's face, marking him.

"Your muscles are incredibly dense," Wrath said, bringing the whip down again on Sloth's arms. "So much that you might as well be wearing armor. Penetrating you with bullets or knives is almost impossible."

Sloth charged at Wrath, but the pyrokinetic fell onto his back, spinning his legs in a windmill motion. Fire flowed out from his feet, and as Sloth raised a fist to slam it down on him, Wrath flipped himself up off the ground, striking Sloth across the face with a kick that sent flames everywhere.

"But you can burn as easily as anyone else."

Wrath dodged back as Sloth swung his fists at him. The two danced around each other's blows for a moment, with Sloth gaining speed the more he moved. Off to the side, Push was startled by just how fast the larger man was moving. Wrath kept one or two steps ahead of him, but Sloth caught up quickly enough that it couldn't be called a real advantage. Sloth seemed leery of Wrath's flame powers now, having been on the receiving end of them enough.

"Wide open!" the big man howled, swinging his fist in a deep arch.

Wrath managed to duck it, however. "Same to you," he countered.

They were inches apart now. Wrath put his palms up against Sloth's chest as the walking tank came back around for another swipe. The point-blank range worked in Wrath's favor, blowing Sloth backward away from him and into the spaceship.

Even then, Sloth got back up, giving Wrath a seething glare. "To hell with this for right now," he growled. "We'll finish this later. I've still got a job to do."

Push felt his jaw drop as Sloth moved into a crouch, then launched himself straight up into the air. The man landed on the top of the spaceship and backed away.

"I'd stay back if I were you," Sloth warned as Wrath moved toward him on the ground. "This thing might go off if you aren't careful."

Wrath actually hesitated, giving Sloth the time he needed to bend back down on the spot where he'd been fiddling with the exposed wires before.

"Ideas?" Wrath asked.

"Can you knock him off the ship without damaging it?" Push asked, moving in closer to where Wrath stood, waiting.

"Absolutely," Wrath replied. "But I would have to go all-out to do it. A blast that powerful would likely fling him way out into the lake, and I thought we were supposed to bring him in alive."

Push wavered a moment. "I could try to hit him with a telekinetic jolt," he said, thinking aloud. "But my punches aren't as refined as yours. I'd probably damage the ship, and it would have the same result."

"I guess that leaves me, then," said Scratch, reaching into his coat pocket. "Funny, I didn't think I'd have to use one of these again so soon."

Push froze as Scratch brought out a black eight-ball. "You're kidding, right?" Push insisted, his eyes going wide. "I can't believe you even brought that with you."

"We were going to be dealing with aliens," Scratch said, extracting his cue stick next.

"What's the eight-ball for?" Wrath asked.

"It's loaded with C4 plastique," Push explained. "The last time he used it, a roof nearly fell on our heads."

"Good thing we're outside," Scratch replied. "Um, you guys might want to cover your ears."

"You'll hit the ship!" Push yelled.

Scratch took aim as Sloth let out a shout of triumph. "I'm not aiming for the ship," Scratch said, tossing the ball into the air.

The crack that filled the air as the cue stick sent the ball flying sounded like thunder. Sloth rose up as the explosive hurled toward him, and calmly reached up with one hand to snatch the ball out of the air.

"Cute trick," he jeered, tossing the ball far back into the water behind him.

"Thanks," Scratch told him loudly. "But that wasn't the trick."

The ground beneath their feet shook as water erupted in a geyser behind the ship. The ship itself lurched forward onto the shore, scattering the three heroes on the ground. They dove for cover out of the way. Atop it, Sloth lost his footing and was saved from falling only by snagging one of the metal extensions protruding from it at the last moment.

"That was," Scratch finished, giving his cue stick a twirl.

"Could have warned us first," Wrath said, getting up out of the dirt.

"Seriously," Push chimed in as Scratch helped him back up.

Scratch opened his mouth to speak, but a loud noise coming from the ship cut him off. An alarm was blaring now. Sloth's eyes widened as the hatch he'd been working on popped clean off. A high-pitched whistling resounded as steam blew out from the vents. Then, a compartment beneath the protective sheet of metal sprang up into view. Push had just enough time to commit the shape to memory before it launched into the air under the power of small rockets attached underneath.

The alarm was still sounding. "It's gonna blow!" Sloth declared, releasing his grip on the ship's edge.

"Run for it!" Push shouted.

"We'll never get up the slope in time," Wrath insisted, even as they raced like mad for the edge.

Push stopped short of where the ground rose and motioned for the others to get in close. "Get behind me," he ordered, bringing his hands up. "And this time, you really will want to cover your ears."

"Is this going to work?" Scratch asked, clapping his hands over his lobes.

"I have no idea," Push admitted. "But we're going to find out. Wrath, if you can keep the flames off us, that would help out a lot."

Sloth had broken into a run, but it was too late. The ship began exploding before he'd taken a dozen steps from it. The blast sent him flying off his feet. The moment the roar filled Push's ears, he planted his feet on the ground, raised both hands, and lashed out with whatever strength remained in his reservoirs. He felt the gigantic force bubble released from his hands collide with the explosion like two trains meeting one another on a track.

Wrath was blowing the flames back as best he could, even as the ship continued destructing. Shrapnel flew around them on all sides, missing the three thanks to the sheer force of will being thrust out from Push's body.

The chaos seemed to go on forever. When it at last ended, Push felt his knees give out from under him. His hands stung, as though he'd been pounding them against a brick wall. A buzzing sound rang in his ears. Sweat dripped from his forehead as he fell to the ground.

Wrath collapsed to one knee. "So much for our spaceship," he mused, looking out toward the lake.

"I'll trade a spaceship for one more day," Push replied, laughing weakly.

The three of them surveyed what was left. Other than a few bits and pieces drifting along the surface of the water, there was nothing. The ground where the ship had rested was scorched, as if to remove any trace of it having been there.

"What do you guys think was in that pod it spat out?" Scratch asked.

"And what happened to Sloth?" Wrath added.

There was no trace of the albino anywhere. Push made sure to look closely in case his body was floating amid the debris. Wrath was doing the same, and scowled in disappointment when nothing showed up.

"Good questions," Push said, slowly getting to his feet. "Things we'll figure out later on, though. For right now, let's go home and get some rest. It's been a very long night."

CHAPTER
TWELVE

IT WAS a long walk back out of the woods. Wrath led the way and managed not to get them badly lost. Apparently, the forest looked different during the day, but Push didn't complain too much. Wrath managed to eventually steer them back to the field where they'd entered from. The goo from the aliens they'd fought was still splattered on the ground, a testament to what they'd experienced.

All three of them were wiped out by the time they got back to the Pussy Wagon. Nobody felt like driving, least of all Push, but Wrath surprised him by extending his hand for the keys when Scratch withdrew them. The ride home was uneventful. Push didn't even bother watching for the shocked looks from people. After everything the town had witnessed the day before, none of the locals had the time or energy to be concerned with a cat-themed truck bearing a suggestive name across it.

Everyone entered the house without a word and made tracks to shower. Push went to his computer first to give an abridged report of the activities of the day before, having neglected to do so last night. After composing it, he then keyed in everything he could remember about the past six hours or so and mailed that report in along with the first one. For a moment, he contemplated what the Association would do when they read about his extraterrestrial encounter. Without the spaceship to prove it, it was possible they would want both him and Scratch back in Chicago for a full psychiatric evaluation. By now, however, he couldn't have given a rat's ass. Emotionally, physically, mentally, and spiritually, Push was completely drained. There was nothing left for him to do but strip down and take a shower before going to bed.

The water was freezing, but Push didn't mind. It felt good to wash off the night's insanity. His costume was a complete wreck, having been covered with alien slime, mud, and cockleburs. Thankfully, there were spares in his new closet. He'd still have to hunt down a decent dry cleaner later on.

Once he felt clean, Push turned off the water, dried off, and climbed under the covers. Letting out an exhausted sigh, he slowly shut his eyes, remarking as the darkness closed in around him at how unfamiliar the ceiling looked.

Sleep evaded him.

Push wasn't sure how long he lay in bed. No matter which way he turned, his body remained on full alert, aware of the small noises echoing through the rest of the house as it settled in for the day. In his haste, he had forgotten to close the bedroom door. Push contemplated getting up, but felt an irresistible urge to stay under the covers. Even still, he could not fall asleep.

Push tried counting sheep, but all he received for his trouble was a head full of imaginary baa-ing. He shifted positions every few minutes, but this made his back feel stiff. Just when he was starting to think he would have to seek relief at the bottom of a whiskey bottle, there came a knock at the door.

"Sorry," Scratch's voice said quietly. "It didn't sound like you were asleep."

"I wasn't," Push said, not turning over.

"Oh." There was silence for a moment. "Can I come in?"

"Sure."

Push kept his head facing the wall away from Scratch. The sound of the door shutting filled his ears, followed by Scratch's footfalls as he padded softly across the carpet toward the edge of the bed.

"Push," Scratch said softly.

Scratch's voice sounded muffled slightly. Push debated turning around then, but froze up completely as he felt the mattress shift. The far side of the bed behind him sank down as Scratch crawled onto it. Without a word, Scratch slid his body up against Push underneath the covers. Scratch's arm curled around the shorter man's abs near his navel, letting the fingers trail over the contours and grooves there.

Push's breath caught in his throat as he felt his best friend snuggle up as close to him as he could. Scratch's head came down to rest on the pillow Push was using, the tip of his prickly chin resting against the back of Push's head. Push felt Scratch's breath tickle against his ear, but didn't dare move away. It was the first time he could ever recall them being this close, and if what was going on underneath the sheets was any indication, Scratch was by no means unhappy to be there.

"This is so nice." The words were let out slowly along with a long, deep sigh. "We should have done this before now."

Push swallowed the lump in his throat as he felt himself relax against the hard body behind him. Slowly, his eyes closed, despite any attempt by him to keep them open. The tension from before swiftly vacated Push's body, and he felt himself drift off.

It wasn't sleep exactly. Push felt himself drifting in and out of consciousness over a period of time, though how long, he couldn't be sure. Several times, he felt Scratch move behind him, though only to bring their bodies closer together. Neither of them changed positions the whole time. Whenever Push felt himself wake up, it was to the sensation of the hairs on the back of his neck stirring in time to Scratch's slow breathing. Their hearts beat in synch with one another. Each time Push felt his heart jump inside his rib cage, Scratch's would thrum against his back in time to it. Occasionally, Scratch's cock also jumped to the same rhythm, though more infrequently.

Scratch had kept his boxers on, and his dick was tucked down one of the legs. Push felt himself wishing it were resting in a more accessible position, but was unwilling to rock the boat. This was the best he'd ever felt, and he wanted to make damn sure it lasted for as long as possible.

Fortunately, Scratch saved him the trouble.

Push was just beginning to drift back into a state of blissful unawareness when he felt Scratch's arm draw back slightly. Without warning, Scratch dragged his hand up to Push's chest and seized one of his nipples.

"You awake?"

Push swallowed. "China would've woken up to something like that."

In reply, Scratch released his hold and brought his hand down to Push's crotch. "Not yet," Scratch noted, giving the low-hanging balls a squeeze. "But definitely getting there."

Push felt his throat go dry. "Scratch," he tried, sounding hoarse.

"Quiet," Scratch barked, though there was a definite note of pleading to his voice. "Don't say anything. I don't want to hear it just yet. I need this to keep going for a little bit longer."

Push frowned into his pillow. "What did you think I was going to say?" he wondered, still baffled by his friend's behavior.

"That we shouldn't be doing this," Scratch stated with confidence. "That we can't do this, because we're friends, and because I'm not gay."

"You're not," Push responded.

Push tried to turn around to face Scratch, but Scratch held him firmly in place. "I am," Scratch affirmed. "Overall, I prefer girls. I don't plan on switching over to an all-beef diet. That's not what this is about."

Push waited, but Scratch left his words hanging in the air. "Okay," he said, feeling even more confused now. "Then what is this about?"

"I'm not sure," Scratch said, running his hand up and down along Push's abs. "But I know it's not really about the fact that I'm straight, or the fact that you're gay. It's about us."

Push tried to turn over onto his back, and found that he could. "You're not making any sense," he said, drawing in a deep breath. "If you don't like men, how does that change us? You're...."

"Straight," Scratch cut in, sounding irritated now. "Yes, I remember that. Thank you for continuously pointing it out. I'm straight, Push. I don't think that much has changed, but I'm pretty sure I also love you."

The words came out so matter-of-factly that Push had to laugh. "I love you too," he replied tentatively. "You're my best friend."

"And you're mine," Scratch affirmed. "I don't just mean that, though. When I look back on it, I think I've been in love with you for a while."

Scratch raised himself until he was resting upright against the headboard. "I've always needed a wingman," he explained, looking down at his feet. "Growing up, there was always someone at my back, someone I felt a little bit connected to. It wasn't until the Association that I really started to wonder about why that was. From the beginning, you were different. It wasn't that I expected to feel this way about you, no offense. At the time, I didn't have any feelings for guys in general beyond just being buds."

Scratch turned toward Push then, and there was a look of absolute fear there. "I figured that, since it hadn't happened so far, it never would. I assumed I was straight to the core. Then we started hanging out with one another outside of work, and something clicked into place. I started worrying about who you were going out with. At first, I was just concerned because…."

Scratch stalled.

"Go on," Push encouraged. Even if he didn't agree with what his friend was saying, it was still strangely fascinating. "I'm listening."

Scratch gulped. "You tended to hook up with a lot of jerks."

Push tilted his mouth wryly. "I was going through a phase," he insisted, knowing full well that wasn't the whole truth. "A very long phase."

"You were grieving," Scratch clarified. "You still hadn't gotten past Jeremy's death."

Hearing the name of his old boyfriend sent Push back through time for an instant. Jeremy, whom Push had met while in his last year of college, just before grad school. The two of them had hit it off right from the start despite having almost nothing in common. Jeremy had been the bass player for a local gay hard rock band. The two dated for almost a year before taking the plunge and getting a small, one-bedroom apartment together.

It had been Jeremy who suggested Push become a superhero. Jeremy had written a song about a villain falling in love with his archrival while drunk on a dare from Push. The next day, in between nursing away a hangover, he'd brought up the idea. Jeremy had been one of the blessed few to whom Push had revealed his secret, and he had not freaked out over it.

"It actually kind of makes the fixation with comics clearer now," he could still hear Jeremy saying.

Push had resisted. All his life, he had just wanted to be normal, and their relationship had been the closest to normal he'd ever had. The idea hadn't gone away, and were Push honest, he'd deliberated over it quietly to himself right after Jeremy brought it up.

What helped had been the beatings. The Capitol district had suffered a rash of gay bashings. The victims were left comatose, and the community was getting panicky. Against his better judgment, Push had gone looking online for costume ideas. His major concern had been coming up with something functional, but there were several sites with many good ideas. In the end, he'd scribbled down a couple of rough sketches detailing what he wanted, scanned them, and e-mailed the designs to an internet cosplay company with an advance payment. In a little over two weeks, his costume had arrived in the mail, and just in the nick of time.

On his first night out walking the neighborhood, Push had found them. It was a group of guys no older than him, probably students at the same university, no less. He'd been scared shitless, but after one pulled a gun, Push had thrown a force bubble at the guy, dropping him in one hit. The rest had scattered, wetting themselves.

There had been eyewitnesses, late arrivals, of course. Thanks to the victim's testimony, the cops were able to track the group down and make arrests. Within a few days, the whole neighborhood was ablaze with the news that the gay community had its first ever superhero, and one with an actual superpower no less. Push had been frantic about his secret getting out, but the people were ecstatic. Someone he'd never met before, a spunky little redhead with cute freckles, offered to design a website for him free of charge. The hit counter on it was in the thousands the day it went live.

For the next couple of years afterward, things were great. Push had found a job working as a grief counselor. The pay hadn't been much, but he and Jeremy managed. People occasionally would donate money or other things to help out if they thought he was struggling.

One day, Push had taken off work early so he could go home and surprise Jeremy with some quick loving before they headed out on the town to go clubbing with friends. Jeremy hadn't answered the phone.

At the time, it hadn't seemed unusual. Push had figured Jeremy was taking a shower and hadn't heard the phone ring. He'd amused himself with thoughts of Jeremy having to shower all over again the rest of the drive home.

Then he'd gotten to their apartment and found the door open.

Jeremy's body was lying sideways on the living room floor. A burglar had broken in and shot him almost point-blank in the head. According to the medics, he'd died instantly.

Not very long afterward, Push had received a call from someone at the Association, offering their condolences and asking if he would be interested in joining their ranks at some point down the road. He'd packed his bags within the week and moved to Chicago.

"It wasn't your fault," Scratch insisted, shaking Push out of his thoughts.

"I know," he said, perhaps too quickly. "Really, I understand that now. I was at work when the burglar broke in. Hell, I'd even taken off work early. It's not like I was running around the city playing hero to other people while he was shot by the bastard. Nothing about it was because of what I was doing. Even the police admitted that was most likely true, and they hated the sight of me."

Push hesitated. "But I still hate myself sometimes for not being there."

"Because you could have saved him?"

"No," Push insisted. "Because I *would* have saved him. Assuming they were right, and it was just a burglar, he wouldn't have stood a chance. I could have blown him straight through one of the walls without blinking."

"I know," Scratch said. "It sucks balls to bones."

"That's why I do this," Push told him. "I don't know that I've ever told you, but that's why I keep doing this. Shit happens. People lose their loved ones in horrible, senseless tragedies. Little kids mistakenly run out into the street despite having loving, protective parents. Life sucks, but maybe if I do what I do, it doesn't always have to be like that. Not every day. Not for everybody."

Scratch smiled in a sad sort of way. "I can't imagine going on after losing someone I loved the way you loved him," he said.

"I didn't think I was," Push admitted. "Going to keep going, I mean. After a while, though, the hard part wasn't getting out of bed every day. It was knowing that I was getting better. It felt like I was getting over Jeremy too fast. I started to wonder if I'd really loved him as much as I thought I had, or was just in love with the whole idea of what we had."

Scratch thought over that for a moment. "I hate that you lost Jeremy," he told Push, moving a little closer to him as he spoke. "He seemed like a tough act to follow."

"He was," said Push firmly.

"Well...."

Scratch didn't finish his sentence. Instead, he reached over and pulled Push toward him, leaning forward at the same time to meet him halfway. Their lips met, and it was like a dam broke between them. Push saw fireworks flash before his eyes as he tasted the warm, wet flavor of Scratch's mouth. The hairs dusting his partner's chin scratched at his face as he kissed Scratch back, but Push wasn't about to complain. They felt wonderful!

Somehow, they lay back on the bed together atop the covers. Push kept his weight from pressing down onto Scratch by holding himself up in a slight push-up position. Scratch gasped, grabbed the back of Push's head again with both hands, and dragged him all the way down as their tongues met one another amid the sauna that was their connecting mouths.

"God," Scratch gasped, between kisses. "Do that thing with your tongue again!"

Push obliged, and felt the mound in Scratch's boxers swell painfully.

"Take them off," Scratch said, the heat in his eyes flaring as he locked eyes with Push. "I want to watch you do it."

Push didn't move, however. "Scratch," he said, breathing hard. "We don't have to do this. You don't have to…."

Scratch cut him off by kissing him hard. "Shut the fuck up!" he hissed, giving Push a hard shake. "I'm not drunk and I'm not confused. I've wanted this for a while now. Why do you have to keep making it harder than it needs to be, huh?"

"What if you can't handle it?" Push asked seriously, still not moving. "What if you freak out afterward? How are we supposed to still be friends after that?"

Scratch reached down and hooked the band of his boxers under each thumb, then yanked hard. His cock sprang free as the boxers slid past, but Scratch kept going. When he was naked, Scratch tossed the pair hard against the wall, then lay back on the bed.

"I can't think of anything else to say," he said with a hard edge to his voice now. "I've done all I can to convince you that I'm not going anywhere, so now it's your move."

Push's eyes widened. "What?"

"Take me," Scratch said, his voice still hard. "Do whatever it is you want, and see if I freak out. Consider it a free pass. You'll get some, and I can finally show you what I mean."

It felt like his stomach had gone on the first plunge of a rollercoaster. "Scratch," Push said, backing away now. "Have you lost your mind?"

Scratch rose up at this, and there was something in his face that immediately let Push know that this had been the wrong thing to say.

"Push," he asked, sounding scared now. "Do you just not want me anymore?"

In that moment, Push didn't think he'd ever seen his friend look so completely vulnerable. The fear on his face was so raw that it made Push's chest ache. His best friend, his partner since their training days, had just laid his soul out for Push, and he was on the verge of shattering it.

"Are you sure?" Push asked, as a part of him he hadn't been aware of unclenched.

"More than anything," Scratch said. "Please, believe that."

Push felt himself smile, then. Whether Scratch was serious after the fact, or their friendship never remained completely the same, he couldn't turn away from what was being offered.

If nothing else, Push thought, as their mouths connected again. *I will always have this one time.*

IT HAD started with Push on top. He'd always been an aggressive lover in bed, but Scratch didn't appear to mind. He'd expected his friend to want to be the pursuer, him being straight and all, but Scratch lay back and allowed Push all the freedom he wanted to maneuver.

Soon, though, Scratch flipped Push over onto his back. "I've been wanting to know what this would be like for a while," he said, keeping his eyes locked onto Push's as he kissed his way down.

Push went rigid as Scratch took hold of his cock in one hand. The tip of his tongue licked at the head tentatively, almost playfully, while the hand began lightly stroking him up and down.

"Tastes pretty good," Scratch said, sticking the tip of his tongue down into the slit. "Not bad at all."

A glob of precum oozed out as a result, to which Scratch lapped up eagerly. The groan that came from him as the fluid hit his taste buds was the single most erotic sound Push had ever heard before. He felt his breath quicken as Scratch attacked his task more ferociously now.

Push felt a jolt go through him as he realized his was the first dick Scratch had ever sucked, and the knowledge nearly made him cum on the spot. Fighting it off, he gasped for breath as Scratch lowered his mouth down onto the treat in front of him with another hungry moan that sent chills over his skin.

Despite being a novice, what Scratch lacked in technique, he more than made up for in sheer enthusiasm. Push didn't even have to warn the man to keep his teeth out of the way, and was surprised when Scratch used his tongue to swirl around the thick shaft near the base.

"Oh God!" Push exclaimed, grabbing Scratch by the back of the head. "Where on earth did you learn to do that?"

Scratch raised up off Push long enough to answer. "I told you," he said insistently, still jerking away at the base. "I've wondered about this for a while. Finally got curious enough to read up on it a little."

Push's eyes bugged out at this, but his surprise was soon replaced by Scratch sinking his mouth down almost all the way to the root of his shaft.

"Fuck!"

Breaths came to Push in short spurts. "Nobody learns that from reading!" he insisted, gripping the sheets.

Scratch raised back up and gave Push a smirk. "I'm a fast learner."

All too soon, Push felt his nuts drawing up. He tried to fight it off, tried to hold out so Scratch could keep sucking his cock forever, but the moment wouldn't be delayed. Push opened his mouth to warn his friend, but all that came out was a mix between a grunt and a low growl.

"I'm gonna…" he managed to get out.

Then his load erupted up through his shaft and into Scratch's mouth like a geyser. Push expected Scratch to spit it out or gag, but Scratch gulped the cum down like there was no tomorrow. Push's balls drew up again, sending another volley into Scratch's waiting mouth. His body jerked as wave after wave of pleasure rocked through him. Stars swam in his eyes and the room went dim. Everything was spinning now.

Push let out a roar as the last drop of cum spurted free. Scratch rose up just in time to catch it in midair. Dazed, Push looked into his friend's face, expecting to see him look back with worry or regrets. Instead, Scratch was smiling as he licked away at his mouth like a cat with cream.

Slowly, as though weakened by the experience, Scratch pulled himself up alongside Push's body until his head rested on Push's chest. There, Scratch reached down and began jerking his cock feverishly. Push reached over with a hand and lightly stroked his friend's hair as Scratch's own orgasm overtook him. A line of fresh cum splashed diagonally across Push's lower abdomen. Scratch kept on jerking himself, sending rope after rope in the same pattern over Push's abs, until they bore his seed in the shape of tiger stripes.

Scratch collapsed against his friend in exhaustion.

"Do I seem freaked out to you now?" he asked, letting out a long, contented sigh.

Push pulled his friend in close and opened his mouth. Scratch, however, wasn't going to wait for Push to give an excuse, and he clasped their mouths together for a long, wet kiss that made Push's toes curl.

"How about now?" Scratch demanded.

"No," Push admitted, regarding Scratch for a moment. "You don't seem freaked out."

"Good." Scratch placed his head back down on Push's chest at this. "Because we need to do this again. I think my cocksucking needs more work."

Push snorted. "You didn't hear me complaining."

"No," Scratch said. "You weren't. I still want to get better at it, though. You've had a lot more experience than me, and started off a lot younger than I did. I've got a long road ahead of me before I'm the best you've ever had."

This made Push smile. "You're the best friend I've ever had," he said meaningfully. "I've wanted to do this for years."

Scratch leaned over slightly so he could breathe in Push's scent. "I want us to be more than just friends from now on," he said softly. "I want us to be lovers."

Push wasn't sure what he'd been planning to say in response, but a knock at the door saved him from opening his mouth and ruining the moment.

It was Wrath.

"I apologize," the pyrokinetic said stiffly, glancing off to the side. "I didn't want to interrupt, but this really couldn't wait any longer."

"We were just…" Push started, but Wrath cut him off.

"You were fucking," Wrath stated matter-of-factly. "Figuratively or otherwise. I'm an empath, remember?"

Push frowned. "What was it again?"

Wrath caught the tick in Push's voice and immediately raised his BlackBerry up to where Push could see. "I got a message from Sloth," he said tensely. "He wants me to meet him alone after midnight tonight."

Scratch had been slowly getting out of bed with the sheet wrapped around his waist when he heard this.

"What the fuck?" he demanded, frowning. "Um, where?"

Wrath turned the screen to face him. "'At the Arcade on Route Nine,'" he read aloud. "'At one o'clock in the morning. Come alone.'"

"Does the message say why?" Push asked.

"No."

"He acted like he wanted to kill you earlier," Scratch said, coming over to stand by Push. "What do you think he wants?"

Wrath sighed. "That," he replied, looking between the two of them, "is what I'm planning on finding out."

SLOTH felt his palms sweat as he stared at the blank screen. His employers had insisted on maintaining anonymity, as always, in case the transmission was intercepted somehow. At the moment, he was finding it hard to control his breathing. His failure was not going to be taken lightly. The real question was how he could smooth this over.

"Where is the vessel now?" one asked anxiously.

"I don't know," he answered. "In the confusion of the ship's self-destruct sequence triggering, I didn't see which direction the lifeboat flew."

"Unacceptable," a crisp, distorted male voice declared. "The project has taken many years to complete. We cannot afford to have it fall into a random person's hands now."

"It won't," Sloth promised.

"The lifeboat was designed as a last-minute precaution," yet another of his employers said. "It cannot fly very far, even while running at top capacity. Odds are the vessel is somewhere close by."

"Agreed," said another.

There was silence for a moment, during which Sloth guessed his employers were conferring privately among themselves.

"Retrieve the vessel," they said at last, after a few more minutes. "Then bring it to us. The plan can still be salvaged, with a few moderate adjustments."

"Understood," Sloth complied. "In the meantime, though, I need some help keeping the spandex club off my ass. It was all on account of them that I lost the vessel in the first place."

Silence followed again.

"What do you require?" one asked hesitantly.

"Let me call in some favors," Sloth suggested. "I know a couple of guys I can count on to watch my six while I hunt down your little boy blue. All that's needed on your end is a few new toys to play with."

The screen flickered as Sloth picked up the jumbled mutterings of two, before the blackout on his computer fell back into place.

"Fill out your request voucher and send it in," the head said at long last. "We are depending on you to keep this discreet."

"I know how to work the back streets," Sloth reminded them, reaching for the key that would terminate the call. "I'll contact you when I know more."

"Keep in touch," one managed to edge out before the transmission was severed.

Sloth leaned back in his chair for a moment, flexing his fingers as he eyed the now dead laptop.

"Playtime, boys," he whispered to himself.

EPILOGUE

Hero Gaiden

Yotaka

THEY had been trying to rape her.

The poor woman was understandably shaken up. Yotaka doubted the costume was helping matters much. Quickly, he sheathed his tonfa in the holsters that rode low on his thighs.

"Ma'am," he said in a firm but soothing voice while keeping his distance, "is it all right if I approach? I would like to check and make sure nothing is broken, if that is all right with you."

The woman considered him for a moment. "Alright," she choked out, fighting a losing battle to keep her breasts covered with the torn piece of her blouse.

"I promise," he assured her, kneeling down slowly. "I'm not here to hurt you."

This seemed to get through to her. "I know," she said, clearing her throat. "I mean, I know you aren't. I just...."

"There's no need to explain," Yotaka assured her. "I understand perfectly."

Aside from some bruises and scrapes, which she would need to get looked at by a professional, nothing appeared severe.

"Can you stand?" he asked her, offering a hand.

The woman started to accept it, an encouraging sign, but then pulled back. "Tobey!" she exclaimed, looking around. "What happened to Tobey?"

Yotaka turned around, still crouched on the hard alley concrete, toward the younger man whom he assumed was Tobey.

"I'm going to check on him," Yotaka told her, standing. "Stay right here. Once I'm done, I'll call a friend of mine on the force, and an ambulance for you and your friend."

"I don't..." she started to say, but Yotaka quickly cut her off.

"You're badly bruised," he insisted pointedly. "And the police need to know what happened. Otherwise, these bozos will just go back out tomorrow night and try this all over again. Even I can't be everywhere at once, and sooner or later, they'll get lucky and pick a place I don't patrol through."

The woman looked around in response to this. Yotaka stepped over the bodies strewn out on the ground haphazardly, mindful to break a few fingers with his boots on his way over to where Tobey was whimpering in pain.

There had been four of them, at least at first, and all of them could have played for the Falcons as linemen. A fifth had been in the shadows with his pants unzipped, watching the scene unfold, when Yotaka arrived. It had apparently taken the man a moment to put his junk away and zip back up. By that time, Yotaka had brought two of them down.

The rest had dropped like flies. Yotaka was small, about five-nine and weighing in at around a hundred and sixty pounds, depending on the time of year. His body had a swimmer's build, taut and lean, definitely not the sort you'd expect to drop five rapists, each of whom made three of him easily.

Yotaka had only studied under one sensei his whole life. The man had called him a genius at fighting, right before he tossed Yotaka out of his dojo and onto the street. Yotaka had never taken the black belt examination in any fighting style. It had seemed like a big waste of his time, especially since it would have just made him an easier target for the police. He'd been fighting for years and had seen the inside of more than one police station because of some jerk with an ax to grind.

Or, in one case, because of a cop who liked to harass queers.

"Tobey," he said gently, reaching the kid. "Can you hear me?"

Now that he had a closer look at the guy, Yotaka saw that Tobey was actually a couple of years older than him.

"My arm," Tobey whimpered feebly. "I think it's broken."

Yotaka whipped out his phone in a single move, causing Tobey to flinch. "It's cool, man," he assured him. "I'm just going to call an ambulance, then get a friend of mine to come down so she can make sure you guys get the help you need."

Tobey mumbled something unintelligible.

"*Nani*?" Yotaka asked in Japanese, before remembering he was supposed to speak English. "What?"

It was an annoying habit from his youth that still reared its obnoxious little head every so often. If Tobey noticed, he didn't seem to mind.

"I said," Tobey whispered shamefully, "I can't ride in an ambulance."

"Why not?" Yotaka asked, as the line rang.

"I'm positive," he explained as Lieutenant Higgs picked up. "I'm HIV positive."

"What is it?" Higgs demanded in a curt tone.

"Nice to hear from you, too," he quipped back at the cranky female cop, his one and only contact on the whole force. "How's the missus and the kids?"

"Stow it, bird boy," Higgs bit back. "What is it this time?"

"Attempted rape victim," he said, cutting right to the chase. "A woman and her friend were jumped outside of an alley by five men built like trucks. I barely got to them in time."

"Great." Higgs let out a long sigh. "And how bad did you hurt them?"

Yotaka looked around the alley. None of the men were moving.

"Never mind," said Higgs wearily. "Tell me where you're at. My partner just turned on the blue lights."

Yotaka gave the address. "Could you please hurry?" he added sheepishly. "I'm going to be late for work."

"Fuck you," Higgs replied before hanging up.

Yotaka made a quick call for an ambulance, then put the phone away and moved to help Tobey up. "Keep your arm elevated," he advised. "And don't worry about the ambulance. They can't refuse to take you in it."

Tobey didn't look reassured.

"Trust me," he said, bringing the guy over by his lady friend so he would calm down some. "I know the cop who's on her way here. If they tried to turn you away, she'd break them in half, then arrest them for being stupid or something."

The woman laughed at this, which got Tobey to give the tiniest smile. "I like her already," she said. "Thanks for helping us."

One of the men on the ground stirred. Yotaka saw this and slammed the heel of his boot down into the back of the scum's head.

"My pleasure."

Higg's patrol car pulled up a few minutes later. Either her partner had driven like a bat out of hell, or they hadn't been far when Yotaka called. Either was likely, and he didn't care enough to deliberate the possibilities. The ambulance arrived a minute or two later. Higgs took all three of their statements, then handed the woman and Tobey over to the paramedics.

"Would it be all right if I came down to the station later to fill the stuff out?" Yotaka pleaded. "I really am going to be late."

"What's the matter?" she asked, cocking an eyebrow at him. "Are the ice caps going to thaw out if you don't grind your ass into some old man's crotch?"

Higgs shot a glare toward the alley. "The bad thing about all this," she said, giving Yotaka a look. "We need another ambulance to get all five of them to the hospital."

"I could have put them in the morgue instead," he pointed out, only half joking.

"Get out of here," she ordered, pointing down the street. "Get to work, and once that's taken care of, go straight home. If I find out you've been roaming these streets again in that get-up tonight, I'll have a SWAT team ready to raid that herpes den by the end of the week."

"I'm gone, Lieutenant." Yotaka gave her a wave as he took off. "Try to get laid on your next day off. It sounds like you could use it."

"Yeah?" she shot back as he disappeared around a corner. "You volunteering?"

The Side Pocket was located in the Midtown section of Atlanta, tucked away in a hard-to-reach spot near the Fox Theater. It was a pub that had been around for several years and thrived to a large degree thanks to word of mouth alone. To get there, one generally had to know the way, meaning its clientele were typically regulars. Nevertheless, even in the middle of the week, its employees could always count on a packed house once things really started going. Today was Thursday, meaning people would be gearing up for the weekend, wanting to squeeze in a little extra fun before Friday.

The alley that led to the pub's front door also arched around sharply to the side, where the employee entrance was located. Yotaka rushed past it, mindful to stay out of the bright overhanging light, and ducked behind a dumpster bin. There, he quietly pulled out the air-tight duffel bag from its secret hiding place behind a false panel on the side of the building and proceeded to change. It was a cold night, so he acted quickly. In a moment, the crime-fighter known as Yotaka was gone, and in his place stood fresh-out-of-college Shinichi Kozunaka.

Shinichi pounded on the back door to be let in.

"Cuttin' it kinda close, aren't we?" Daniel asked, cracking the door to see who it was.

"Lemme in," Shinichi insisted, squeezing through. "I'm late."

"No, you're just barely right on time," Daniel replied, closing the door and locking it after him. "The crowd really hasn't shown up yet, so it's just Brandon and Riley out on the bar for right now. Juan Lee hasn't even come out of his office yet."

"He's probably still snorting coke," Shinichi mused, changing out of his clothes again. "The man can't face the night, or the fact that he's gay, without at least six lines in him."

Daniel laughed as Shinichi tossed his clothes in his locker. "You got that shit right. So, ready for another long night of bumping and grinding?"

"As ready as I'll ever be." Shinichi yanked up a pair of tight boxer briefs that were two sizes too small for him. "Let's roll."

Daniel didn't move. "I thought Juan said he didn't want you wearing the ones with the Batman logo on them anymore."

"He did," Shinichi said, continuing on toward the door. "But the others are still at the cleaners, and the last time I wore something from the bin, they tore right in the middle of Led Zeppelin's 'Sympathy for the Devil', and the cunt who got hit in the face by the elastic threatened to have me arrested for indecent exposure."

Daniel was right in that the crowd hadn't shown up yet. Side Pocket didn't cater much to the female persuasion, but every once in a great while, somebody would get wind of the place and come to see what it was all about. Two women were sitting on either side of an older-looking man at the bar, cheering as they watched Riley do his stuff. Shinichi hated to admit it, but the boy had the moves. He was almost as good as Shinichi had been when he first started.

It had seemed like a good enough idea at the time. College was expensive, and his family had never been very big on support, at least where he was concerned. Shinichi had known he was facing a lot of long, hungry nights without so much as a cup of instant ramen if he didn't find work soon. This was back when the recession was just starting to creep in, back when the job listings in the newspaper hadn't gotten quite as thin. However, the police record that somehow still hadn't been expunged prevented Shinichi from finding work, until a roommate confided in him that there was a place where he could make two or even three hundred dollars a night.

Shinichi had been sold.

It helped that he was handsome. That was at least a part of it. Shinichi was not blind to the fact that he turned heads wherever he went.

It was just a matter of fact. His skin was smooth, his face ever so slightly square, with the right measure of leftover baby fat to give him an adorable, puppy-dog expression. His eyes were dark enough to look thoughtful without seeming spacey, but the hair was what made him stand out. Somewhere back a generation or three ago, a Scot-Irish had married into the Kozunaka clan. It was the shameful secret they had all been forbidden to speak of until he arrived, a glaring mixed bag of genetics.

Shinichi's hair was long, hanging down in feathered waves along the sides of his face, adding a slightly cocky vibe to his expression. It made the girls swoon. Being Japanese-American made him a chick magnet by default. There were moments when he wished the female anatomy held a greater interest for him. With the way women were always tripping over themselves as he walked past, he could have probably talked them into doing some seriously freaky shit.

Of course, given that he had an eight-and-a-half-inch cock that was almost as wide as his wrist, it was a wonder he didn't give up dancing and go straight into doing porn.

Shinichi avoided the bar altogether and went straight for one of the pool tables. Side Pocket had something of a theme. The bar was where guys usually danced, but the pool tables were reserved for semi-private shows. This area was separated from the bar by an arch, which kept it out of view from the entrance. Thus, customers could ask for a little extra from dancers shaking their balls above the billiards, provided they tipped handsomely for it. If the place was slow, though, a dancer could commandeer a table in the hopes of drawing a few patrons away from the liquor.

It wasn't always easy, but Shinichi had been doing this for a while.

A figure way on the other end of the bar moved, and as the lights flashed on and off, he saw that it was Brian. Shinichi seriously considered stepping off the table right then and there, but then remembered that the rent would be due soon. Calling Brian a regular was a bit of an understatement. He'd been a faithful attendee of Side Pocket for nearly three years now and, during that time, had zeroed in on Shinichi like a smart missile. Nearly every night, Brian could be found lurking in some part of the bar, usually far away from the crowd, and doing things with one of the dancers that would have been considered indecent in most other settings.

Shinichi continued to dance as he watched Brian march around the bar toward him. It was because of Brian that he hadn't been hurting for money much. For whatever reason, Brian was fixated on Shinichi. Shinichi, of course, knew he was good-looking, but the Side Pocket didn't exactly stock their shelves with second-rate merchandise. For a while, longer than he cared to admit, Shinichi had worried the man was some kind of stalker. Shinichi could take care of himself, but there was always the lingering fear of a knife coming at his back in the dark while he wasn't looking. According to his official record, which Higgs had been kind enough to show him once he'd explained the situation, Brian was a divorced man working as a teacher at a local middle school. Aside from a shoplifting incident in his teens, the man didn't have so much as an outstanding parking ticket. Higgs' advice had been for him to not give the guy any personal information or details about his life, enjoy the windfall, and report anything that seemed dubious to her.

Shinichi had taken this to heart.

Brian was waiting by the corner of the pool table now, watching Shinichi like a hawk through those narrow glasses of his that made it look as though he were always squinting. Shinichi ignored him for a moment, continuing his dance for the empty side of the room. All too quickly, Brian reached into his pocket and pulled out a wad of bills, all twenties. Shinichi saw them, because Brian had wanted him to, and slowly made his way over to where his patron stood waiting.

"Hi," Brian said, as Shinichi scooted himself up to the edge on his knees. "Long time, no see."

"Yeah." It had been all of two nights since Brian's last visit. "How have you been?"

"Teaching sucks," Brian stated flatly. "Let's go sit in a corner together and talk."

"Talking," of course, meant that Brian wanted to give him a hand job. Shinichi slid down off the table in the most provocative way possible and marched over to a nearby stool, giving Brian a good look at his ass in the process.

"So what did you want to talk about?" he asked playfully as Brian took a seat on the high stool.

Brian patted his lap. "Come up here with me," he asked, a pleading tone to his voice despite the handful of cash in his grip.

Shinichi obliged, adjusting himself to where the curve of his ass rested against the bulge in Brian's worn, faded pants.

"How are the students?" he asked, leaning back into the late-thirties man while his arms reached around to lock behind Brian's neck, pulling him in closer.

"Lazy," Brian answered, breathing in Shinichi's scent. "Stupid. Incompetent. I don't want to talk about them right now. Tell me how things have been with you."

Brian's hand reached into the band of his briefs and began tugging impatiently at Shinichi's limp cock. Shinichi groaned, more for show than anything, but the man seemed to appreciate the gesture all the same.

"The same as usual," he answered, keeping things light. "Get up, come to work, dance around in my underwear for the adoring public."

Brian gripped his slowly inflating dick in response to that. "Do any of them tip as good as I do, huh?"

Shinichi sighed. "No one tips as much as you," he assured the man, and in his mind, it didn't exactly sound like a compliment. "You'll always be my favorite."

Shinichi began grinding his ass into Brian's cock while the man's hand continued its attempt to get him hard. It wasn't for nothing, in the end. Shinichi thought Brian was kind of sweet; possessive, and horribly lonely, but not a bad person. The best thing for them both was to keep things at a professional level. He'd known that long before the sudden turn of events in his life a little over a year ago.

"Let's go to the back room," Brian said suddenly, tucking Shinichi's cock back into his shorts. "I want to be alone with you."

The back room, as Brian liked to refer to it, was an incredibly narrow hallway with four rooms placed alongside one another, each not much bigger than a bathroom stall. To get to it, one had to go through the restroom area, a design flaw if Shinichi had ever seen one. The entrance was a door frame located past the row of urinals covered by a black curtain, and past said curtain was a very large black man named Tony who had muscles in places even professional wrestlers would consider unnecessary.

Tony was there to collect the back room entrance fee and ensure none of the dancers got hassled by customers who felt they were entitled to something without having to pay for it. Shinichi had once proven Tony's services unnecessary when a customer had refused to take no for an answer. The old manager had politely asked afterward that Shinichi leave the brutal crippling of miserly jerks to the guy they hired for such tasks.

The standard fee for the use of a room was a hundred bucks an hour, which the house automatically kept. Anything that went on inside the rooms, the customer paid for and the dancer got to keep. Thus, the rooms were highly coveted; a few of the regulars memorized what schedules their favorite dancers worked and came in when they had the early shift to snatch a room up before they were full.

At the moment, the rooms would be empty, meaning they wouldn't have to listen to anyone else getting off through the paper-thin wooden panels. Brian handed his hundred to Tony without even looking at the guy as they passed through the curtain. Shinichi felt a pair of eyes on him from behind as he started forward, and looked back to find a young man watching him curiously while he pissed in the urinal.

"Ask the bartender," Shinichi said plainly, letting the curtain go. "He can fill you in."

Brian was waiting in the metal chair for Shinichi with the door wide open, his foot tapping impatiently against the floor. Shinichi closed the door behind him, locked the latch in place, and stripped out of his Batman boxer briefs.

"What did you have in mind?" he asked, surprised to see Brian still clothed.

Brian, it just so happened, loved to touch. His hands seemed to crave feeling another man's flesh the way a druggie needed a new fix. Brian would often start out running his hands along Shinichi's body and through his hair, completely ignoring his cock at first. Aside from him being dressed, tonight was no different. Shinichi leaned back in the man's lap and let him do his thing. All in all, Brian didn't have a terrible touch to him. He was more take than receive, but there was concern buried underneath for Shinichi's pleasure as well. Shinichi hadn't become aware of this until recently, and it made taking the man's money a cold choice.

Next came the blowjob. For this, all Shinichi had to do was stand perfectly still while Brian went down on him. It was the easiest part of their time together. Every minute or two, he would remember to let out a soft moan of encouragement. Shinichi loved head in general, so his method for dealing was to close his eyes and simply enjoy what was happening, forgetting about every other aspect of the situation for the moment.

The last part was the tough one, though. Brian hastily stripped out of his clothes and sat back down on the chair, wincing slightly at how cold it was. There was lubricant and rubbers on a corner shelf behind them. Shinichi prepped Brian first, slipped a condom on, then lubed his ass up liberally. Brian wasn't a large man, but Shinichi knew from experience that even the average dick could be painful to take, especially with the position they were forced to assume. Thanks to the gel, the head of Brian's dick slid into his ass with almost no resistance.

Shinichi heard himself groan then, and not just for Brian's benefit. "Oh yeah, baby," Brian hissed out, seizing Shinichi by the hips. "Ride me."

THE remainder of the night passed without incident. Brian paid Shinichi in two wrinkled one-hundred dollar bills and five twenties. By the time their hour was over, the pub had started to pick up speed. Jerry, Timothy, and Adrian had arrived along with Miguel, and the four of them were manning the top of the bar for a circle of drunken patrons. Shinichi took a quick break to clean up, get himself a water, and cool off. He rarely drank alcohol, and never while on the clock. Shinichi had witnessed first-hand the dangers of dancing four feet off the ground while inebriated.

Since the others had the bar covered, he decided to take to the pool table again in the hopes of attracting some more paying customers. Pretty soon, he had two more offers to go to the back. Sadly, Tony informed them that the rooms were all full when they got there. One went back to the bar, while the other agreed to wait and paid Shinichi to dance more on top of the pool table.

Brian watched from a distance, scowling every few minutes at Shinichi's new playmate, but did nothing. After a while, he got up and left. Shinichi wasn't too worried, though, since this whole scene had played out more times than he could afford to count.

Finally, after a long, sweaty eight hours with only the one break, it was time to call it a night.

Overall, Shinichi was happy. He'd raked in a good bit of money, enough to cover the rent, pay one or two bills, and put the rest aside for his retirement nest. There was even a chance he and Allen could go on a date soon.

Shinichi had worked something out with the old management when the man's nephew had gotten into a bit of trouble selling drugs. It was actually worked into the owner's contract that he be allowed to use the small shower stall built in the management office. Of course, the minute the ink dried, Juan Lee tried to rein in on that part of the deal. Shinichi's response had been to break the guy's wrist, then phone a lawyer friend from his fraternity days to confront the man about it.

The lawyer had admonished Shinichi for using violence, but then brought up several embezzlement accusations that he'd found in Juan Lee's records. So, in the end, Shinichi was allowed to resume showering before he left work every morning.

Once he was clean, Shinichi said goodnight to a handful of the other guys and sneaked behind the bin to change back into his costume. The day was just starting, but there was time for a quick patrol on his way home.

Thankfully, it was an uneventful run.

Shinichi smelled something wonderful cooking as he turned the key to unlock the apartment door. Allen stuck his head out of the kitchen entrance as he came down the hall and smiled.

"You're just in time," the forty-nine-year-old man said. "I made lasagna."

"So I smell," Shinichi said.

Their two-bedroom apartment felt wonderful after the night Shinichi had endured. Quickly, he stripped out of his costume, having taken the hidden entrance no one else in the complex knew about to avoid being seen. Once it was laid up neatly in the closet where their washer and dryer were stored, to be cleaned later, he went to their room for a change of clothes.

Allen Silvermane had no qualms about his lover being naked. The man spent a lot of his work day in the same state, or some degree of it, at least. Allen was a Sacred Intimate, sort of like the companion from that TV series *Firefly*. The two had met one day on the bridge over Lake Clara Meer in Piedmont Park, and for Shinichi, it had been love at first sight. He'd been patrolling through the neighborhood per a friend's desperate request and had ended up saving Allen's life from a couple of muggers.

That was Allen's version, at least. He'd been attempting to talk them down, but when that hadn't worked, the badass daddy had come out to play. Yotaka had jumped in, thinking a man his age would need help, but all he'd done was kept the others off Allen's back while he took their leader apart. Allen always believed in trying the nonviolent approach. That wasn't to say he couldn't handle himself, though.

After that night, they'd been inseparable. A mutual friend had spilled the beans and given Allen his phone number. Within a few days, they were sleeping together. A little over a month after that, Shinichi moved in with him.

Shinichi had never liked lasagna until Allen started cooking it for him. The man could make dirt taste good. Shinichi savored the smells as his arms wrapped around his man from behind.

"I missed you," he breathed out.

"I missed you too," Allen said, setting the hot pan down on the stove before turning around to face him. "Tell me about your night."

Shinichi sighed heavily. "A girl was nearly raped," he began. "The friend who was with her had a broken arm. The poor guy was afraid he wouldn't be allowed to ride in the ambulance because he was HIV positive."

Shinichi had to pause a moment before continuing. "I didn't even get her name. I'll have to go down to the station and sign some stuff soon."

"We can go later," Allen offered, knowing how much it would mean to him.

"Thanks," Shinichi whispered. "Brian was at the pub tonight again."

"We know how much he adores you," Allen replied lightly, rubbing the top of Shinichi's head affectionately.

"I think he wants to pretend I'm in love with him," Shinichi said, feeling miserable. "The more I see him, the worse I feel for taking his money. It's stopped being a business transaction for me. I'm starting to think I'm making it worse by leading him on."

"You can't help everyone," Allen reminded him. "This guy, Brian, is older than you and ought to know better than to make your time together into something it's not. If he can't accept that, it isn't your fault. If it weren't you, it would be someone else, and probably someone not as adept at defending themselves."

Shinichi's eyes flew open. "That's true," he mused.

Allen squeezed him tightly.

"I just feel so useless sometimes," Shinichi moaned. "Four years of college and then graduate school to become an engineer, and I'm still shaking my ass to make ends meet."

"Did you ever hear back from the company you applied to?"

Shinichi shook his head miserably. "They don't have any openings for right now," he mumbled. "The economy still hasn't bounced back, no matter what people keep insisting on the news. I also heard back from the Association before I left for work. My petition to be promoted to a second-class ranking was denied. It looks like I'll be busting heads on the street for a little while longer."

"I know at least one person who appreciates what you do," Allen said knowingly, giving Shinichi a smile. "If you hadn't kept those two off my back that night, I'd be dead."

Shinichi smiled at his lover's gratitude. "It just sucks," he groaned. "I'm gay, but I don't have a superpower to my name, so those bastards at the top don't see me as worthwhile. Unlike their little blue pet who can knock cars over with his hands from a mile back. You know, he blew me off once at this fundraiser they dragged me to?"

Allen chuckled. "Come on," he said, turning Shinichi around. "The lasagna can wait for right now. I know someone who needs a full-body massage."

Shinichi expected Allen to take him to the spare bedroom where all of his equipment was stored, but Allen steered him to the left toward their bed. Once there, he slowly stripped Shinichi out of his clothes, one piece at a time, until he was nude. Patting the bed, he motioned for Shinichi to lay facedown on it, then began systematically rubbing down each and every muscle.

Allen had a gift with his touch. There was a power, a primal magic to the way his fingers dug into another man's flesh. At his command, a body moved like putty underneath him. Shinichi had laughed the first time Allen told him he could bring a man to climax without going near his dick or balls, and challenged him to prove it. An hour and six orgasms later, he'd been too out of it to register the "I told you so" Allen gave him.

Shinichi didn't have to let himself relax under Allen's ministrations. His body responded automatically and shut down to let the man in to work. Within minutes, he was whimpering for more. Allen let out a low chuckle and obliged.

When Shinichi felt Allen draw back, he didn't protest. They had done this before, and he knew what to expect now. Allen was already naked when Shinichi turned over and raised his legs up. Their bed had come with a small cabinet built into the headboard. Lubricant and condoms were stored there for easy, quick access. Allen suited himself up, then applied a good amount of lube to his dick and Shinichi's asshole to make the first couple of inches easier. Allen had an incredibly fat shaft, especially near the head. Shinichi threw his head back into the pillow as he felt that first inch enter him.

"Go slow," he pleaded softly. "Please?"

"Always," Allen promised, rubbing a hand up and down Shinichi's chest reassuringly.

Once the whole thing was in, he knew everything would be all right. Allen took him to the same place he always did when they were together, coupled in a way that most could only dream about. Allen moved flawlessly in a rhythm that shook Shinichi to his core. Their gasps rang out over the walls as the pleasure between them built. Allen's cock was made for his ass, just like Shinichi's asshole had always needed Allen to fill it. The two were inseparable, and in this moment, nothing else mattered but the feel of their bodies crashing together like waves against the shore.

Allen always made sure to bring Shinichi to climax twice before losing his own load. When the second wave finally died down, Allen pulled out and removed the condom. Shinichi clumsily reached for Allen's dick the moment he felt it leave him.

"Let me," he begged. "Please, I want to do it for you."

Allen smiled, a twinkle sparkling in his eyes as he lay back on the bed next to Shinichi, and moved his hands away so his lover could go to work. It didn't take long for Shinichi to bring him to climax.

"I love you," Shinichi gasped, once the hair on his boyfriend's chest was spotted with cum. "Gods, I love you so much I think it might kill me sometime."

"You need someone to take care of you," Allen said matter-of-factly.

"I need you," Shinichi countered, snuggling up next to him. "You're my hero, remember?"

Allen laughed and placed a kiss on Shinichi's forehead. "Even heroes need someone to save them every now and then."

Allen got up long enough to wrap the lasagna in foil and put in the refrigerator. He was back in a flash and curled up against Shinichi's backside. The two slept on their sides, with Shinichi wrapped in Allen's huge arms for safekeeping.

Around noon, Shinichi awoke with a start.

"It's okay," Allen whispered in his ear, holding him as he trembled. "Was it the same dream as before?"

Shinichi swallowed hard and caught his breath before answering. "No," he said, his voice shaking uncontrollably. "I wasn't back home.

This was different. There was a girl, and she needed my help, but everything was changing…."

"It's okay," Allen promised as Shinichi choked up. "There's no one here but us. Here, lie back down."

Allen wrapped his arms around Shinichi as he leaned back again. "Lie still," he said, placing kisses along Shinichi's neck. "Everything will be all right. I'm here, Shinichi."

Shinichi went back to sleep with those words still ringing in his ears.

"I'm here."

J.L. O'FAOLAIN was born the youngest, with four older sisters, in the backwoods of the Deep South. Those that have braved getting to know him have attributed this to being the root of his growing insanity. A teased bibliophile in his youth, O'Faolain spent his years prior to getting published as a cook, laundry man, delivery boy, grease monkey, and retail stocker. He has a plethora of skills and abilities, none of which would work well on a job application. In his spare time, O'Faolain enjoys weightlifting, philosophy, deconstruction, reading, writing, porn, and the Internet in general. Aside from becoming a successfully published author, he would very much like to pilot a giant robot while Two-Mix's "Rhythm Emotion" is playing in the background. Either that, or travel the world in a dirigible. In short, the general consensus by all, including himself, is that he is a mighty strange fellow.

Section Thirteen from J.L. O'FAOLAIN

http://www.dreamspinnerpress.com